Cracked Island

By
Chris Kohler

Keith Publications, LLC
www.keithpublications.com
©2015

Arizona
USA

Cracked Island

Copyright© 2015

By Chris Kohler

Edited by Ray Dyson
www.raydyson.com

Cover art by Elisa Elaine Luevanos
www.ladymaverick81.com

Cover art Keith Publications, LLC © 2015
www.keithpublications.com

ISBN: 978-1-62882-112-3

If you are interested in purchasing more works of this nature, please stop by
www.keithpublications.com

Contact information: keithpublications@cox.net
Visit us at: www.keithpublications.com

Printed in The United States of America

Dedication

In memory of Peter Welle, a friend to Haiti, a friend to mankind, and a friend to me. You are missed by all.

Acknowledgements

I am most appreciative of my agent, Diane Nine, for having faith in my writing and for sharing my vision of Haiti as a wondrous setting for a novel. I thank everyone I shared time with in Haiti. Many of you are encapsulated in my characters. In particular, I thank my wife, Charlee Sue, who not only has shared most of my life, but also experienced much of Haiti with me. I am most grateful for her encouragement, editing prowess, and typing so many versions of this novel.

Chapter 1

Melons

The barkeep popped the cap to a frosted bottle of Prestige and slid it across the mahogany counter. Tim snatched the local beer, guzzled a healthy measure, and slammed it back to the hard surface. "Thanks, Leonard. You read my mind." He took another gulp. "What's left of it."

"The usual tab?"

"Not tonight. I'm limiting myself to just this one."

"As you say, Mister James." The lanky Haitian straightened his bow tie and buttoned his white jacket, all the while fixing his gaze upon his lone patron. He turned away without further word, picked up a dish towel, and wiped the recently rinsed glassware in preparation for the late-night crowd soon to bring life to the dead joint.

Tim shrugged off the skepticism laced in Leonard's eyes. *What the hell…it's the man's job to serve miserable slobs of the likes I've become.*

He reached for his beer, thought better of it, and turned his attention to the variety of liquors on the top shelves, more to kill time than out of curiosity. Rums from all corners of the Caribbean took front stage so tourists could experience for themselves that the nationally distilled product ruled supreme. He enjoyed a tropical rum drink as much as the next bar stoolie, but found beer provided a needed level of sustenance to accompany the numbness he sought, yet seldom achieved until he passed out.

"Well, well, look who's all gussied up tonight. Must be a special occasion."

Tim clenched his teeth upon hearing the contrived French accent of Bertram DuMarche. The parasitic asshole had impeccable timing when it came to dousing the slightest spark of a positive mood swing.

"I can't remember the last time I've seen you looking so suave and debonair." DuMarche released a crooked smirk and pointed to the resort's casino adjoining the bar. "Perhaps you'd like to join me tonight for a game of chance?"

"I don't want to bore you with the long answer, Bertram, so let's just leave it with the short one. Fuck off."

"No need for such language, my good friend. It is unbecoming of someone looking so fine and fancy. I'd come to believe you didn't even own a razor. Now, you wouldn't be thinking about skipping out of the country before paying off that little sum you owe me, would you?"

Tim's lips parted to something short of a hairline crack. That's exactly what he planned to do. He owed Bertram over fifty thousand dollars and, even though his employer garnished half his monthly wages to repay the debt, with the accruing interest being well in excess of credit card rates, the principal remained virtually the same. As usual, Bertram took to making it his business to know everyone else's. *I only need to stave this bastard off another day.*

"My hope is, if I can clean up my act, I might get my old job back." He straightened himself on the leather stool. "That's the only way I see to pay you off in a reasonable time."

Bertram's fake grin uncurled. "Good thinking. I'll even put in a word for you with management, but you best display exceptional behavior for the next few weeks to demonstrate you're truly off the sauce. I'd been hoping this day might come, my dear friend."

"Believe me…it's here."

Bertram nodded and meandered out to the casino in search of fresh prey.

Tim stared into his beer. *Half empty? Half full? Does it really matter?* Long ago, he conceded his ever-mounting dependence on the bottle had precluded further management of the beach club's dive operation. He remained clueless, though, as to why they kept him on as a maintenance man. It is at times like these when most individuals take a moment to reflect on how and why they became mired in such a crap-filled abyss. Taking stock in his life seemed simpler. *Money? Zilch. Friends? Vanished. Siblings? None. Parents? Dead. Wife? All of the above.*

Alone and penniless pretty well summed up his life. Of course, when he threw into the mix the outlandish chunk of dough he owed Bertram DuMarche, all the parts for a clusterfuck of epic proportions had been cast. But that mattered little now, for he felt confident some scrap of the train wreck called his life would soon be righted or, at the very least, he would incur a change of scenery.

****

Absent the haze from excess booze, Tim tossed about most of the night, and then rose well before his alarm sounded. He skipped breakfast, which he generally slept through anyway, and bounded out to the parking lot with his prized carved mask and other belongings not previously packed into his 1964 Land Rover. His sole means of transport had been cobbled together by a mishmash of spot welds, baling wire, duct tape, and a prayer. It persevered as long as he didn't forget to add a quart of oil every month or so. For today, in addition to its thirst for oil being quenched, the spark plugs had been re-gapped, the tires fully inflated and, for a sweeping change, the fuel gauge read full. It responded by smoldering to a grumble at the second turn of the ignition. He stiff-armed it into first gear and fishtailed out of the club's parking lot. The spray of sand and fragmented seashells pitched in his wake served as a fitting farewell.

His outlook brightened the instant he rolled onto the two-lane *la Route Nationale Numbre Une*, the main thoroughfare connecting Haiti's northern coast to its capital, Port-au-Prince. Other than Bertram DuMarche, he figured not a soul would be the least bit unhappy to see him flee this godforsaken island. In truth, his so-called bar friends would be pouring *gratis* rounds to celebrate no longer having to drag his sorry ass back to the broom closet masquerading as his room.

His attention shifted into overdrive when he approached a rise in the pocked roadway and spotted a round, green object rolling in his vehicle's path. He swerved at the last moment to miss it. He slammed his brakes. A second green object didn't enjoy the same luck.

Directly ahead, dozens of watermelons tumbled out of a flatbed truck, its rear supporting railing had sloughed what remained of the rust piecing it together. The trucker screeched to a halt, which triggered even more melons to topple to freedom. A bevy of dilapidated vehicles, aft and fore, jammed into a tangled web, obliging the irate drivers into an incessant round of horn blasts, a fitting soundtrack for the circus about to unfold.

The offending melon trucker slung his door open, leapt out, and scurried about to retrieve his rolling cargo, but not before a horde of women and children sprouted from nowhere and snatched more melons than most could lift, let alone lug away. The trucker stormed into the growing throng, reeled off all manner of *Créole* obscenities, only to become stymied when the melon-toting thieves morphed into an indecipherable swirl of motion.

Sweat streamed down Tim's square-jawed, sunbaked face. He had little choice but to linger within the bustling commotion and amuse himself with the ensuing debacle. Some moments later, a scrawny old woman ambled along on the back of an even scrawnier burro, partly obstructing his view. She puffed on a corncob pipe and, although her clothes and appearance conveyed utter raggedness, she carried herself with an air of dignity. She spotted him with his bright complexion, shaggy blond hair, and sea-blue eyes—all features difficult to miss in Haiti. Despite two years of exposure to the tropical sun, he hardly tanned, mostly just burned and peeled, after which the process would start all over again.

The woman remained stone-faced, removed the pipe from her mouth, and blew out a rivulet of smoke. She barked the traditional salutation when a Haitian encounters a Caucasian. *"Blanc."*

He smiled and nodded. The woman meant no offense. He grudgingly grew to respect Haitians, particularly their capacity to endure endless hardships and repeated heartaches, a trait he wished would rub off on him.

4

Another skeleton of a woman, wearing a feed sack for a dress, materialized. She foisted a melon in his face. "Please, sir, buy a melon from me. Only one dollar…five *gourdes*. A good price for you."

He shoved the melon aside. "*Non, merci*," exhausting most of the French he knew.

"*Cheri*, only one *gourde*. Almost free." She again shoved the melon to within an inch of his face.

He pushed the melon aside, this time with more force. "Look, I'm not interested in a melon. Besides, didn't you just steal it from that truck over there?"

He figured his blunt accusation would surely send her on her way. Instead, the melon plopped onto his lap. He sighed, pulled a wadded-up *gourde* from his front trouser pocket, and dropped it into her grimy hand. He held back a chuckle when he saw her scamper back to the fray to filch another melon.

A deluge of women and children witnessed the transaction and wasted no time in descending upon his trapped vehicle. Despite the absence of any semblance of air conditioning to lessen the unrelenting heat of the Caribbean sun, he rolled up his windows and blankly stared ahead, determined to avoid all eye contact, lest he inadvertently show interest to the melon-bearers swarming about.

The mob dispersed as suddenly as it appeared once all the melons surviving the melee had either been reloaded onto the truck or liberated by the peasantry.

He seized this opportunity to veer around the obstruction, using the right-hand, unpaved shoulder. His unwanted melon somersaulted from the comfort of his passenger seat to the rust-encrusted floor, which he made no effort to retrieve. Weightier matters occupied his mind.

His odds for escaping this ravaged country he had grown to despise, odds previously seeming so insurmountable, recently improved. A highly-respected Port-au-Prince attorney, a Mister G. Vincent Bennett, agreed to take his case. It should be a cinch for this hotshot lawyer to yank him out of his self-dug pit. They would meet tonight for dinner at a hotel in Pétionville, a crumbling suburb of the even more decrepit capital. The attorney indicated when they first spoke over the phone, all Tim needed to do was provide some minor details, fill out a few forms, and in a matter of weeks he would be free to leave the country. *Free to leave the country? No, it would be more like an escape—an escape to reclaim my self-respect—to reclaim my life.*

He inched along for several miles behind a caravan of ramshackle, open-air trucks, each spewing out a flume of gaseous tar. Along with being overloaded with some combination of produce, livestock, and charcoal, nearly every truck carried a contraband topping of peasants, all of whom, he gathered, aspired to find better lives in the big city. Taking advantage of the slightest of openings, he leap-frogged past the convoy, one rattletrap at a time, and then picked up speed for several miles before being forced to shift into low gear behind a sluggish *tap tap*—the Haitian rendition of public transportation. The *tap tap*, a canopy-covered pickup with two facing bench seats in its bed, boasted a brightly painted kaleidoscope of religious scenes and inscriptions across every visible surface. Evenly divided upon the benches, a dozen or so zombie-like passengers sat. The driver, heedless of the apparent lack of space, stopped twice to pick up additional fares. Tim marveled at how the new arrivals managed to melt into places, despite those previously seated having relinquished mere slivers.

Traffic plodded along at a burro's pace. His relentless urge for a beer mounted in his parched throat, but he contented himself with a few swigs of lukewarm water from a metal canteen. Of late, one beer always led to another, but for this day he found the strength to retain sobriety. His stomach knotted when his thoughts turned from the road to the singular presence nearly always comprising the whole of his mind—Sarah. He fondled his gold wedding band with his left thumb, loosened his grip on the steering wheel, and visualized her seated next to him in her customary slouched position, her long, slender legs crossed at the ankles. Tears welled in his eyes as he fought the compulsion to re-live the events he so fervently attempted, but so utterly failed, to purge from his mind.

Paradise burned into ashes in a single, horrific night. The two years since passed in a state of total torment.

Mired in a recurring nightmare, he didn't initially register the sudden upheavals of the earth rippling around him, nor the deep fissure in the road, still expanding, and scarcely a few car lengths ahead. He slammed the brakes and jerked the vehicle to the shoulder and into an imposing rock outcropping. The force of the impact flung him flat onto the blistering, wobbling pavement. He struggled to turn his head to the side and, before consciousness slipped away, found himself facing a cracked melon.

****

The rustling of bottles and canisters on the shelves, not to mention the ground shaking, caused Madeleine McCoy to lose her concentration. When calm returned a few minutes later, she assumed the commotion to be just another earth tremor, although maybe a bit more prolonged than usual. After all, being located on La Gonave, Haiti's largest outer island and, thankfully, miles from the hustle and bustle of Port-au-Prince, didn't provide immunity to shifts of the earth's core.

Nothing comes easy in Haiti, she reminded herself. Calamities can crop up in the blink of an eye, whether from the depths of the earth, or the far reaches of the sky. She tucked the memories of her recent struggles into the black box of her mind, where they joined a number of other unpleasant experiences, and then returned to completing her inventory of medical supplies. She paused and gazed about the children's clinic with a rare feeling of satisfaction. Everything was finally coming together.

Chapter 2

Heavy Clay

The short, stocky *blanc* shut the door to his palatial Port-au-Prince office and rattled the handle to make sure it locked. He paused to admire the brass nameplate adorning the door, repeating the inscription to himself, *G. Vincent Bennett, Attorney at Law.*

He looked like he stepped off the set of an old Humphrey Bogart movie shot in a steamy, tropical setting. His everyday attire consisted of a white, slightly wrinkled, linen suit, with a matching sweat-stained, narrow-brimmed hat. A thin, black tie, black belt, and black shoes served as the sole contrasts in color to his suit, hat, and starched shirt. He looked, talked and, in particular, acted like a highly respected attorney—for in Haiti, perception is reality. Where else could Vinny Berkowitz, a two-bit con artist from Queens, resurrect himself from the mob's hit list to become an attorney at law?

To his own surprise, he rapidly became established in the Port-au-Prince legal community. After duping the law firm of LeClerck, DuBois, and Fontainebleau into believing he was a Yale-educated attorney, he found himself being swept up to handle matters where an American's presence would prove beneficial. He excelled at handling the lucrative overseas divorce trade and, after Maurice Fontainebleau was killed in some unfortunate episode with governmental henchmen—the notorious *Tontons Macoute*—became a full partner. Haiti may be a hellhole for peasants, but for the rich within the ranks he soon joined, the island nation provided a life of splendor.

He strolled out onto *Avenue Delmas,* which fronted the LeClerck, DuBois, and Bennett law offices. A gaunt boy wearing only ragged shorts and one shoe stood watch over his freshly washed luxury sedan. The thirteen-year-old possessed the unwritten franchise for holding parking spots, as well as washing and guarding all vehicles parked in front of the law firm. Vincent knew the boy only by his first name, Hermaine. Two younger boys were in his employ, but Hermaine personally handled all transactions.

"*Bonjou, Monsieur* Bennett." Unlike most street urchins, Hermaine politely waited to be paid for services rendered.

He returned Hermaine's greeting and forked over two *gourdes*, double the going rate. Hermaine amply reciprocated this largesse with specialized services. Vincent always received the prime parking spot, no one dared touch his sedan lest they be severely chastised, and it received the first washing while the water in Hermaine's single bucket still possessed a hint of transparency.

Vincent started the engine, turned on the air conditioner, and shifted into gear. Snaking through the busy streets of Port-au-Prince, he turned onto *Avenue John Brown,* which led to the lush, hilltop suburb of Pétionville. He had a scheduled afternoon meeting with a regular client, Richy Richardson, and a dinner meeting with his newest client, Tim James, a young American employed at the beach club in Saint-Marc. Unlike Mister Richardson, Vincent didn't expect to collect much of a fee from the second client, but if things worked out with Richy as planned, this James fellow might prove useful.

He turned his white vehicle sharply between the iron-gated entryway of the equally white hotel. The Victorian-style building, complete with gingerbread ornamentation, stood as one of Pétionville's finest. After he parked under the partial shade of a palm tree, the hotel's bellman rushed over to open the door of the sedan. "Welcome, Mister Bennett, it is very good to see you once again."

He acknowledged the white-uniformed Haitian with a nod before bounding up the steps to the main veranda. After admiring the brilliant hues of the bougainvillea, contrasting colorfully with the white exterior of the hotel, he surveyed the pool and spotted two female bathers. Since neither wore tops, he assumed them to be European. A neatly dressed waiter interrupted his shameless gawk.

"Good day, Mister Bennett. We have been expecting you. Your party has already arrived and is seated at your usual table."

He strolled over to the corner table overlooking the pool where a sixtyish, wrinkle-faced man, in equally wrinkled attire, gulped a bottle of Prestige. Another empty bottle rested on the table, along with an ashtray brimming with butts, some still burning. The man's ample belly suggested beer had long been a dietary staple.

"Hey, Vincent, thought you forgot me."

"Not a chance, Richy. Got caught up in traffic. Too damn many goats, chickens and, oh yeah, Haitians, cluttering up the roadways, but I'm here now."

"Would Mister Bennett like his usual?" the waiter asked.

"The usual…yes." Before he could take off his hat and wipe his receding brow with his handkerchief, the waiter returned with a squatty glass of rum-on–the-rocks.

"You drink that shit straight?" Richy asked.

"This shit, I'll have you know, is five-star Barbancourt, the best and smoothest rum in the world. I still can't believe it's distilled right here in Haiti. If this is shit, then I guess people aren't far off when they say I'm full of it. Anyway, we're not here to talk about my drinking habits, are we?"

"No, indeed, we have more important matters to discuss."

"Did you bring it? I think it's about time I see it for myself, don't you?"

Richy pulled a neatly folded handkerchief from his inside jacket pocket and placed it on the table. He rotated his head to either side to rule out onlookers before sliding the cloth bundle across the table.

Vincent performed an identical reconnaissance before unfolding the handkerchief. His eyes widened at the sight of a fully-engraved, crescent-shaped, gold amulet. "This is incredible. What do you figure it's worth?"

"It depends. In today's gold market, it's worth a couple thousand or so, but as a pre-Columbian artifact, it's worth tens of thousands more."

"How do you know it's pre-Columbian?"

"Just look at it." Richy's voice grew louder. "It has the same engravings as all the broken pieces of terra cotta I've been dealing in these past couple years. Believe you me, the slaves didn't bring gold with them when they were shipped here from Africa. This amulet is pre-Columbian."

"Shhh…don't tell the whole world. Tell me again, how did you come into possession of it?"

"Didn't I tell you all this in your office last month?"

Richy had, in fact, blurted out everything in their earlier meeting, which unbeknownst to him, Vincent recorded on tape. "Of course you did, but it's not like I took notes. I just want to make sure I got the facts straight. Must be the lawyer in me." Oftentimes, he felt as if he actually was a lawyer.

"Basically, I slip everything through customs with my shipments of woodcarvings and primitive paintings. The only things those customs guys in Miami seem to be concerned about are drugs and maybe endangered species. Once I get the stuff into Miami, I wholesale it to a distributor, Alomar Enterprises. No muss. No fuss."

Richy finished the second Prestige and motioned to the waiter for another. "About six months ago, my contact with Alomar, Ricardo Colón, informed me he had a buyer from somewhere in South America who would take as much as I could supply and pay a premium. Needless to say, I put the word out to my guys to start hauling in everything they could get their stinking paws on."

He paused as the waiter arrived with his beer and removed the two empty bottles. He took a few gulps, waited for the Haitian to get out of hearing distance, lit a cigarette, and took a deep puff. "I heard rumors of vast amounts of terra cotta littering the countryside on the island, out in the middle of the bay. La Gonave, they call it."

11

"Yeah, I've heard of it. Supposedly, it's one bleak piece of real estate."

"I sent one of my guys over there to line up a few peasants, mostly farmers, to scoop up whatever they could find. I paid by the weight. A *gourde* a pound. It's amazing what twenty cents will buy you in this country. I never imagined getting a chunk of gold like this. Lucky for me, it was totally covered with dried mud and looked like terra cotta. Hell, I knew it wasn't clay the second I picked it up."

"How do you know where it came from?" Vincent intended to squeeze out every nugget of information he could.

"We labeled each box with the name of the pea brain that brought in the artifacts. Ti Bon Baptiste was the name in this case. He farms a small plot of land outside the island's main village, Anse-à-Galets. I sent one of my guys over to ask him where he collected his broken pottery. The farmer was hesitant at first, but opened up after being paid ten *gourdes* as an advance on future purchases. It turns out there is a cave in the hillside behind his farm. He won't go inside because he thinks it's haunted by spirits or something."

"Why didn't you just send your men into the cave to check it out?"

"Are you kidding? My guys are Haitians, too. They won't step foot in some damn cave full of ghosts, zombies, or what have you. Besides, I don't want them to know about the gold. You can't trust a Haitian with pocket change, let alone gold."

Richy took a swig of beer and slammed his bottle on the table. "You're the only one I trust to tell this to."

Vincent maintained a straight face, but inwardly chuckled at what an imbecile he was dealing with. "You'd be wise to keep it that way. Why do you think you need my help?"

"Dealing with broken clay pots is one thing, but gold is another ball game. I need someone with your education and sophistication to cut a deal with Alomar." Richy wiped the sweat from his face. It grew redder with each gulp of beer. "We're looking at a golden retirement, my friend."

"What makes you so sure there's more gold in the cave? Maybe this amulet is just a trinket some clumsy Indian lost."

"First of all, only a *Taíño* chief would wear such an amulet. Secondly, I have good reason to believe this is just the tip of a golden iceberg. It all goes back to good ol' Christopher Columbus."

"Christopher Columbus?"

"Yeah, Christopher Columbus. It seems when he first arrived on this island five hundred and some odd years ago, the Indians were covered with gold. Gold around their necks. Gold stuck in their noses. In their ears. You name it, they were covered."

Vincent straightened himself on his chair and fantasized as to how much gold there might actually be on this otherwise godforsaken excuse of a country.

"After returning to Spain," Richy continued, "Columbus' main argument to return was his stories about all of the gold he saw. Queen Isabella couldn't wait to get her hands on it. She sent Columbus right back, but when he arrived the second time, he couldn't find a single Indian adorned with even an ounce of gold. Historians figured Columbus fabricated the story about the gold so he could squeeze another voyage out of the queen."

"It's obvious there was at least one gold amulet." Vincent found it harder to maintain his disinterested composure.

"There's a helluva lot more than that, my friend. It seems, back in the early nineteen sixties, some anthropologist figured the Indians hid all of it in caves after realizing the Spaniards had more than a passing fancy for their gold ornaments."

Richy took a swig of beer and added another butt to the ashtray. "This anthropologist guy went on an expedition to the small island off the northwest coast, called *Ile de la Tortue* and, sure enough, after snooping around for a few months, he came across all kinds of gold ornaments stashed away in a cave, exactly as he predicted. They did a write-up in a major magazine, exonerating our good man, Christopher Columbus." Richy drained his third beer.

"What happened to the gold this guy found? He must be richer than shit."

"That anthropologist didn't give a hoot about the gold. All he cared about was publishing an article in some journal no one reads and speaking at meetings only other anthropologists attend. All the gold went to the government, supposedly placed in a museum to be enjoyed by the masses. No one has seen or heard about it since. Rumor has it Papa Doc, who controlled everything on this island back in those days, melted it down and stashed it in one of his Swiss bank accounts."

Richy could wait no longer and motioned to the waiter for another beer. After one big chug of the new brew, he ended his discourse. "So, the way I see it, if Indians hid gold in caves on *Ile de la Tortue*, then why not in caves on *Ile de la Gonave*?"

"Why didn't someone long before you think of this?" Vincent asked.

Richy shrugged. "I suppose because they never had the good fortune to actually stumble upon a gold ornament."

Their triumphant grins disintegrated the instant the underground eruption began.

Chapter 3

White Powder

Ti Bon Baptiste eyeballed the single-engine plane approaching his farm at a low altitude. Much to his astonishment, it dropped a cluster of small objects onto his recently cleared corn plot. He watched the plane fade into the horizon and then raced to his field where he found thirteen packages scattered about, each weighing about five pounds. He quickly concealed them in the nearby acacia shrubs, well aware of the many eyes in Haiti, even on this desolate outer island of La Gonave. He then sprinted to the one-room mud hut housing himself, his wife, Marie Joseph, and their five children. He was alone this morning. His wife had taken their infant boy and the two girls to the market at Nan-Café. The two older boys attended school at the Greater Evangelical Mission.

He fastened the wooden shutters of the hut's single window, grabbed his wife's other dress, and darted out the door. He dashed straight to the packages, wrapped the dress around one of them and, in exaggerated nonchalance, carried it to his hut. He repeated the charade until he secured all the packages into the safety of his tiny abode.

Sitting on the dirt floor with the packages evenly displayed in a circle around him, he savored the moment. He had experienced few such pleasures in his twenty-six years. Clutching the package nearest to him, he used his teeth to cut the twine tied around it, unwrapped the brown paper, and discovered a cardboard box secured by duct tape. Smiling, he admired the box, thinking how thrilled his wife would be to have it and the others to store food, additional valuables, or to use for bartering. He took a deep breath, opened the box, and found several clear plastic bags sealed with rubber bands. The bags contained a white powdery substance.

His chest swelled with joy. The bags and rubber bands would be extremely useful for storing his seed. His wife could use others for keeping weevils and flies out of their stored food. *How perfect the day will be if this white powder turns out to be edible.* Food was always scarce in the Baptiste household.

He slipped off the rubber bands sealing each of the bags and felt quite pleased with himself for not having broken a single one. He poured a small amount of the powder into his cupped left hand and sniffed it. It did not smell like anything. He stuck his tongue into the powder and tasted it. It had no taste he recognized as food. Each of the packages contained the same thing.

Eager to surprise his wife of eight years with the wealth of boxes, plastic bags, and rubber bands, but without the distraction of the worthless white powder, he emptied the contents at the back of his house. He could hardly contain his glee when some of the floury substance puffed up against his hut. He knew a good thing when he saw it.

****

Marie Joseph loved market day at the mountainside village of Nan-Café. There, she could purchase nearly anything needed. She relished the opportunity to gossip with her friends about the latest happenings and scandals, with today's exchange centering upon *Soeur* Madeleine, a *blanc* who took over the children's clinic at Anse-à-Galets. Her father established the clinic, but poor *Père* Thomas died of a heart attack three months ago. *Soeur* Madeleine came to Haiti several years earlier to work at her father's side, but after he passed away, she promptly left for the States. Everyone assumed the clinic would be no more. To the delight of nearly every native inhabitant on La Gonave, *Soeur* Madeleine returned, had a new roof placed on the clinic, and would soon re-open its doors.

The gossip continued as to how a woman, who moreover was not married, could possibly run the children's clinic. The women exchanged much speculation concerning her marital status, including what man or men might be in her life. They all agreed that because of her training in America they would not hesitate to take their sick children to see her. Each made a point to convince one another that how *Soeur* Madeleine conducted herself in her private life remained absolutely of no concern to them.

When the mid-day hour arrived, Marie Joseph surveyed her straw basket containing all the day's purchases—about one pound of rice lying loose on the bottom, a small crumpled paper bag filled with black beans, two dried fish, and a sliver of fresh goat meat placed inside a used envelope discarded by some wealthy *blanc*. She shook her head in dismay, for twelve *gourdes* didn't go as far as it once did.

The gangly, mahogany-skinned mother balanced the basket on her head without disturbing her son, Ti Ti, who suckled on her left breast. Six-year-old Premíse and seven-year-old Colette each carried on their heads five-gallon plastic pails recently filled with water from the community well. The proud, slender Baptiste women, along with a contented Ti Ti, cheerfully trekked back to their home. Along the way, the rumblings of the earth, lasting only a few minutes, prompted the travelers to give thanks and praise to the spirits below.

****

Marie Joseph froze in stunned disbelief a few hundred yards from their farm. There, right before her very eyes stood the most splendiferous sight she had ever seen. During her absence, the Baptiste home had miraculously turned brilliantly, blindingly white.

Chapter 4

Mostly Dead

Sprawled face-up on a concrete slab, consciousness crept through Tim James' veins, leading to spasms of pain mushrooming across his half-stripped body. His eyes stung with the seepage of accumulated sweat. Gloom surrounded him. He sensed flies crawling on his face, but couldn't summon the strength to swat them. Forcing his head to the side, he came face-to-face with an open-eyed corpse. He jerked his head to the opposite side and received an equally gruesome greeting. Flies lit for the ceiling— beetles and rodents darted for cover—the instant his scream pierced the morgue's silence.

He popped to his feet. A wooden object, his carved mask of all things, fell off him and banged on the floor. Scores of cadavers encircled him. His lungs clogged with the steaming stench of putrefying flesh. He frenziedly searched for any means of escape. Scanning each damp block, he spotted a single door at the far, right-hand corner. Not seeing any unobstructed paths, he grabbed his mask and then leapt over rows of bodies toward the sole exit to the chamber—a chamber now seeming more narrow and crowded with eye-bulging corpses.

He wrenched at the doorknob. It stubbornly resisted. He tried again and then again. Only after he inadvertently turned the handle counterclockwise did the rust-encrusted door squeak open.

In an equally dim-lit hallway, he encountered two pretzel-bodied undertakers dragging another body to join the others. They dropped their inert cargo and bolted out a side door. He chased after them, but the terrorized morticians blended into the moonless night.

Blindly, he darted down the vacant roadway, bludgeoned his bare feet on the rough cobblestone, and thereafter scarcely managed a limping trot. Once his eyes fully adjusted to the star-studded darkness, he discovered a paper tag tied to one of his bloodied toes. The sight triggered a chain reaction of shock, trembling, and dry heaves.

His fog of terror began to lift as he pieced the horrifying puzzle together. He had been on his way to Port-au-Prince, rattling across the potholed, two-lane *la Route Nationale Numbre Une* in his beat-up, four-wheel drive vehicle. He hazily recalled the earth ripping apart, but dismissed the bizarre image and concluded a vehicle racing from behind must have slammed into his, knocking him unconscious in the midst of some melon melee—another remembrance making little sense. Apparently, he'd been declared dead by some incompetent physician and carted off to the city morgue to be buried in an unmarked grave with all the homeless peasants who recently met their demise.

His stomach wrenched at the realization—had he not regained consciousness he would have been buried alive.

Chapter 5

Clinic

Madeleine spent most of the day checking and re-checking her inventory of medicines, vitamins, and various sundries. Tomorrow, after a three-month hiatus, she would re-open the newly christened Dr. Thomas McCoy Children's Clinic. It would not be a day too soon for many of the families of La Gonave. She anticipated a legion of mothers and scores of sick offspring lining up at the clinic's door long before the sun would rise. Despite being a highly-trained nurse practitioner, she reluctantly accepted that many of the illnesses among the natives, exasperated by chronic malnutrition, would exceed her ability or available medicines to treat.

Darkness rolled in by the time she completed her inventory and returned to the cottage once occupied by her late parents. The five-room residence resembled a Florida beach house, with its combination of concrete blocks, tin roof, hurricane windows fitted with screens, and Mexican tiles throughout, all serving to provide a homey and cool atmosphere. Adding to its charm, each room boasted rattan and mahogany furnishings, along with colorful splashes of primitive paintings her mother, Pamela, periodically purchased from skilled craftsmen on her monthly forays to Port-au-Prince. The screened porch proved, by far, to be the family's favorite place to congregate. She had many fond memories of playing cards with her parents, chit-chatting about the events of the day, or quietly relaxing in the cool evening breeze, the latter pastime being all the porch could now offer.

Being ever the optimist, her father had the entire house wired and plumbed for utilities. "Someday, we'll be damn glad I did this," he would always say. That day had yet to arrive. The only stable source of electricity on the island resided within the walls of the Greater Evangelical Mission, powered by a diesel-fueled generator operating twenty-four hours a day. Running water remained an unknown luxury to every inhabitant of La Gonave.

Along with the cottage, she inherited its young housekeeper, one of her father's first patients. Yvette stood five feet tall fully stretched and weighed a dozen pounds shy of one hundred. Her flawless, cinnamon complexion and sharp facial features revealed a French slave master in her ancestry. Her cropped, woolly hair had the appearance of a poodle's coat recently groomed. Despite a day spent cooking and cleaning, her long, white and blue polka dot dress remained as spotless and wrinkle-free as when she first arrived early that morning.

When Madeleine entered the cottage, the petite Yvette greeted her with a unique emphasis placed upon the last syllable of her name. "Good evening, *Ma-da-leen*."

"*Bonsoir*, Yvette. I mean, good evening." She learned, long ago, Yvette preferred to speak in English, both of them being fluent in each other's native language.

"You are working much too hard, *Ma-da-leen*. You should have had your dinner two hours ago."

"I know…I know, but there was so much that needed to be done at the clinic."

"The work will wait. It always does."

"Yes, but this needed to be finished before tomorrow's opening."

Yvette accepted the explanation with a sigh and pointed to the kerosene-lighted dining room table. "Please, *Ma-da-leen*, won't you sit down so I may serve you dinner? I prepared one of your favorite dishes, curried chicken and honey-covered yams."

Madeleine felt shameful for once again having a decent meal before her when most others in Haiti did not. She consoled herself by recalling her father's often spoken phrase, "You must eat well to heal well."

She strolled to the candle-lit bathroom where a bowl of tepid, soapy water rested on a wooden stand. After dampening a washcloth, she wiped the day's accumulation of dried perspiration and grime off her brow. She inherited her mother's green eyes, auburn hair, and high cheekbones, along with her father's tall, thin build, being only four inches shy of his six-foot, two-inch frame. Upon gazing at her reflection in the dim room, she wondered if the shadows cast upon her face remained during the glaring light of a Haitian day. Although only twenty-eight, her reflection in the mirror eerily resembled the aged mother she remembered. After cleansing her body, if not her mind, she released the barrette in her hair and gently shook her head, allowing her long locks to cascade to her narrow shoulders. She added a hint of blush to her pale cheeks. Before blowing out the candle, she glanced back into the mirror and felt relieved to see an image she recognized as herself.

After dinner, she took the lantern and migrated to the front screened porch to enjoy the cool breeze. On the stand next to her caned-back rocking chair rested a cup of steaming hot chocolate and a slice of coconut custard pie, her favorite dessert. She poked her head through the opened front door and interrupted the young maid's cleaning. "Yvette, you're being much too good to me and you're going to make me fat."

Her comment resulted in another scolding from her petite housekeeper. "You need to put some meat on those bones of yours. You're starting to look like a Haitian peasant. *Père* Thomas would not approve."

The last statement, regularly brought into conversations whenever Yvette felt the need to reinforce her position, left Madeleine with no rejoinder. "Yes, you're right, Yvette. *Père* Thomas would not approve."

After grudgingly taking pleasure in the pie and hot chocolate, she gently rocked her chair in synchrony to the faint throbbing of *Vodou* drums echoing from the hillsides. Unlike most *blancs*, she fully accepted *Vodou* as being the essence of Haitian culture. "When it comes to religion," *Père* Thomas was fond to say, "Haitians are ninety percent Catholic, ten percent Protestant, and one hundred percent *Vodou.*"

A tapping at the outside screened door interrupted her tranquil repose. She got up to open it and instantly recognized the imposing figure of Mildred Sponheimer, the founding director of the Anse-à-Galets Greater Evangelical Mission. Everything about Mildred reminded her of an overgrown swine. Mildred's stocky legs narrowed to undersized feet and her spherical torso presented identical profiles from every angle. Her pumpkin-like head seemed to rest directly on her shoulders as if its massive weight had collapsed her neck. She did not hold Mildred Sponheimer in the highest regard.

"*Bonsoir*, Mildred, *intérieur venez, s'il vous plait*." She deliberately spoke in French, knowing full well that in nearly thirty-four years in Haiti, Mildred had not learned a single word of it, the country's official language, or *Créole*, the language of the people.

"Miss McCoy, it's me, Mildred Sponheimer. Is it all right if I come in?"

She chuckled to herself when the stout mission director acted as if she had not heard the foreign greeting. "Yes, please be my guest. Can I get you something to eat or drink?"

"Thank you, but I've already eaten."

"To what do I owe this pleasure?"

"Just a social visit. I've been meaning to welcome you back to La Gonave. We're all so very pleased to have you here again. The clinic your father started is so badly needed by our poor Haitian brethren."

She recalled her father's cautions concerning Mildred Sponheimer. "No visit will ever occur without a hidden agenda."

Although motioned to take the opposite seat, Mildred plopped onto Madeleine's rocker and scanned the surroundings. "Doctor McCoy surely built a splendid cottage. I've always admired it. You should be quite comfortable here."

"Yes, I'm sure I'll remain every bit as comfortable as were my parents."

"Oh? I didn't realize your mother was all that comfortable here."

Fully aware very little happened among the *blancs* on La Gonave that Mildred did not make it her business to know, she replied, "She was happy to be at my father's side."

Mildred lowered her bun-crested head. "I'm sorry. It must be painful for you to talk about your late parents. That was thoughtless of me. Shall we change the subject? I've been curious as to how you'll be funding the clinic. What are you calling it now, the Doctor Thomas McCoy Children's Clinic?"

"Yes, I've re-named the clinic in honor of my father."

"That is certainly appropriate and a very fitting memorial, I must say." Mildred pursed her porky lips. "I suspect it must be very expensive to keep a clinic in supplies when it has historically served so many needy. Were you fundraising back in the States these past three months?"

Painfully aware of how expensive running the clinic would be, and with her meager finances already stretched after paying the last installment on the new roof, she concluded a slight exaggeration to be in order. "Father left a sizable endowment to run the clinic for some time to come. I spent the last three months getting his estate in order."

"Is that so?" Mildred's tone exposed a measure of disappointment. "I'm so happy to hear that," she rapidly added. "If there's anything the Greater Evangelical Mission or I can ever do for you, please do not hesitate to ask. Will we be seeing you in our church this Sunday?"

Although raised a Presbyterian, Madeleine made it a habit to attend various Christian churches. "Yes, I would be pleased to attend services this Sunday at your church. I plan to rotate to a different church each week."

Mildred took a deep gulp. "Even the Catholic church?"

"Yes, I will attend Catholic services. The Catholic faith does represent the vast majority of our poor Haitian brethren." She purposely inserted some of Mildred's own words.

Mildred catapulted her more than ample body out of the rocking chair. "I must be going. Oh, and Miss McCoy, you do realize Catholics allow *Vodou* rituals to be conducted as part of their ceremonies? Quite non-Christian, I dare say."

She fought back the urge to roll her eyes. "I'm aware Catholics allow drums to be played during their mass, but I don't believe the playing of drums necessarily equates with *Vodou*."

"Listen to those drums coming down from the mountains. In Haiti, drums mean *Vodou*. Please be careful, Miss McCoy. A single and attractive white woman such as yourself needs to be very diligent in following the word of God. *Vodou* is devil worship. I'm very concerned about you being here alone. Good night and please consider coming to our church every Sunday. Our doors are always open to you, Miss McCoy."

"I won't be here alone much longer."

"Oh?" Mildred pulled away from the screened door.

Madeleine immediately regretted blurting out the unsolicited information. Now she felt obligated to continue. "A Methodist minister from New York has arranged for a graduate student to help me maintain the clinic in exchange for room and board. He will be conducting anthropology research on La Gonave. They will arrive this Friday."

"A Methodist minister? You know, I founded the Greater Evangelical Mission here in Anse-à-Galets more than thirty years ago. You could have come to us if you needed help. My offer still stands if this Methodist situation doesn't work out. Other churches, although often well intentioned, don't have the commitment to Haiti mine has."

Mildred stormed off before Madeleine could respond.

****

A lingering Yvette poked her head out the door opening. "Will *Ma-da-leen* be requiring anything else of me this evening?"

"No, Yvette, I'm fine. You'd best hurry home now. You've stayed much too late."

Only after the young Haitian disappeared into the darkness did Madeleine settle back into the solitude of her rocking chair. She relaxed late into the night to the rhythmic beat of distant drums.

Chapter 6

Client

Not accustomed to being kept waiting, G. Vincent Bennett fidgeted the time away under candlelight on the hotel's veranda. A glass of rum-on-the-rocks kept him company. His newest client, Tim James, had already missed their evening dinner appointment by over two hours. Possibly one of many casualties, he gloomily considered, of the immense earthquake having struck just hours before.

His earlier meeting with Richy Richardson played out exactly as planned. Calculated greed replaced skepticism the moment he laid eyes on the amulet. The matters of determining if more gold artifacts existed in the cave of Ti Bon Baptiste, gaining possession of them if they did, and negotiating their sale to Alomar Enterprises, were now in his able hands, along with a retainer for ten thousand dollars. To augment his earnings, he negotiated one-third of the profit for all gold discovered and sold. Of course, under certain scenarios, all the profit could be his. Regardless, he figured to make a handsome sum off this venture.

Now this damnable earthquake might screw up his plans, but he would work around it like he had every other shit-ass roadblock thrown his way. After all, he already heard the building housing his law firm went largely unscathed. His own house, like most of Pétionville, waltzed through virtually untouched. *There is certainly a God for those deserving one.*

He knew very little about Richy Richardson. All expatriates, with the possible exception of some missionaries and the like, have sad tales as to how they found themselves in Haiti. That was certainly his case.

The waiter disrupted his solitude. "Can I bring you another drink, Mister Bennett?"

"Sure, why not? I have another hour to kill. Make it a double."

"Certainly, Mister Bennett."

His attention returned to Tim James. He learned a couple days before of the troubled young man through the manager at the beach club in Saint-Marc, a distinguished-looking Brit with a wispy moustache who called himself Sir John Winston. Vincent instantly concluded Sir John was to royalty what he was to the legal profession and dismissed the absurd title as harmless. After all, the man did represent the only high-profile resort in Haiti.

Their short conversation spun through his mind.

"The resort I represent finds itself with a personnel problem requiring your legal expertise," Sir John had said.

"And what problem would that be?"

"We have in our employ a young gentleman by the name of Mister Tim James. His unseemly behavior has become quite the embarrassment to the resort. A situation my employers no longer find tolerable."

"So, why not fire the bum and be rid of him?"

"Truth be told, the situation with this chap is a tad complicated."

"How so?"

"Mister James commenced his service with the club about three years ago. We hired him to head our dive operation. He subsequently lost his wife in a tragic accident, an accident from which the club could, as I am sure you could confirm, be sued for certain aspects of negligence. Mister James has not, up to this moment, pursued any legal action against the resort."

"Tell me, what's the problem? It sounds like you have a loyal employee on your hands."

Sir John repositioned himself on the leather-cushioned chair. "I wish that were so. I'm afraid Mister James' failure to seek legal recourse has more to do with his sorry state of mind than loyalty to his employers. You must understand that since this unfortunate episode involving his spouse, Mister James has become nothing less than a bloat. This sad state of affairs forced the resort to relieve him of his duties with the dive operation. He now serves in the maintenance department."

"You mean he's a janitor?"

"That would be a less gentle way of putting it."

"Where do I come in? This doesn't sound like much of a legal problem to me. If he hasn't sued the club by now, he probably never will. Why not cut him a severance check and send him packing to the mainland with a one-way ticket?"

"As I previously mentioned, the situation regarding this young man is rather complicated. In addition to his propensity toward inebriation, Mister James has amassed a considerable debt of a gambling nature. His creditor, a chap by the name of Bertram DuMarche, not exactly a gentleman I might add, managed to procure his passport as collateral and filed documents with the U.S. Consulate to officially record his debt. *Monsieur* DuMarche has certain political connections preventing this James fellow from being issued a replacement passport until his debt is cleared. With accruing interest, Mister James' debt now exceeds fifty thousand American dollars. In his present capacity as a maintenance man, that isn't likely to happen any time soon."

"No, I guess not. How about family? Maybe someone stateside would be good for a loan."

"A most unfortunate situation. Mister James has no siblings or surviving parents. He hasn't a soul to turn to."

"That's too bad. What do you have in mind?"

"Your services are being solicited to secure Mister James' departure from Haiti, legal or otherwise."

He liked the sound of this. "That could get very expensive."

Sir John did not hesitate. "The club is prepared to pay any reasonable fee to have this matter resolved. However, there is one non-negotiable stipulation."

"What would that be?"

"You are to retain Mister James in your, shall we say, custody, until he has departed Haiti safely. Matters could end rather tragically if he were to fall into the hands of the bloke to which he is indebted."

He always loved it when matters could end rather tragically for clients. He immediately turned the conversation to his fees. "I require a five-thousand-dollar retainer, in cash. You will be billed for all incidental expenses. We're probably looking at ten to fifteen grand when all is said and done."

Sir John didn't flinch. "The five thousand dollars will be delivered to your office Wednesday morning. I assume you would prefer payment in small denominations?"

"Tens and twenties will be fine."

****

Vincent summoned the waiter and handed him a piece of paper, along with a five-*gourde* tip. "Please give this note to Jacques Michel. Tell him I'll be back in the morning."

"Certainly, Mister Bennett."

He stood and stretched his creaking bones. It had been a long day, maybe longer for most others in Haiti, but that was their problem. He was not totally surprised his new client turned out to be a no-show, the earthquake notwithstanding. If the lout didn't make an appearance by morning, he would simply send a couple of his people to collect him, assuming he was still in one piece. After all, drunkards are never hard to find and, as everyone knows, God watches out for them and fools. *This clown is surely both.*

Tim James' case did strike him as a bit peculiar. He wondered why the club was so eager to be rid of him. They could simply let this gambling thug eliminate their problem. Sir John did not come across as the sympathetic type, either, but whatever the resort manager's motivation might be, he felt certain about two things. The club's money, in U.S. greenbacks no less, would spend as well as anyone else's and, better yet, as for the troubled Mister Tim James, he fit perfectly into what could very well prove to be the most lucrative score of his scam-filled career.

"That son-a-bitch better be alive, damn it."

Chapter 7

Ebony Man

Embalmed in fear, Tim wandered the dim passageways of Port-au-Prince and found himself deep inside the visceral labyrinth of *Cité Soleil*, the infamous slums. Entire families dwelled in any structure they could find, with even burnt-out cars and cardboard boxes serving as homes for many. Without warning, countless Haitians sprung from the shadows and surrounded him, the ivory whites of their eyes fixed squarely upon him, a lone *blanc* daring to encroach on their miserable milieu.

He sucked at the humid, tepid air in shallow, rapid pants. He felt his veins throbbing across his temples—metering his pounding pulse. Fear overrode his capacity to flee. More slum dwellers, emerging one by one from their ghostly shadows, formed an ever-tightening noose around him and, in unison, chanted, "*Blanc…Blanc…Blanc.*"

A towering figure—taller, darker, and even shinier than the others—emerged from the pack. The Haitian's skin glistened like the finest ebony. The others retreated to their shadows in deference to him.

He attempted to face the Haitian, but dropped his eyes upon experiencing the fire in the man's piercing, haunting stare. Tim's bare and bloodied feet sank into the caustic muck beneath him. The pungent odor of human excrement, only partially obscured by the fumes of the charcoal fires, permeated his lungs.

Desperate for daylight, he stole a glance at his wrist to catch the time, but a chalky strip of skin where his watch had been reflected his sorry plight, not the hour. Somehow he still had his carved mask, his sole keepsake of his parents. His eyes locked shut as he rubbed his left ring finger with his thumb to confirm what he already knew—his wedding band had been stripped from his finger—the last vestige of Sarah, gone.

Despite the ghastly situation, all but thoughts of Sarah fled his mind. He became entombed in one of his countless bouts of irrepressible depression. The apparition before him seemed all too real. Sarah's long, golden curls danced in the tropical breeze. Her full crimson lips and heart-shaped face provided a natural poutiness that drove him, and every other man, wild. He lost himself in her luminous cobalt eyes, reached out, only to see her fade away before he could feel the comfort of her gentle, loving embrace. Even with the passing of two tortuous years, he could not accept how everything had gone so wrong. Whatever fate should befall him now could never match the depths of horrifying despair he had already endured. The unsolved circumstances continuously replayed in his addled brain, the night his beautiful bride vanished.

He raised his head to meet the imposing Haitian's stare and calmly said, "I'm lost. I need your help."

The ebony figure released a satanic smile. His eyes widened and then narrowed again—that penetrating stare. He peered across to the gathering peasants. He uttered something in *Créole* that elicited a round of snickering. He returned his glare to Tim. "So the white man comes to the slums to see how we live?" His accent sounded more Jamaican than Haitian.

"I'm lost," Tim said again. "I have no idea where I am or how I got here."

The massive Haitian snatched the rawboned arm of an aging wench and held her in front of him. "Perhaps you come to sample our women?" Everyone laughed when he repeated his comment in *Créole*, including the remnant of a woman, who exposed a mouth devoid of teeth.

Appalled, Tim only managed to mutter, "No...No...No..."

"Ah, maybe it is the young girls the white man covets? Or, maybe it is the young boys?" When the ebony-skinned man once again translated his comments to the amassing horde, a more hostile howling emerged.

"What are we to do with you?" the spokesman asked. "Perhaps we might ask you to dine with us? We could offer you a splendid meal as you are accustomed to having in your mansion in Pétionville. Oh, but you see, we have no such food here. We hardly have any food at all. Perhaps you would like to eat one of us?" He translated this last statement with more zeal, much to everyone's merriment.

Tim squeezed his eyes shut, only to open them to the same horrid scene. "Please, I'm lost. I don't have any money on me, but I'll pay you tomorrow if you get me to my hotel."

Hushed whispers provided an unpleasant echo to his pleading.

"You have us believe you have no money? All white men are rich. Where is your money?"

"I don't know. I was in an accident. Someone must have taken my wallet. They took everything. My watch…my…my…everything."

"But you have money at your hotel?"

Clutching at this first positive chord in the conversation, he blurted out, "I can get money for you tomorrow. I'll give you a hundred dollars if you get me to my hotel in Pétionville." He did not have a hundred dollars to his name, but desperation has no price tag.

Although they may not have comprehended the exact amount, the word *dollars* appeared to be appreciated by all. The murmuring ceased and the slum dwellers scampered back into their shadows when their leader barked a resonating command.

The massive Haitian glared at him, but smiled after a moment, displaying a white keyboard of teeth—one capped in gold. He beckoned to a small boy, ten years old at most, to come forward. "This is Antoine. He will take you to your hotel. It is still in one piece, unlike most of our dear city. Tomorrow morning, I will come to there to collect my hundred dollars. You will not disappoint me?"

What did he mean by "still in one piece?" He would worry about that later. "I won't disappoint you. Just get me the hell out of here. My name is Tim James. I'll—"

"What name you call yourself means nothing to me. I know who you are…what you are…as do many others."

Tim felt the pierce of the huge Haitian's stare long after Antoine led him by the hand through the amorphous mass of *Cité Soleil*. It seemed no one slept and everything had run amuck. Fires, large and small, flamed in every direction. A Caucasian being ushered through the slums of Port-au-Prince piqued the interest of all they encountered. In some quarters, peasants lined the thin lanes between their tin can houses chanting the ubiquitous chorus— *blanc…blanc…blanc*—as they passed by. Some tried to stop the mismatched pair, either out of curiosity, or to demonstrate some self-vested authority. Antoine simply snapped a few words and they were instantly allowed to pass. The only words Tim discerned were those he surmised to be the imposing man's name, Octave Polynice.

After a time, his battered bare feet turned crippling. Antoine, himself shoeless, displayed little concern for his cohort's pain until it slowed their progress to an unacceptable pace. They came to a stop at a small wooden shanty and Antoine shouted something to the occupant inside. A bent-over fossil of a man brought out a bald tire and motioned for Tim to show his feet. The man positioned a small, thin board against one of Tim's bloodied feet to record its measure, and then placed the board against the tire and cut two equal lengths with a sharpened strip of rusted steel. After rounding the front edges, he made two parallel incisions on the top inside corner of each piece and attached loops within the incisions to allow the makeshift sandals to be fastened.

With Antoine yanking at his arm, Tim could barely mumble *merci*, as they trudged off into the darkness. They paid nothing to the old man and it seemed no remuneration had been anticipated.

He expected to encounter some semblance of civilization once they entered downtown Port-au-Prince, but Antoine displayed an uncanny ability to select one abandoned avenue after another. Many buildings stood in shambles. They eventually wandered onto a particularly gloomy cobblestone road where he managed to make out the familiar sounding road sign, *Rue de l'Enterrement*. They trekked down the deserted avenue and stopped before a huge stoned edifice, much of it crumbled. He recalled seeing a picture postcard of the ancient landmark, *la Cathedral Nationale. What in the hell happened to it?* On the opposite side of the church, in stark contrast, a moon-colored concrete wall loomed, much of it also collapsed. He could see Antoine's eyes widened, for behind what remained of the yard-thick partition dwelled the dead.

After pausing to contemplate their limited options, they forged ahead at a more rapid clip. They approached the far corner of the cemetery wall when a mass of shadows sprung toward them. He felt his hand gripped with all the force Antoine's nearly fleshless fingers could muster. The faceless shadows merged into a solitary fog, engulfed the helpless duo, and soundlessly ushered them into the graveyard.

Trembling, hand-in-hand, they meandered amongst the graves, avoiding all eye contact with their ghostly captors. They encountered a vault towering above the surrounding tombs. A bonfire at its base burst into blinding flames. They sank to their knees under the silent urgings of the shadows behind them. Other shadows positioned themselves near the blazing fire and began to pound drums at an earsplitting beat.

A dozen or so young women adorned in white, cotton dresses seemingly rose out of graves, formed a procession, and danced in synchrony to the pounding drums. A colossal, jet-black figure stepped out of the flames. His monstrous shadow loomed behind on the stone vault. He wore no shoes, only trousers ripped halfway up his calves, a red bandana around his sweat-oozing bald head and, fastened around his neck, a silver cross that reflected the radiant flames. Inexplicably, he had not burned.

Entranced, they remained kneeling. The mysterious Haitian clutched a burning ember from the bonfire with a bare hand, slithered to within an arm's length of them, stopped, opened his mouth, and inserted the flaming rod. He spat out a mouthful of glowing shards and unleashed a demonic smile punctuated by a gold-capped tooth.

Tim's jaw dropped. *It's him—the Ebony Man.* He glanced to his side. Antoine had vanished.

"Welcome to my other world," Octave Polynice said with an accompanying snarl.

Tim knelt deathly still. His heart pounded in tandem with the thundering drums. The drummers intensified their pulsating beat. Octave slithered near the bonfire where one of the white-clad women handed him a bottle half-filled with a clear liquid. He smeared it over his chiseled chest and arms, then reached down and grasped a burning ember. He placed it against his heart, setting himself ablaze. Whenever the flames subsided, he drank from the bottle and spewed the liquid onto his massive torso, causing the flames to flash anew. He unleashed a laugh heard by all—a laugh heard by the dead.

The drummers stopped.

"*Bonsoir, Legba,*" the Ebony Man roared. "*Bonsoir, Damballah. C'est moi, votre domestique*, Octave Polynice. *Papa Legba, ouvri barrière pour nous. Ago yé.*"

The women formed a circle around their leader and chanted, "*Damballah, nous p'vini.*"

Tim understood none of the words, but knew a *Vodou* ceremony had commenced. He had seen numerous *Vodou* shows at the beach club, but those were simply acts put on for gullible tourists. This, he sullenly grasped, could be nothing short of the real thing.

The women again danced and chanted as the drummers recommenced a rhythmic pounding. The Ebony Man, no doubt a powerful *Vodou* priest, continued to spew flame-flashing liquid over his sweat-oozing body. The dancing continued while he gyrated in and around the bonfire. After a time, one of the girls fell on the ground, writhing and screaming, as if she had been set ablaze. She ripped off the top of her dress and exposed her perspiring breasts. The other girls tightened a dancing circle around her, the *Vodou* priest, and the ceremonial fire. The piercing drumbeats intensified in never-ending increments.

Tim rose to his feet, the mask left on the ground and, in a state of sheer delirium, broke through the procession. He stood before the half-naked girl. The drummers stopped. The dancers stopped. The possessed girl sat up, now calm in her bewilderment. Octave

Polynice vacated his flames, approached the offending *blanc,* and discharged his penetrating stare—a stare Tim returned with equal force.

No one noticed the ceremonial cock, previously tethered to a branch anchored in the ground, break free. With mystical force, as if blasted from a cannon, the fighting bird struck Tim across his left temple, sending him, once again, to the dark and lonely domain of the unconscious.

Chapter 8

Cross

A collage of open-eyed corpses, bonfires, and demonic images danced through Tim's dreams. He forced his eyes open the next morning certain even worse horrors awaited him. Relief poured out in a long breath when he found himself in the comfort of a Caribbean-blue room, neatly appointed with hand-hewn mahogany furnishings, complete with a ceiling fan, although it whisked no life-renewing breeze across his aching body. Selected memories began to emerge as he struggled to determine if his ordeal the past night had simply been a terrible nightmare brought about by cheap Haitian rum.

He swung his legs over the side of the bed and rubbed his face with both hands to hasten the flow of blood and consciousness. Light peeking through the nearly closed window shade told him it must be midmorning. Painful spasms spiraled up his body when he rose to his feet. He shuffled to the window and flipped the blind open. The room overlooked a concrete courtyard with a lavish landscape of bougainvillea, frangipani, and hibiscus, all brilliantly in bloom. In the right-hand corner a lone flamboyant's mandarin-orange blossoms flamed in the breeze. He paused to absorb the carousel of colors, the sunlight, and the feeling of safety provided by the concrete walls enclosing the courtyard, assuring himself the scenes popping through his mind could only be remnants of a convoluted, horrific dream.

He glanced around the room. His gaze instantly fixed on a far corner where a pair of makeshift sandals constructed from sections of old tires had been tossed. His stomach turned to stone as more vivid and detailed scenes of his hellish night permeated his mind. *Holy shit.*

He rushed to the bathroom, flicked up the light switch, only to learn no power existed, and faced the shadowy mirror. A bruised and filthy likeness returned his stare. He squeezed his eyes shut, visualizing a glossy, black giant of a man with haunting eyes and a devilish smile filled with flawless ivory teeth, save for one capped in gold. Tim's eyes widened at the startling realization that around his neck dangled the silver cross belonging to none other than the Ebony Man.

A sharp rapping at the outside bedroom door jolted him. He regained some of his composure at the second volley of knocks. "Yes, who is it?"

"Mister James, I am Jacques Michel, the assistant manager of the hotel. I apologize for disturbing you, but you have a visitor, Mister Vincent Bennett. Should I ask him to return at another time?"

He had virtually forgotten why he came to Port-au-Prince. The sooner he could see his attorney and take care of whatever paperwork needed to be done, the sooner he could get the hell out of Haiti. "No. I need to meet with Mister Bennett. Please let him know I'll be down to the lobby in a few minutes."

"As you wish, Mister James."

He hurried back to the bathroom. After his hellish night he needed to clean up. After showering in cold water, he searched the room for something decent to wear. What remained of his clothes, shredded and bloodstained, emitted putrid odors. He looked inside an oversized armoire and found a white terry-cloth bathrobe with the hotel's name embroidered on the upper front pocket. It would have to do.

Clean, but unshaven, he limped down the mahogany stairway to the main lobby about twenty minutes later than promised. Wearing only a white bathrobe and a silver cross around his neck, he hobbled barefoot to the registration desk where he located a white-uniformed Haitian he assumed to be Jacques Michel. "I'm Tim James. Can you show me to Mister G. Vincent Bennett?"

Jacques Michel made a head-to-toe inspection of him before answering. "Certainly, Mister James. Right this way."

He led him to a corner table on the veranda, where a pudgy man, a couple notches past middle-age, stared blankly into a half-full cup of coffee. Jacques Michel interrupted the attorney's meditation. "Excuse me, Mister Bennett, this is Mister James to see you."

The attorney's initial expression of bewilderment turned to one of concern.

"What in God's good name happened to you? Got caught in the earthquake, no doubt."

"I guess you might say I had a bad night." He had no desire to recount the horrid ordeal he experienced. Knowing nothing about any earthquake, the mention of one did start to make some sense of things.

"I would guess so. Please, take a seat."

He sat across from the lawyer. A waiter appeared.

"You look like you could use a good breakfast," Vincent said. "Please order something. It's on me."

A stiff drink instantly came to mind, but he thought better of it. "A cup of coffee would be fine. Black."

"You can warm mine up too, please," Vincent said to the waiter.

The waiter left to fetch the coffeepot from the charcoal stove.

"Where are these papers I need to sign? I can't get off this damn island soon enough."

The attorney returned a jaded expression. "I'm afraid there's been a little snag in your paperwork, Mister James."

"What do you mean? A little snag?"

The conversation paused as the waiter returned with their coffee.

"Your case is a little more complicated than I first anticipated," Vincent said. "It seems this matter of you being over fifty thousand dollars in debt is making things rather difficult. Now, this damnable earthquake is causing some added inconvenience."

"Earthquake? How bad?"

"Nothing to worry about. This is Haiti. Shit happens."

He didn't give the earthquake further thought, but concluded being battered and half-dressed did not provide the makings of a good first impression. "Look, I know I don't have the money to pay your fees right away, but once I get back to the States, I'll be good for them, with interest."

"My legal fees are not the problem, Mister James. I decided to take your case *pro bono*. I feel a certain obligation to help fellow Americans who get themselves into jams here in Haiti. You certainly fit that description."

He felt a rare fragment of relief. Life had not been kind to him. Haiti had been cruelest of all. *Is my luck about to change?* "I don't know how I can ever thank you enough, Mister Bennett."

"Please, don't mention it. The law profession is not about making money. That was one of the first things I learned at Yale."

"What do I do? I'll do anything, laws or no laws."

"Calm down, son. Don't forget I'm a lawyer. I took a sacred oath to uphold the law. On the other hand, here in Haiti, laws are always subject to interpretation. With the proper payment of, shall we say, facilitation fees, anything is possible."

"But these…ah…facilitation fees, sound like it could get expensive. I can't expect you to pay these fees and I sure as shit don't have the money."

Vincent finished his coffee and motioned to the waiter for a refill. "The facilitation fees are the least of your problems."

"What do you mean…the least of my problems?"

"What I mean is this gentleman you owe the fifty thousand dollars to *is* your problem. He is not going to take kindly to you skipping out of the country without paying your debt."

"What do you suggest?"

"I think I have a solution to enable you to cover the costs of the facilitation fees, while at the same time keeping you out of sight."

"What do you have in mind? Like I said, I'll do anything."

Vincent glanced around the veranda and said in a hushed tone, "This may sound strange, but I want you to hide out on the big offshore island called La Gonave. Do you know it?"

"La Gonave? Yeah, I know that island. I used to dive all around it. I never stepped foot on its shores, though."

"I'm sure I don't have to tell you that La Gonave is even more destitute than most of the Haiti you've already experienced."

"Believe me, what I've experienced of Haiti can't get any worse." He fought to block a vision of the Ebony Man's demonic stare. "I can hack anything if I know it will eventually get me the hell out of here. How do I get there? Where will I stay?"

"I have everything arranged. You will, of course, need to remain *incognito*. Your name will be Tom Jamison. You'll pose as a graduate student from Syracuse University working on your master's thesis in anthropology. You'll be working as a maintenance man for a children's clinic in exchange for room and board. This will be in return for the opportunity to conduct your research. It's a perfect cover."

"But, I don't know beans about anthropology." He scrunched his forehead, feeling certain this plan was doomed to failure. "What am I supposed to be studying?"

"You won't need to know beans about anthropology. You only need to act as you do. You would be surprised at how few questions people ask when you come across as if you know what you are doing. In my profession, I have to constantly be on guard for charlatans."

He felt a little more at ease, but still had concerns. "What will I tell people I'm doing?"

"No problem, my good man. This is all you need to know. Before Columbus, *Taíno* Indians inhabited this area. The Spaniards, and later the French, felt obligated to enslave them. They did not treat them very well and eventually they all died. The French later brought in African slaves to do their dirty work. You know the rest of that story. Anyway, there is a lot of smashed, pre-Columbian pottery strewn all over La Gonave. You can tell people you're collecting samples and sending them to Syracuse for more detailed analysis. Of course, you'll inform them you'll be returning the artifacts to a Haitian museum after you've written your thesis. That's all the information people will need, or care, to know. Just act like you're some sort of intellectual highbrow."

"What if someone asks to see some of these artifacts? What do I do then?"

"Actually, to make your charade appear legitimate, I already arranged for you to collect artifacts from the opening of a particular cave not far from where you'll be staying."

"Will I basically just be biding my time over there at this children's clinic?"

Vincent's expression turned more serious. "Not at all. First, the artifacts will go to the Port-au-Prince Museum of Pre-Columbian Art. Fortunately, it sustained minor damage from the quake. I happen to be one of the museum's founding directors. The museum will pay a finder's fee for the artifacts. That should more than cover the costs to get your exit documents in order. Who knows, maybe you'll even make enough to pay off some of your debt. Secondly, you'll be doing a great service to the needy children of La Gonave by helping to maintain the clinic. I'm always looking for small ways to help those who cannot help themselves. I prefer to do this without drawing any attention to myself. I have lived here in Haiti for the past fourteen years because I have a deep commitment to its people. I'm going to tell you something only a few of my closest associates know."

Remaining silent, Tim straightened himself on the wooden chair.

Vincent bowed his head and paused for a moment. Taking a deep breath, he raised his gaze to the ceiling, as if being able to see to the sky, before turning to Tim. "In addition to my law degree, I hold a Doctorate of Divinity. I am an ordained Methodist minister."

"You're a minister *and* a lawyer?"

"I know. It's an unusual combination. Some people might even call it an oxymoron. I have to tell you all the same, it has allowed me to serve those in need, both physically and spiritually. By the way, I like that cross you're wearing."

Chapter 9

Blessed

No man could be more proud that night than Ti Bon Baptiste. Spread out on his straw mat with one arm around his wife and the other cupped behind his head, he continuously replayed the events of the previous day. When Marie Joseph returned from the market, her reaction to seeing their house whiter than bleached coral surpassed even his wildest expectations. Speechless, she circled the house with Ti Ti cradled in her arms. Meanwhile, he stood silently in the doorway, fighting back a grin. After making her last dizzying circumference, his wife stopped in front of the house, handed Ti Ti to Premíse, and swallowed Ti Bon up in her arms. Before she could speak a word, he let it slip there were more surprises inside. He insisted they wait until the boys returned from school, so the entire family could share in this joyous occasion. While the girls danced around the house, he and Marie Joseph, along with the ever-sucking Ti Ti, relaxed in the shade on the east side of their home.

****

Returning from school, Piérre and Jean stopped at almost the identical spot their mother and siblings had before them. They glanced at each other, both wondering if they had somehow gotten lost and walked to the wrong house, when their sisters raced toward them with screams of delight. The four children, hand-in-hand, ran to their parents' outstretched arms.

Ti Bon proudly bade his family to enter their home. In the center of the nearly empty, single room, thirteen cardboard boxes—and a like number of plastic bags and rubber bands—had been meticulously arranged. Ti Ti broke free from the arms of his overwhelmed mother and crawled to the closest box to use as a plaything. Marie Joseph snatched her infant and then asked Ti Bon to take the other children outside to play so she could contemplate the various uses of the objects before her.

The Baptiste family dined on their week's supply of meat that night, celebrating the good fortune having graced them. With a judicious amount of embellishment, Ti Bon recounted the story about how he came into possession of the packages of white powder and ended by giving orders the story was not to be shared outside the family. Their neighbors could simply wonder how they came upon their new-found wealth.

Once night fell, and with his wife's warm body pressed against him, Ti Bon listened intently until he could discern the soft breathing of each of his five healthy children. With a smile firmly entrenched, he joined his family in slumber.

****

The Baptiste's sparkling white abode attracted a number of villagers the next morning, some curious, others envious, but all duly impressed. Rumors ran amuck as to how the Baptiste's could afford such an ostentatious improvement to their dwelling. Although most came to gawk, a few neighbors sought Ti Bon out to see if he could also whiten their homes. He calculated he had enough powder left to coat six or seven huts, and after considerable haggling, a charge of ten *gourdes* for coating each hut was agreed upon as fair compensation.

While he went into the whitewashing business, Marie Joseph bartered with the cardboard boxes, plastic bags, and rubber bands. She kept two of each for herself and gave one set to her sister, Michelle. Altogether, the white powder and packaging netted sixty-seven *gourdes*, one live chicken, two papayas, and a coconut.

Marie Joseph handled all the family finances, and with the money they just earned, their cash position totaled two-hundred-eighty-three *gourdes*. After nearly two years of scrimping and saving, they finally accumulated sufficient wealth to purchase uniforms so Premíse and Colette could attend school with their brothers. The school itself cost nothing, but the entire family was required to regularly attend services at the Greater Evangelical Mission Church and contribute one tenth of their weekly income. Considering most weeks passed with little or no earnings, this seemed like quite the deal.

Reassured of the accuracy of her cash count, Marie Joseph took a mental inventory of their other forms of material wealth. The two-acre farm, inherited when Ti Bon's father passed away, remained their largest asset. The roughly six-acre parcel had been equally divided among three surviving sons. Ti Bon, the eldest, had first choice and wisely chose the section with the residence. Both brothers promptly sold their plots and moved their families to Port-au-Prince to find employment. Not hearing from either brother for several years, Marie Joseph assumed their lives must be too grand to be bothered with poor relatives living on La Gonave. She sometimes regretted their choice to stay on the farm.

Recently, her husband made some additional money by selling broken bits of pottery he found on their farm. She felt blessed to be married to such a good provider. Besides cash, their liquid assets consisted of one sow and now a complement of three chickens. The scraggy sow, which the children affectionately called Bon Bon, weighed about one-hundred-fifty pounds. It essentially served as their savings account and could be counted on to produce one or two litters each year. With piglets selling for fifty *gourdes* each, the sow proved to be quite the moneymaker. If in immediate need of a cash influx, it could always be sold alive or slaughtered for market.

Marie Joseph surveyed their domicile with feelings of great accomplishment, but accompanying her excitement a growing sense of anxiety arose, for tomorrow she would have an audience with the Greater Evangelical Mission director, the most powerful *blanc* on La Gonave. They were blessed, but there were more blessings to be had, should Mildred Sponheimer be disposed to grant them.

Chapter 10

Minister

Despite the turmoil in the quake's aftermath, the money arrived by special courier at the law offices of LeClerk, DuBois, and Bennett early Thursday morning. Beaming, Vincent spread the greenbacks in neat bundles across his glass-topped desk. Sir John proved to be a man of his word, even under the worst of circumstances. It all was there—five thousand dollars. He could not imagine a more pleasing sight, except of course, even bigger piles of dough or, better yet, piles of gold.

He opened his wall safe and stacked the loot inside. Earlier, he turned over to the firm's accountant the ten thousand dollar check from Richy Richardson. He had to share Richy's advance with his partners, but not the club's cash. That is how the game played out in Haiti and that is how he played it even before arriving at this desolate island.

After securing the lock of his safe, he strolled across the hall to gloat about the Richardson account. He tapped at a partially-opened door, poked his head inside, and spotted Rinchard LeClerk, senior partner, seated at an ornate desk. Rinchard's rarely used grin indicated word of the sizable check had already spread.

The obese Haitian rose to his feet, his grin still firmly entrenched, and extended his right hand. "Vincent, my good friend, please come in."

The partners clasped in mutual triumph.

Rinchard repositioned himself on the comfort of his leather-cushioned armchair. "Please, Vincent, take a seat."

"Thanks, Rinchard. I can only stay for a moment, though."

"This new account looks to be quite lucrative for us."

He noted Rinchard's emphasis on *us*.

"What legal matters does this case involve? An ugly divorce?"

He instantly concocted another story, not intending to mention a word about the gold amulet or, for that matter, his club caper. "Not this time, Rinchard. It appears my client has gotten himself into a little fix with customs agents in Miami. Something to do with exporting leather goods contaminated with anthrax."

"That's nasty stuff. I assume your client also failed to list the items in question on his export declaration?"

"Indeed, that's the case." He returned Rinchard's knowing nod. "I will handle that transgression in the usual fashion."

"Of course, but what of the Miami litigation? How will that be handled?"

"I need to retain the services of an attorney licensed in Florida for that." He maintained a dummy law office in Miami for such occasions as this. He would be writing checks from the firm's account to himself for services never to be rendered.

Rinchard's grin turned south. "That will cut into our profits."

"Can't be helped."

"No, I guess it can't."

"By the way, Rinchard, I'll be out of the office for a few days. I have some legwork to do on this Richardson account, along with some other caseloads that have been backing up. I'm also hoping we can score some contracts with the U.S. government. Money will be streaming in for earthquake relief. There must be some legal problems cropping up where we can be of service."

Rinchard sank back into his cushioned desk chair. "You are a busy man, Vincent, and, I must say, always thinking."

"That I am."

****

The armed guard opened the metal gate, allowing Vincent to drive into his walled enclave at the outskirts of Pétionville. Like nearly all expatriates in Haiti, including most missionaries, he imprisoned himself in the comfort and safety of a fortress. He pulled up in his driveway and inspected his gardener toiling at his daily assigned task—thwarting the lush foliage's never-ending effort to revert into an uncontrollable jungle.

After parking his car, he sauntered across the stone sidewalk, opened the carved mahogany door, and entered the marble-tiled foyer. He spotted his live-in maid mopping the kitchen floor while humming a *Créole* tune. "Hattie, I'm home."

Hattie continued at her chores without a glance in his direction.

He gazed around his home with pride. Only the finest of Haitian paintings decorated his gleaming white walls. His hand-hewn mahogany furnishings, ornate even by an aristocrat's standards, were all made to order. He truly lived in splendor.

A winding marble staircase led to the master suite. He entered the room, stood before a full-length mirror, and practiced looking ministerial. The transformation from bogus attorney to bogus minister took all of five minutes.

"Dearly beloved, we are gathered here today..."

Chapter 11

Crossing

Tim slept, mercifully without terrorizing dreams, from Wednesday afternoon until a few minutes shy of the noon hour the next day. Soon after awakening, he discovered a bundle of khaki clothing neatly folded on the chair next to the armoire. A pair of hiking boots, size eleven, rested underneath the chair, replacing his bald-tire sandals. A small, canvas satchel and a safari-style hat sat perched on the ornate dresser. He unzipped the shoulder bag, finding inside an ample supply of toiletries, underwear, and socks.

He was impressed by the thoroughness of G. Vincent Bennett, or Reverend Vince Burkholder, as he'd requested to be addressed henceforth. The minister's explanation for his name change seemed no more bizarre than any other oddity occurring in Haiti.

"I know this may sound strange," the minister told him, "but my life has become simpler with two separate identities. It seems, no matter how hard I try, I can't convince people I can be a crackerjack attorney while maintaining my sacred vows to Christ our Savior, so I quit trying."

He shaved, treated himself to a prolonged shower in cold water, and then donned his new wardrobe. He mocked himself in the full-sized mirror attached to the inside door of the armoire. "So, this is how an anthropologist is supposed to look?"

He had a candlelit table to himself that evening for dinner in the otherwise crowded hotel restaurant. A multitude of news reporters and relief agency staff had already rushed in from the States and elsewhere. Several Haitian diners glanced in his direction. They conversed amongst themselves in hushed tones. He figured they were poking fun at his silly outfit.

"Would you like to start with a cocktail, sir?" a sable-skinned waiter asked, his coffee-bean eyes fixated on the silver cross fastened around Tim's neck.

He figured cold brews would be hard to come by on La Gonave and felt obliged to imbibe. "I'd like a beer."

"Foreign or domestic?"

"Make it a Prestige."

After downing a second Prestige with his dinner of spiced chicken and rice, he mulled over the conversation he had the previous day with the affable attorney. Hiding out on La Gonave struck him as quite the clever scheme. Bertram DuMarche and, for that matter, the Ebony Man, would never dream of looking for him there. He felt as if his tide of misfortune had finally begun to ebb. *How can I go wrong with an attorney, an American no less, who is also an ordained minister?*

He charged the meal and beverages to his room, as instructed by his attorney. *When you're penniless there's no need to stand on pride.* He owed over fifty thousand dollars to an unscrupulous gambler, but the hundred dollars he owed to Octave Polynice concerned him most. He exhausted every frightful fate imaginable by the time his head hit the feathery pillow late Thursday night.

****

Tim stiffened when a series of short raps rattled his door. He realized morning had arrived at the second volley of knocks.

A familiar voice emanated from the other side of the door. "Mister James, I have been requested to wake you. I have brought coffee. Mister Bennett will arrive in thirty minutes to take you to your destination."

Upon hearing Jacques Michel's voice, he released his swallowed breath, jumped to his feet, and opened the door. He took the tray, gulped down the tepid coffee, but only ate a single bite of the cold, hard toast. He felt renewed. *Today will be the start of my escape from this hellhole.* He threw on his clothes, gathered his new belongings, and bounded down the stairs with hardly a hint of a limp.

He passed through the front door of the hotel and spotted Reverend Vince Burkholder leaning against a white luxury sedan and holding a small bible at his side. The minister wore a long-sleeve white shirt, black trousers, and black shoes. His white socks completed his clerical ensemble.

A collection of street vendors, intent upon selling all varieties and sizes of woodcarvings, encircled Tim the moment he stepped out into the parking lot. He raised his hands in the air. "Sorry. I'm not buying anything today. I have no money."

One of the vendors understood English and translated the *blanc's* assertion of being penniless to the others. All animated much amusement. The English-speaking vendor spoke for the group. "You have on new clothes, new boots, and new hat. Of course you have money. We are just poor people trying to earn a living. We lost everything in the earthquake. Please buy something from us. Look at this fine mask. I carved it myself. Ten dollars. Please, take it."

The newly varnished mask looked all too familiar. "You didn't carve this. Where'd you get it?"

The Haitian grinned. "Take it. It's yours. *Monsieur* Polynice wanted you to have it back."

"Thanks." He took it and then glanced about—no Ebony Man in sight. *Thank God.*

Jacques Michel, standing on the hotel's veranda, ordered the pesky throng to vacate the premises. The street vendors, including the one who had given Tim the mask, unleashed a medley of indignant replies before scattering to their stations outside the gate. The minister strolled over to Tim only after the crowd had completely dispersed. "Good morning, Mister Jamison."

He felt uneasy being addressed by his bogus name. Doubts surfaced whether he would be able to pull off this ruse. "Good morning, Reverend Burkholder." Speaking the minister's name didn't feel right either.

"I trust, young man, you had a good night's rest?"

"I don't remember a thing. I must have slept like an old dog. So, ministers get to drive fancy cars just like attorneys?"

"In Haiti they do. Hop in, we have a boat to catch."

The shiny, luxury vehicle pulled out of the hotel gate. The street vendors spotted Tim slouched on the leather passenger seat. They pointed at him and unleashed a round of jeers until the vehicle passed from sight.

The two-hour drive to Saint-Marc proceeded without further incident, although not being behind the steering wheel made him feel all the more vulnerable to Haitian drivers and their mob mentality. Now, in the aftermath of the earthquake, everything had tumbled into even further disarray. He wondered if any of them could manage to drive without blasting his or her horn at the sight of every vehicle, pedestrian, chicken, or rock encountered. He wished they would use their brakes as liberally.

The minister pulled in front of a concrete dock with a wooden sloop bobbing at its end. An undersized, unidentifiable motor hung from the boat's transom. Its prop barely extended below the water's surface.

"This isn't exactly a luxury liner, I must admit," the minister said. "I made arrangements with the Nazarenes for this boat. The boat over there could get us to La Gonave in thirty minutes. It belongs to the Greater Evangelical Mission. As it turns out, these particular missionaries aren't much into sharing."

Tim peered across to the adjoining dock where a thirty-foot yacht sporting twin inboard/outboard motors dwarfed the native sailing vessel. The motorcraft exuded the luxury style he'd become accustomed to when he worked as the dive master and environmental educator at the nearby beach club. Two years had passed since he held that position, but it seemed like twenty.

His gaze shifted to a spindly Haitian standing in front of the sloop. The man's head, shaved well above his ears, sported a matted flattop about the width of a hand. His sole attire consisted of a pair of ragged, cut-off shorts drooped halfway down his bone-protruding hips. He had not seen the man standing there when they first arrived, nor had he seen him get out of the wooden craft.

They slid out of the car and approached the partially clad sailor.

"Welcome," the Haitian said. "I am Cristophe, the captain of the boat. I will be taking you to La Gonave today."

Tim never ceased being amazed at how well so many Haitian's spoke English. He recalled how Leonard, a waiter at the club, spoke five languages, all fluently and self-taught.

"I'm Reverend Burkholder," the minister said. He wrapped his pudgy right arm around Tim's shoulder. "My companion here is Mister Tom Jamison. We appreciate you taking us to the island."

"It is my pleasure," Cristophe said, a congenial grin blooming across his face. "I understand you came to assist the Doctor Thomas McCoy Children's Clinic. *Père* Thomas saved two of my children. All of La Gonave was greatly saddened by his passing. God be praised, his daughter has taken over the clinic. Please, let me help you with your bags."

****

The twelve-mile crossing of the La Gonave Channel, under the sweltering heat of the midday sun, took three glacial-paced hours. The tattered sails remained taut, but the puny motor's propeller popped out of the water with the passing of every wave. The minister, ignoring Tim's counsel, perched himself on the windward bow, where he promptly experienced a battery of waves crashing over the gunwale. He crab-walked aft and leeward to join them, oozing water through his ministerial garb like a bloated soaker hose.

Halfway out into the channel, a pod of dolphins emerged on either side of the sloop, materializing like crescent-shaped torpedoes, skipping in and out of the sparkling, indigo water. Apparently tiring of this game after thirty minutes or so, they disappeared into the depths of the azure sea as suddenly as they appeared. As the foreboding island loomed closer, Tim realized today was his first time aboard a vessel since that unthinkable night over two years ago. His stomach knotted when his thoughts turned from the sea to Sarah. It had been love at first sight. He previously had worked as an instructor for a small, dive shop in Key Largo, when Sarah, gorgeous beyond belief, waltzed into his life to register for one of his SCUBA courses. He promptly jettisoned his self-imposed prohibition of dating students, and three months later the newly dive-certified Sarah became his wife.

When he first arrived with his new bride in Haiti nearly three years ago, he thought he found his personal paradise. Less than two years after completing an undergraduate degree in marine biology at Florida International University, he obtained the job of his dreams—the dive master and environmental educator at the swanky beach club. The resort on the outskirts of the village of Saint-Marc, in a lush, tropical setting miles away from the squalor of Port-au-Prince, provided excellent pay and benefits, top-of-the-line boats and diving equipment, and all the sensational perks one associates with resort living.

Taking a job in Haiti seemed like a fate fulfilled. He'd long felt an urge, more like a pull, to travel there. It probably had something to do with the carved mask. It came from the island, or so his parents had said, but he never knew how they came to possess it—even why they would own such a thing. Whatever, it represented his sole physical reminder of them.

Sarah shared his excitement when they first arrived. The club manager, Sir John Winston, met them at the former François Duvalier International Airport. He'd been easy to spot, clashing with the swarm of Haitians waiting to greet arriving passengers, by virtue of being the only Caucasian. The fiftyish, medium-built British expatriate would cut quite the figure in any crowd. Standing over six-feet tall, his slicked-back, raven mane and matching pencil-striped moustache contrasted with his ivory skin as much as his silky black slacks and chalky, four-pocket guayabera. After a brief exchange to reacquaint themselves, Sir John whisked them off to the resort in the opulence of an expensive sedan, all the while expounding with his impeccable accent upon the virtues of being a member of the club family. Tim and Sarah soaked in every word, hardly noticing the multitudes of destitute peasants spilling onto the streets, or the absolute wretchedness in which these people lived.

The newlyweds found, in the early months, work to be play at Haiti's raucous club. He spent his days running the dive operation, supervising three dive leaders, and conducting all the diving certifications, along with sharing his passion for underwater photography with the resort's guests at least two evenings each week. Sarah, for her part, served as an activities coordinator, specializing in assisting Spanish-speaking guests.

Sir John initially remained non-committal when Tim made the condition he would accept the position only if the resort also hired his wife. Sir John's hesitation disintegrated the instant he met her. "Sarah possesses all the qualifications we seek in an employee at the club," he later confided. "She's exceptionally attractive, bilingual and, despite being an American, having previously lived in Latin America as a daughter of a wealthy and influential diplomat, provides her with that certain *je ne sais quoi* necessary to properly serve our clientele."

Tim's grin vanished. "What about me? I'm an American. I'm not bilingual. I've never even stepped foot outside of the US of A before."

Sir John, cracking a sly smile, simply said, "For adventure, our guests do prefer Americans."

His mind continued replaying events of the early days of their marriage. Sir John had taken a special liking to his *all-American, blond-haired newlyweds*, and arranged for their schedules to be as compatible as possible, so they could enjoy the romantic ambiance that is the club's trademark. At some point, Sarah became disgruntled with her job, the club and, in particular, Haiti. He dismissed her unhappiness, assuming she simply needed more time to adjust. Initially, Sarah shared his enthusiasm for underwater adventures, but even that waned with time. By their first anniversary, intense arguments replaced heated lovemaking and, with Sarah constantly threatening to desert Haiti with or without him, he found himself spending more time with his dive leaders.

Meanwhile, she gravitated to anyone with whom she could converse in Spanish.

Their marital relationship progressively deteriorated over the weeks, when one day Sarah abruptly rushed into his arms. With tear-filled eyes, she begged for forgiveness—begged to return to nuptial bliss. Thereafter, they regularly shared long evening strolls along the white, powdery beaches, often followed by late nights of searing passion. Together, their lives became a magnificent fairytale—a fairytale ending much too quickly and much too tragically.

****

A fog of grief engulfed him and, with no crutch of alcohol to lean upon, Tim summoned the will to shirk free of his despair by concentrating on the island ahead, its jagged edges rising nearly three thousand feet above the sea. La Gonave appeared to be virtually devoid of trees, a bald mountain roughly twenty-by-sixty miles in size. He wondered how it could support the nearly one hundred thousand Haitians the minister mentioned lived there.

Cristophe lowered the main sail upon approaching the mangrove-fringed, protected harbor of Anse-à-Galets—the ramshackle village being La Gonave's finest. In stark contrast to the mangroves, a concrete dock towered over the water's surface. A weathered brass placard imbedded into a piling advertised the World Bank as the monstrosity's proud sponsor. The dock could virtually accommodate an ocean-going vessel, yet the shallow harbor limited it to serving wooden sloops and other small, native craft. Opposite the dock, a sandy beach provided a landing for a fleet of ancient dugout canoes, although no trees large enough to be put to such use remained anywhere in sight.

A heap of discarded conch shells bejeweled a corner of the beach, with most of them lacking the characteristic lip signifying the mollusk's sexual maturity. Tim had grown accustomed to witnessing such unmistakable evidence of over-exploitation in Haiti. The fishers would not have conch to sell much longer. Considering the consequences to both Haitians and the environment, this saddened him.

His gaze drifted to a wooden cross, no taller than a man, standing like a sentry over the sandy shore. An odd assortment of beads and leather braids dangled from its splintered limbs and rustled in the salty breeze. "Is that a Catholic cross?"

Cristophe hesitated before answering. "The cross…it is *Vodou*."

Chapter 12

Soeur Madeleine

Tim lifted himself to the dock with only slightly more effort than it had taken Cristophe. After witnessing several failed, comical attempts from Reverend Burkholder, Tim and the captain lowered themselves back into the sloop. They clasped their hands into the shape of stirrups and hoisted the minister up until he could bend his upper torso over the dock. With the bulk of his weight resting upon the concrete slab, they pushed his flabby legs up and to the side and simultaneously rolled him onto his back. With no apparent embarrassment, the minister struggled to his feet, wiped the dust off his now dry clothing, and said to Cristophe, "You should consider getting a ladder or something."

"I will put that on my list," Cristophe said, and then smiled.

Tim retrieved the mask, his one piece of luggage, and the minister's three. One of the minister's cases weighed as if filled with lead.

"Please wait here," Cristophe said, "while I run to the clinic to inform *Soeur* Madeleine of your arrival."

Within minutes of his departure, both *blancs* oozed torrents of salt-laden sweat. Tim wiped his brow with his forearm. He frowned at the stark surroundings. "Is it my imagination, or is it even fuckin' hotter, I mean, frickin' hotter here than on the main island?"

"It's hot, all right," the minister said. "I've been in saunas cooler than this. By the way, I appreciate the effort you're making to watch your language. I've heard it all before and I'm not particularly sensitive to it, provided the Lord's name is not taken in vain, but I suspect the missionaries around here might take some offense."

"How do you know this Sister Madeleine, anyhow? Is she a nun?"

"I don't actually know her, but I do know she's not a nun."

He squinted and then turned to the minister. "What do you mean, you don't know her?"

"We've never actually met. I made all the arrangements through various clerical contacts. By the way, she thinks I'm from New York. I don't know how she got that impression, but to avoid confusion, I suggest we keep it that way."

He nodded his head. "Okay, you're a minister from New York. Tell me, what *do* you know about her?"

"In the first place, like I said, she's not a nun. The sister bit, or *Soeur* in *Créole*, is a title of respect and affection."

He didn't care for the sound of this. "You're telling me she's the queen bee around here?"

"Not at all. That title goes to Mildred Sponheimer, the director of the Greater Evangelical Mission."

"I suppose they call her…what did you say…*Soeur…Soeur* Sponheimer?"

"Wrong again, my friend. Like I said, it's a title of respect and affection. From what I gather, Mildred Sponheimer gets the respect, but not the affection."

"They both sound like two lovely ladies to me." He wondered what fine mess he managed to get himself into now. He had more than his fill of missionary spinsters on the main island turning their noses at him as if he were some sort of low-life.

"Hey, by the looks of the dust cloud up ahead, I'd say our ride is coming," the minister said. "It's time to put on a happy face for…how did you put it…oh yeah, the lovely lady."

An open-air Jeep Wrangler rolled up onto the dock and pulled alongside them. The driver—a white female with long, auburn hair gently twisted into a knot, and wearing a calf-length dress much too loose fitting for her tall, slender frame—hopped out to greet them. She wore no make-up or, if she did, dust caked it over. No amount of dust could obstruct her high cheekbones or detract from her emerald eyes, accentuated by bold eyebrows. Tim's preconceived impression of Madeleine McCoy vanished. This sister was stunningly attractive.

"Hi, I'm Madeleine McCoy. You must be Reverend Burkholder. And you must be Tom Jamison. I'm so happy you both made it to La Gonave safe and sound. Please, grab your things and jump in. I'm sure you're not use to heat, La Gonave-style."

"That we're not," the minister said. He hurtled himself into the passenger seat, leaving Tim to stack their luggage onto the back bench seat and squeeze himself into what little space remained.

The short drive to the children's clinic crossed a parched salt flat. The dried, chocolate-colored mud cracked into inch-wide fissures giving it a jigsaw puzzle appearance. Dozens of mud huts, resembling monstrous mushrooms, sprouted from the scorched landscape. Mothers, many nursing infants, sat against the outside walls in what little shade the thatch-roof overhangs afforded. Half-naked children bounced about everywhere and many raced to the path of the vehicle to gawk at the *blancs*. One of the boys, his hair an odd shade of orange, wore only a ratty tee shirt, barely obscuring his bloated belly. The gathering mass of children waved and giggled as the *blancs* passed by.

"How can people live like this?" Tim asked no one in particular. "This is even bleaker than I imagined. Look at that hut over there. It's made out of cardboard. I guess that's one advantage to living some place that rarely sees rain."

So as not to be overheard by Madeleine, the minister turned to him and said softly, "Hopefully, you won't have to be subjected to this wasteland for more than a week or two."

That didn't sound intolerable to him. After two unimaginable years of agony, what is another week or two? His gaze turned to Madeleine. The tortoise-shell barrette clasping her luxuriant hair threatened imminent release as they vibrated across the rugged terrain. Her lengthy, slender neck provided a hint of an alluring figure concealed beneath an unworthy dress. *A guy could almost forget about all this misery around here, simply by looking at her.*

Chapter 13

Mission

The Baptiste women ceremoniously attired themselves in their Sunday best. Today being Friday, they would meet with Mildred Sponheimer. Marie Joseph spent the better part of the morning washing and braiding the girls' hair, all the while instructing them on the answers to regurgitate to a litany of probing questions sure to be asked.

After first dropping Ti Ti off with her sister, she marched Premíse and Colette in single file to the mission where a towering stone wall separated the religious compound from the desolate world outside. A metal gate, wide enough to permit vehicles to pass, served as its sole entrance. An armed, square-faced guard, uniformed in starched, military khaki minus the insignias, blocked their path and queried them as to their business. She proudly informed him her two sons attended the mission school and she had brought her daughters to meet *Madame* Sponheimer for the purpose of enrolling them, as well. She felt certain the guard would be impressed. Only well-to-do residents of La Gonave could afford to send their daughters to school.

The guard, still expressionless, bade them to enter. He pointed his World War II-vintage carbine toward the administrative building at the core of the compound. Maintaining their column with military precision, the mother and two children marched to the concrete-walled edifice, halting at its lone doorway. She conducted a final inspection of the girls, straightened the white bows fastened to each of their braids, corrected their posture, and reminded them to answer questions precisely as they rehearsed.

Taking a deep breath and holding her head high as if dangling from a string, she rapped two times at the thick, metal door. The clanging of two bolts unlatching preceded the door squeaking open. Her mirror image, but fifty pounds heavier, stood at its side. After Marie Joseph explained the purpose of their visit, the plump woman, who introduced herself as Rachelle Legand, beckoned them to enter and led them past a metal desk and two matching file cabinets to a second door, this one wooden.

She tapped at it lightly.

A muted voice came from within.

Rachelle cracked the door open and poked her round head inside. After an exchange of several words, all in English, she motioned for the Baptiste women to enter. A chill blowing from an air conditioner in the wall engulfed them. She and her two daughters stood shivering at attention and stared wide-eyed at the imposing *blanc* seated in a cushioned chair behind an ornate mahogany desk. The mission director, wearing a white cardigan matching her paleness, motioned for them to sit. Unaccustomed to chairs, they awkwardly positioned themselves only halfway upon the caned-back seats.

The stocky *blanc* removed her narrow-rimmed reading spectacles and shuffled a stack of official-looking documents onto her otherwise naked desktop. "Welcome to the Greater Evangelical Mission. I am Mildred Sponheimer, the director. It's always an honor to meet with members of our congregation. To what do I owe this pleasure?"

Rachelle translated the director's greeting into *Créole*. Marie Joseph made her introductions, stressing that Piérre and Jean were, as they spoke, attending class at the mission school.

Mildred duly displayed approval after Rachelle relayed Marie Joseph's response. The mission director crossed her arms over her ample chest and asked, "Am I to understand you also wish to enroll your daughters in our school?"

After Rachelle made the translation, Marie Joseph nodded her head in the affirmative.

The mission director's face hardened. "You are aware we have very simple, but strict rules that must be adhered to? Your daughters cannot attend our school unless they wear uniforms. There can be no exceptions."

Marie Joseph pulled a wad of crumpled and grimy *gourdes* from her worn straw pocketbook. Holding their family's life savings in the palms of her hands, she proudly stated she came prepared to purchase the uniforms this very day.

Mildred released a faint smile. "You must also agree to contribute ten percent of your family's income to the church each and every Sunday."

She agreed without hesitation and resolved to make necessary adjustments in weekly expenditures to assure that God would receive His due. Pleased with the progress of the interview so far, her stomach clenched upon learning from Rachelle the remainder of the interrogation would be directed at Premíse and Colette.

The girls' eyes widened despite their mother's calm facade and reassuring nod. Although confident she drilled her daughters in proper responses, her pulse raced. Time crawled. After all, they're only children. *They can slip up.*

The mission director questioned the girls concerning their understanding of Christianity, Almighty God, and the importance of the Greater Evangelical Mission. She posed a number of leading questions relating to their beliefs in *Vodou* and, after hearing convincing responses that they had forsaken all pagan beliefs, she left the confines of her overstuffed chair and patted each upon the head. She cracked a horizontal smile and rendered her verdict. "You have two lovely Christian daughters, Misses Baptiste. I am pleased to inform you they have been accepted into the mission school."

Before Marie Joseph could utter a response of gratitude, Mildred continued with further instructions. "There's something else I must ask of you. I want you to volunteer to work one day each week at the Doctor Thomas McCoy Children's Clinic. However, under no circumstances are you to reveal that I, or the mission, have in any way been involved in your decision to volunteer your services."

Although puzzled, she promptly agreed to the condition.

"God will continue to bless you and your family, my child," Mildred said, and motioned to Rachelle to show them to the door.

"Incidentally, I want you to meet with me each Friday morning so you can tell me how everything is going at the children's clinic."

Chapter 14

Motorcycle Men

Two men riding identical blue motorcycles streaked to the Baptiste home, creating a cloud of burgundy dust in their wake. They skidded to a halt and revved their engines. Wearing new jeans and spotless white T-shirts, both were overdressed by La Gonave standards. A thick, gold chain dangled around the neck of the larger of the two. Neither man was a native of La Gonave. Ti Bon felt certain of this, for he had never seen them before.

He wondered who these strangers might be and for what purpose they came to his home. *Could they be governmental officials, Attachés, or Tontons Macoute by some other name*? Relieved to be the only one at home this morning, he went about his daily chores in hopes they would leave without disturbing him. When it became too obvious to ignore them any longer, he approached and planted a quizzical expression on his otherwise dour face.

The man with the gold chain stood a couple inches over six feet and carried one hundred pounds in excess of Ti Bon's, all of which appeared to be muscle, not fat, the latter being the norm among wealthy Haitians. Greeting him by name, the imposing stranger introduced himself as Marcel, but did not bother to introduce his peasant-thin companion, who silently scanned the premises with steely eyes.

"What is it you want?" Ti Bon asked, mustering a voice of authority.

"We have come to collect our packages."

His throat sank to his stomach. "Packages? What packages?"

"The packages mistakenly dropped on your farm from an airplane."

"I know of no such packages." He attempted a smirk of nonchalance, but failed miserably. "These packages must have fallen someplace else."

"The packages were dropped on your farm. You have them. We want them back."

"What was in these packages I do not have?"

The silent man whispered something to Marcel. Fearing they were on to him, Ti Bon's eyes widened and his muscles experienced a measure of premature *rigor mortis.*

"How did your house become so white?" Marcel asked.

He attempted a shrug. "I painted it."

"You painted it with what?"

"Paint. White paint."

The silent man, a lighter complexion than Marcel, sauntered to the hut and wiped his right index finger on the wall. He pointed the finger to the air, revealing a white residue for both Marcel and he to see, before inserting it into his mouth. He eyed Marcel and nodded his head.

"You used a white powder on your house, not paint," Marcel said with a certainty that could not be brushed aside.

Although petrified, Ti Bon managed to maintain an outer semblance of calm.

Marcel's glare turned hostile. "This white powder…do you have any of it left?"

"No. I used it all on my house and those of my neighbors."

Sweat beaded upon Marcel's brow and his predatory eyes narrowed. After a deafening pause, he asked, "You have no white powder left?"

He shook his head and said, "I used it all."

Marcel's eyes, matching his sable skin, barreled down like a pair of cannons. "You're in serious trouble, little one. We could buy all of La Gonave with what this white powder is worth. We'll search this lump of mud you call a home to see for ourselves if you're telling the truth."

He attempted to block their path, but with an effortless slap of his hand Marcel knocked him to the ground and then entered the hut. The silent man swaggered over to where Ti Bon lay, kicked him in the groin, and followed his partner inside. After several minutes, the two thugs stormed out of the hut and marched over to where he remained on the ground, grimacing.

"You must pay for this theft," Marcel said.

"I have nothing."

"You have nothing? Then we'll take nothing." Marcel's scowl sent a silent order to his partner.

The steely-eyed man pulled a silver revolver from his back pocket, strode over to where Bon Bon stood tethered to a scrub tree, and shot the helpless sow between her eyes. Bon Bon slumped to the ground without releasing as much as a squeal.

Ti Bon remained plastered to the ground, certain he would be next. Marcel, towering above, ordered him to stand.

He struggled to his feet, accepted his fate, and began to pray.

The gunman dragged Bon Bon's carcass to his motorcycle and hoisted it across the handlebars. He returned to where they stood and, with a ghoulish sneer, waved his pistol in Ti Bon's face.

"The pig is a down-payment on the fifty thousand *gourdes* you owe us," Marcel said. "That's only a fraction of what the white powder is worth. If you fail to pay us in full within seven days, we'll take your wife and daughters and peddle them off as whores in Port-au-Prince. As for your sons, we'll sell them to sugarcane plantations where they'll toil their lives away as the miserable slaves they deserve to be. When we're through, you will, as you said, have absolutely nothing."

The silent man slammed the side of his pistol across Ti Bon's face, hurtling him to the ground. The two men rode away as abruptly as they arrived. A trail of Bon Bon's blood marked their path.

Chapter 15

Evening Breeze

Madeleine wore a long dress only slightly less drab than the one she wore earlier in the day. Her sandals did not measurably add to her stature. She hummed a *Créole* tune while setting the table with the bone china her mother carefully carted to Haiti, this being the first occasion for its use since months before her father's passing. She braided her newly washed hair down her back.

Yvette busily prepared dinner in the kitchen. She noticed Madeleine's cheery disposition and the rarely used fine place settings. "Your guests must be very special."

"Yes, they are. The Reverend Burkholder has come all the way from his church in New York to see how he can help our clinic. He arranged for a graduate student to assist us with maintenance. His name is Mister Tom Jamison."

"Is this Mister Tom Jamison handsome?"

She paused to mull over Yvette's query. Her first impression of Tom Jamison was not overly positive. She anticipated a scholarly, clean-cut guy, five years her junior, rather than an over-the-hill fraternity jock sporting scrapes and bruises from some bar room fight. His tall, athletic physique, coupled with short, cropped, blond hair contrasted by fair skin only slightly bronzed by the sun, would provide sufficient enticement for most women. *More than one prom queen has undoubtedly succumbed to his charms.* She detected a hint of sadness in his eyes, which matched the sky, even though his voice and mannerisms intimated the inner strength of a man who had experienced much in life, both good and bad. There existed a certain familiarity to Tom Jamison that deeply puzzled her.

"I really didn't pay much notice," she finally said. "I suppose he is in a rough sort of way."

"Shouldn't you be wearing your Sunday dress, *Ma-da-leen*?"

She paused, bent her head down, and gazed up as if peering over bifocals. "The Reverend Burkholder is a very important visitor. Mister Jamison is going to be our handyman. I want tonight's dinner to be pleasant for the both of them. That's all. Shouldn't you be checking on dinner?"

Yvette smiled and returned to her duties without uttering another word.

****

Reverend Burkholder and Tom Jamison arrived at the McCoy residence Friday evening at precisely seven. Madeleine met them at the doorway. "Welcome. Please, come in. You're right on time."

"Thank you. Mister Jamison and I appreciate you inviting us for dinner."

"Please, don't mention it. It's not like we have a cafeteria at the clinic. I expect you to have all your meals here. Please, take a seat. Dinner is almost ready."

After the minister's short and sweet blessing over the meal, the threesome shared light conversation. Talk of the earthquake soon took center stage.

"Is there something else I can get for you, Mister Jamison?" she asked, noticing he hardly touched his food. "It didn't occur to me to ask either of you what you might like for dinner. We're a little limited in what we can offer."

"The dinner is fine," Tim said. "Excellent, actually. I'm having trouble getting these emaciated children out of my mind. Things appear worse here than on the main island. That's all."

"I know exactly how you feel." She found his sensitivity mildly surprising. "Even after all these years, I sometimes find it hard to eat, as if my not eating would help these people. You really must eat, Mister Jamison. You'll need all your strength to cope with the hardships of La Gonave."

"Please, call me…ah…Tom."

"It is perfectly normal for a layman to lose his appetite after the grim sights we were subjected to today," the minister said. "I, of course, have long-since become accustomed to witnessing the deprivations so many of our poor brethren are being subjected to in this world. We must do all we can to help them. Starving ourselves isn't the answer. Could you pass me some more of the rice, please? Everything is delicious."

"The reverend is right, Mister Jamison…I mean…Tom. I can't express my appreciation enough to the two of you for your willingness to help our clinic."

"It's our privilege, Miss McCoy," the minister said.

At the completion of the meal, she suggested they retire to the front porch. "I believe Yvette has coffee waiting for us there."

The three moved out to the screened surroundings. She took her customary position on her rocker. The minister and Tim sat across from her.

"You get a nice breeze through here," the minister said. "It's rather pleasant."

She crossed her arms, feeling chilled, as the euphoria of previous family times descended upon her. "It is nice. I'm not sure I could survive La Gonave if I didn't have some relief from the heat each evening." She shifted her gaze to Tim. "What do you think of Haiti, Tom? Are you looking forward to your work here?"

He cleared his throat. "Haiti seems like a nice enough place if you can overlook the squalor its people must endure. I have to admit, I wouldn't be here if it weren't for my research."

"What kind of research will you be doing, Tom?"

"Nothing fancy, just digging up some old pottery."

A sharp rapping at the outside porch door interrupted them. "Yoo-hoo, Madeleine, are you home? It's me, Mildred Sponheimer."

She rolled her eyes upon hearing Mildred's shrill, unwelcome voice. "Please, come in, Miss Sponheimer."

"Oh, I didn't realize you had company. Maybe I should come back another time."

"Nonsense. Please, let me introduce you to my guests, Reverend Vince Burkholder and Mister Tom Jamison. This is Mildred Sponheimer. She's the director of the Greater Evangelical Mission here on La Gonave."

The reverend rose to his feet and reached for Mildred's hand. "It's a pleasure to meet you, Miss Sponheimer. I've heard many wonderful things about you."

She expanded like a puffer fish. "I simply play a small part in the Lord's work."

Tim extended his hand to Mildred. "Nice to meet you, Miss Sponheimer."

She avoided contact, returned an inaudible greeting, and then turned to the minister. "I understand from Miss McCoy you're a Methodist minister. It's so unfortunate we don't have a Methodist mission here on La Gonave. You must come to our church on Sunday. Perhaps you would like to say a few words to our congregation?"

"I would be honored to, Miss Sponheimer. Unfortunately, I'll be heading back to Port-au-Prince first thing Sunday morning."

"Oh? I don't think so. I just heard a tropical wave is expected to pass through here tomorrow afternoon. The sea will be much too rough to cross the channel for at least a couple days. As you know firsthand, Port-au-Prince is in shambles. Thousands of marines, bless their hearts, are arriving as we speak to quell any and all riots the natives feel they're entitled to initiate."

The minister sat in stunned silence. His face became a portrait of glumness.

"So it's settled. I look forward to seeing all of you in church. I really must be going now. It was a pleasure meeting the two of you. Good evening, Miss McCoy."

Madeleine re-opened the conversation. "It still should be nice enough tomorrow morning for Tom to check out his research site. The farmer who owns the land with the cave will be by shortly after breakfast to take you there. I was hoping I could tag along."

"Sure," Tim said. "It should be fun. We'll just be reconnoitering the area."

"Wonderful."

The minister pushed himself to his feet. "Please excuse us, Madeleine. Tom and I must be going. We have a big day ahead of us. Thank you so much for dinner. It was fabulous."

"It certainly was," Tim said. "Thank you."

"Don't thank me. Yvette's the cook. I'll pass your compliments on to her. Breakfast will be at seven. I hope you find the bunkroom at the clinic comfortable. Let me know if you need anything."

"I'm sure everything will be fine," Tim said. The minister nodded his head and the two men departed.

Madeleine returned to the kitchen to help Yvette put away the dishes. Once the last plate had been placed in the cupboard, Yvette singingly said, "The handyman is very handsome."

Chapter 16

Dreams

Ti Bon mentioned nothing to Marie Joseph about the two thugs demanding payment for the white powder he found and innocently put to good use. With little questioning, she bought his explanation that he bruised his face slipping on some rocks on their hilly farm. In her excitement over the successful encounter with the mission director, his wife didn't even notice Bon Bon missing. He managed to feign pride and pleasure as Premíse and Colette modeled their new uniforms—nearly all their family savings invested in this wardrobe. Would the two men accept the uniforms as partial payment of his debt? Would they demand his farm? Force his wife and daughters into a lifetime of prostitution? Enslave his sons in the cane fields? Leave him with nothing? Why had he told these strangers he had nothing? He was wealthy. He had a lovely wife and five healthy children. He even owned his farm.

After his spouse and children retired to the safety and comfort of their straw mats, he latched the wooden shutters of the hut's sole window and double-checked the door was fastened, thus preventing entrance to any evil spirits intent upon creeping inside. After assuring himself each of his children breathed effortlessly, he soundlessly crawled alongside Marie Joseph and kissed her soft cheek. She stirred slightly, but did not awake.

Tormenting thoughts filled his mind. He could not imagine obtaining such an outlandish sum as fifty thousand *gourdes,* unless he allowed himself to consider the spirits might intervene. He prayed to *Damballah*, the most powerful of the other world, but after a time his thoughts wandered to the meeting he would have in the morning with *Soeur* Madeleine and some visiting *blancs*. He would be paid handsomely for simply showing them the cave on the hillside above his corn plot. A smile crossed his face. *Perhaps the spirits already answered my prayers.* Relieved, he joined his family in slumber.

The spiritual world visited Ti Bon's dreams. The two henchmen returned for their money, transformed themselves into serpents, spiraled up his legs, and then to his neck. The scaled creatures tightened their grips. A colossal figure approached from the shadows. The serpents released their holds and slithered into the darkness. Filled with fear, Ti Bon faced the imposing intruder—a gargantuan wearing a shiny black tuxedo and a matching top hat. The whites of the intruder's eerie eyes glared out as the sole facial features not blending into his skin and attire.

The dark figure bellowed, "Beware of the cave."

With the warning still echoing into the night, the colossal phantom unleashed a jack-o-lantern grin. One of his teeth, capped in gold, glittered in the light of the full moon. He dissolved into the shadows without further word.

****

Less than one mile away, Tim tossed with discomfort in body and mind on a lumpy bed in the bunkroom of the Dr. Thomas McCoy Children's Clinic. To his annoyance, the minister snored at full volume on a second bed a few feet away. Even though he felt he'd finally distanced himself safely from the twin evils—Bertram DuMarche and Octave Polynice—torturing thoughts seeped into the chasms of his mind. He had his ample share of girlfriends throughout high school and college, but Sarah had been his first and only true love. He fell for and married her without ever fully knowing her. Their time ran out much too rapidly. Sadly, time never returns. He began to accept what had been before the unthinkable. He would move forward and create a new life for himself. *But can I?*

He succumbed to sleep—his slumber far from restful. He dreamed of being on a beach late at night. The white sand glowed in the light of the full moon and the sea sparkled with phosphorescent microorganisms flashing with the passing of each rippling wave. A ravishing woman swam nude a few yards offshore, her golden locks streaming alongside her voluptuous body. She beckoned him to join her. Mesmerized, he waded fully-clothed into the warm water. Regardless how far he ventured, she remained an elusive distance away. The sea soon rose above his head, forcing him to bob up and down so he could only catch a glimpse of the taunting apparition at the crest of each wave.

Sarah's shrill laugh pierced the mist-filled air.

****

Two men woke in the shadowy night to the resonating pulse of island drums. One man was black and the other white. The black man found solace in the rhythmic beat. The white man felt only fear.

Chapter 17

Possessed

The minister rose Saturday morning shortly after a menagerie of roosters and mangy dogs made their presence known. His thoughts raced through his sordid scheme. He spotted Tim shuffling about the clinic in a daze. "What's the matter with you?" he asked with an eyebrow raised. "Didn't get much sleep last night?"

"I've had better," Tim said, "that's for sure. Didn't you hear those drums?"

"Drums? What drums? I slept like a baby."

"There were drums echoing off the mountains."

"Let's not forget this is Haiti." The minister was amused by the concern in Tim's voice. "What did you expect? It's not the club where the only *Vodou* ceremonies performed are for drunken tourists. Ignore that stuff. We have a big day ahead of us. We're going spelunking."

"Spelunking? You didn't say anything before about any spelunking. I thought all we had to do was peek inside the entrance of some cave and grab whatever broken pots were handy. I don't even have a flashlight."

"Don't worry about that," the minister said with a toothy grin. "I brought flashlights, extra batteries, even rope, if we need it."

"Rope? What are you talking about? I agreed to pretend I was an anthropology graduate student, not some great-white, spelunking explorer."

"Now don't get your bowels in an uproar." The minister realized he would soon have to feed him a larger measure of information as to their true purpose for coming to this miserable island. "We're just going to do a little reconnoitering, as you put it. That's all. Where did you come up with that word, anyway?"

"It seemed to fit."

"It sure does. Remember, you're just playing a role. If you don't take this cave exploration seriously, how do you expect anyone else to believe you're really an anthropologist? I don't need to remind you you're in grave danger on the main island, do I?"

"No, you're absolutely right." Tim lowered his head. "I'll toe the line from here on."

"That's the spirit. Let's go get some breakfast at Sister Madeleine's." Noticing a smile crossing Tim's face, he concluded another sermon might be in order. "She sure is a fine looking lady. Don't you go letting that pretty face of hers cloud your mind as to why you're here."

Tim returned a puzzled look. "At this point in time, I'm not interested in any lady, no matter how attractive. I'm just interested in getting the...let's see, how should I put it...the H, E, two-sticks out of Haiti."

That was the sort of answer the minister hoped to hear. "Let's get a move on. I need to fill you in on a number of details regarding this cave exploration."

****

The breakfast conversation centered upon the cave and what it might contain. Tim, for his part, sounded like an exuberant graduate student. Reverend Burkholder felt bemused. *Yes, there's a little con in everyone.*

Ti Bon arrived a few minutes after they finished breakfast. Madeleine offered him something to eat, but he steadfastly refused. Her fluency in *Créole* astonished the minister. A blind man would swear she was a native.

Madeleine introduced Ti Bon, who appeared to be in his late twenties, about five-feet, ten-inches tall, and no more than one-hundred-forty pounds. A grimy, cloth bandage ringed his forehead. The soiled and tattered *Life is Good* T-shirt did not reflect his current disposition. Before greetings could be exchanged, the

Haitian demanded one hundred *gourdes* in payment to lead the group to the cave.

Madeleine translated the ultimatum.

"I thought we agreed earlier to fifty?" the minister said.

Madeleine's lips curled into a partial smile as she shook her head from side-to-side. "If fifty *gourdes* is what you agreed to, then that's what you should pay. Haitians barter on everything, but it's unusual for them to renege on a deal once it's made."

She spoke to Ti Bon. Her voice conveyed a level of sternness this time.

Based upon the tone of his response, the minister assumed the Haitian hadn't budged from his original demand. "Look, I'll pay him what he wants, but tell him not to plan to come back to me for any more. I'm a charitable man, but I believe in spreading my charity around." The time had arrived to get this show on the road. In any event, incidental expenses would be charged to Sir John Winston or Richy Richardson. Better yet, he would give both identical bills.

****

Although not yet eight o'clock in the morning, the reading on the thermometer exceeded one hundred degrees. With sweat streaming down his face, Tim took notice of Madeleine and Ti Bon sauntering about without showing the slightest sign of discomfort. The short stroll to Ti Bon's farm took an extra ten minutes to allow for the out-of-shape minister to catch his breath.

The Baptiste family awaited the cave explorers. Each of them stood with perfect posture in front of their sparkling, white home. Their faces remained expressionless until Madeleine's greeting, "b*onjou','*" caused them to blossom into a bouquet of grins.

The proud father introduced his wife and each of his five children. Ti Bon's spouse, who stood nearly as tall as her husband, shared his flawless complexion and lean physique. Excluding their plump infant, Ti Ti, the children exhibited signs of emaciation, although their bellies did not appear severely distended.

Jean rubbed the blond hair on Tim's right arm. Piérre and his two sisters, Premíse and Colette, soon joined in the fun. Tim remained motionless, feeling like an over-sized, stuffed animal while a pair of children ran their hands up and down each of his arms. He turned to Madeleine and said, "I seem to be the center of attention here."

Madeleine chuckled. "Haitian children love to rub soft and furry arms. They would do the same to your legs if you were wearing shorts."

Ti Bon barked a command to his children. They backed away, giggling. Only when Tim joined in their laughter did their father's authoritative demeanor wane. He remained grinless while exchanging a few words with Madeleine.

"Ti Bon apologizes for his children," Madeleine said. "You're the first blond-haired Caucasian they've ever seen." She mimicked the children by lightly rubbing his left arm.

The minister paced about during the extended exchange and then broke into the conversation. "Okay, let's get this show on the road. Where's the cave?"

Madeleine pointed to a clearing of baked, red earth on a nearly sixty-degree incline. "It's up that hill…beyond the field. Ti Bon will take us there now."

The steep hillside reminded Tim of a quip he'd once heard. While farmers in America fear falling off their tractors, Haitians have to contend with falling off their farms. He noted the barren field. "What's planted there?"

Madeleine posed the question to Ti Bon and translated his response. "Ti Bon says he planted corn, but mostly what grow are rocks."

Everyone forced a smile.

Despite his two-year drinking binge, Tim remained in reasonably good shape, although he proved no match for Madeleine. She reached the entrance to the cave several paces ahead. Respectfully, Ti Bon traipsed up the hillside at the minister's sluggish pace.

As Tim arrived, Madeleine released an impish smile and asked, "What *Taíno* treasures do you think we'll find inside?"

Her mention of treasure rattled him. He learned about the *real* treasure from the minister just before breakfast. "I'll be happy if we find some broken pots. We better wait for the minister. I know he wants to see an anthropologist in action."

"What sort of research will you do today?"

"I'll be limiting my exploration today to the first one hundred meters or so." His tone exuded a measure of scholarship. "I won't collect any artifacts today. I'll need to catalog everything once I start collecting. That part is tedious and not too exciting."

He paused to reflect on how easily deceitfulness came to him. For the past two years he'd been nothing short of a drunken lout and now he managed to transform himself into a sober fraud. He couldn't decide which version of himself he found more despicable.

Madeleine peered inside the cave's opening. "What can you tell me about the Indians that inhabited this area?"

"They obviously expended a great deal of time and energy making terra cotta pots and figurines." Not wanting the conversation to continue any further, out of fear his charade would unravel, he hollered to the minister, "Hey, we don't have all day. Don't forget, there's going to be a tropical wave coming through here this afternoon."

"We'll be right there," the minister gasped. "I'm not as young as you two are, you know. Thanks for waiting."

Tim had been floored by the conversation he had earlier in the day when Reverend Burkholder confided the artifacts they would search for were made of gold, not clay, as Tim had initially been told. The minister explained that museum officials long suspected gold artifacts might be found in caves on La Gonave, but did not have the finances to mount an expedition. If he and the minister should find any gold it would be necessary for them to maintain absolute secrecy to prevent the cave from being ransacked by unscrupulous looters. All the gold artifacts would be deposited in the museum and, being a board member of the Port-au Prince Museum of Pre-Columbian Art, the minister/attorney indicated he would handle the transfer himself. He also said Tim would be handsomely rewarded by the museum, possibly enough to retire his debt so he could finally escape Haiti. Tim beamed at the mere thought.

Once the foursome reached the opening to the cave, Tim took control and gave directions on how they would proceed. With caution, he led them through the five-foot high, three-foot wide opening. The cavern's dimensions, shortly thereafter, increased measurably. The path appeared clear, except for a few rock overhangs dipping from the ceiling. Feeling like an anthropologist, he spotted a few fragments of terra cotta pots and pointed them out to Madeleine.

A tucked-away memory that he once toyed with the idea of seeking an advanced degree in underwater archaeology startled him when it surfaced. He dropped the notion the instant he met Sarah. His only thought from that point on had been to share a life with her in an exotic locale. *If only I had stayed in school, I could have made something of myself and Sarah might still be at my side.* Not wishing to rehash one rotten choice after another, he allowed the sullen thoughts to plunge to the abyss of his mind. He knew they would resurface another time.

After roaming another thirty feet or so, the cave sharply turned to the left, obscuring all light from the entrance. In the excitement, no one apparently noticed Ti Bon dripping with sweat and shivering until the Haitian dropped to the floor of the cave and began to convulse.

Madeleine shined her light at his writhing body. "Stop, everyone. Ti Bon's been possessed." Her last word ricocheted down the mountain's rock-lined throat and waned to nothingness—swallowed deep within.

They gathered around the Haitian, who shook as if having an epileptic seizure. "We need to get him out of here," Madeleine said.

They carried Ti Bon, who continuously spewed disjointed words, back to his home. They placed him on a straw mat stretched across the hut's earthen floor. Marie Joseph, cradling Ti Ti, shooed the other children outside before motioning for the minister to sit on their one wooden stool. She and Madeleine knelt alongside Ti Bon. Scarcely a breath of air passed through the Baptiste's single window.

Unable to stand erect in the puny hut, Tim hovered in a hunched position. "What's he saying?"

"It's not him talking," Madeleine said. "It's the *loa*."

The minister uttered his first words since leaving the cave. "What in heaven's name is a *loa*?"

"*Loa* is *Créole,* for spirits," Madeleine said. "There are many spirits, or *loa*, in *Vodou* culture. Apparently, we disturbed one or more of them. I'm surprised Ti Bon agreed to let us enter the cave. He must have known it's their home.*"*

The voice emanating from the peasant farmer intensified—his cadence now a chant. Marie Joseph, eyes wide, pressed her infant son to her bosom.

"The spirits are very angry," Madeleine said, her voice quivering. "They will not let our intrusion go unpunished. We could all be in danger."

"You don't really believe in all this mumbo-jumbo, do you Madeleine?" the minister asked, reverting to his courtroom alter ego.

"It doesn't matter what I or, for that matter, you believe. Ti Bon believes it and I do know when a Haitian says spirits are going to punish someone, something bad inevitably happens to them. Call it superstition. Call it mumbo-jumbo. Call it anything you like, but things happen here only Haitians can explain."

"I have to tell you, Madeleine, as a minister of the Christian faith, I find all of this preposterous. There are no such things as cave spirits, or *loa*, or whatever you called them. Mister Jamison has important research to conduct. He can't suspend his activities every time a Haitian becomes overwrought with this superstitious nonsense."

Vividly remembering his cemetery experience with the Ebony Man, Tim became filled with other thoughts. "Maybe I can find another cave. Or better yet, I'll just rummage around the hillsides looking for artifacts. I can't see disturbing these cave gods any further."

"That won't be enough to appease the *loa*," Madeleine said, still on her knees and wiping sweat from Ti Bon's brow. "We have to find a way to cleanse our souls and re-enter the cave in their good graces. It's the only way Ti Bon will find redemption."

"Okay," the minister said. "If we have to cleanse our souls to re-enter the cave, I'll lead us in prayer to the Lord our God."

"That won't do," Madeleine said.

"What do you mean that won't do? Of course it will. I'm a Methodist minister."

"We're not dealing with the Christian faith in its entirety here. This is *Vodou*. We need to be cleansed by a *houngan*—a *Vodou* priest."

"You want us to see a witch doctor?" Tim asked, re-living his encounter with the Ebony Man and the relentless pounding of *Vodou* drums. "Those people are dangerous."

"Not a witch doctor. A witch doctor is called a *bocor*. We need to see a *houngan*. They're as religious as Reverend Burkholder."

Tim could see Reverend Burkholder didn't look relieved by her answer.

"Religious in what way?" the minister asked.

"They're Christians, just like you and me. I assume you're also a Christian, Tom?"

"I sort of am, although I haven't been practicing it much of late."

"A *houngan* is a *Vodou* priest," Madeleine said. "They're invariably Catholic, the main Christian religion in Haiti. *Vodou* is a conglomeration of Christian and African beliefs. When you think about it, even as Christians we're asked to take an awful lot on faith. What's the big deal that Haitians have a few more spiritual entities in their lives? That doesn't make them less Christian. Maybe it makes them more?"

"Okay, what do we do next?" the minister asked.

"Ti Bon will know what to do once he comes out of the possession."

"When will that happen?"

"Possessions rarely last more than an hour or so. Whatever is required of us will have to wait for at least another day. The tropical wave is going to be fierce tonight. The *loa* will be venting their anger."

Chapter 18

Une Grande Ondée Oest

The storm, brewed in sub-Sahara Africa, raged with unrelenting winds by the time the trio of *blancs* returned to Madeleine's cottage. The sky, having transformed from polished silver to a foreboding and lusterless pewter, discharged a barrage of thunderbolts rumbling across the sea and rocking the exposed island. Villagers scurried like ants to secure their possessions, including livestock, inside their huts. The angry winds came to a halt, much like a saber-rattling cavalry pausing in anticipation of a bugle to signal a charge.

"You both better stay in my house tonight," Madeleine suggested, her eyes locked on the hostile horizon. She slowly inhaled the sultry air. "My father built this cottage to last. It has survived two hurricanes unscarred. I don't have the same confidence in the clinic. Hurry and get your things. *Une grande Ondée Oest* will be upon us at any moment."

"*Une grande* what?" Tim asked, still perplexed by the strange events earlier in the day.

"*Ondée Oest*...tropical wave to you. They come in all sizes and this one is going to be close to hurricane force."

"Let's go, Tom," the minister said. "We better get our stuff."

A sky tarnished to blackness collapsed with pelting rain as Tim and the minister sprinted to the safety of Madeleine's home. The violent blasts of air sent rippling sheets of rain seeping through the tightly squeezed hurricane shutters. Scrub trees growing alongside the cottage clawed at the metal window casings, sounding like wild animals seeking refuge inside. The three huddled on the sofa against the living room wall farthest from the windows. Conversations became pointless in the ensuing pandemonium. The storm sustained the assault until the early hours of morning and then mercifully withdrew. Madeleine lit an oil lamp, illuminating a floor thinly coated with water.

Tim broke the aura of silence. "Wow. That was some storm. Those must have been one-hundred-mile-an-hour winds. I can't believe any of these mud huts will still be standing."

"You'd be surprised what those huts can withstand," Madeleine said. She lit a second lantern.

"All the same, I'm glad we were in your house. Your father built it?"

"He didn't actually build it, but he did oversee its construction."

"Why were you so worried about the clinic?" Tim asked. He opened a shuttered window to peek outside. "Isn't it built just as well?"

"I'm afraid not." Madeleine joined Tim at the open window. "It was built by a group of volunteer students from Grand Rapids, Michigan. They did the best they could with the materials they had at hand. It's been somewhat of a struggle to keep it in one piece."

Tim noted a touch of anxiety in Madeleine's voice and that her face had paled. "Maybe we should go check it out now? See if it's okay?"

"That can wait till morning. There's nothing we can do tonight, anyway. You two can sleep here in the living room. One of you can take the sofa and I have a cot I can pull out."

The minister spread himself out on the sofa. "Don't go to any trouble for us."

"It's no problem. Tom can't very well sleep on the wet floor."

Tim did not feel the least bit fatigued. "If you have a mop, Madeleine, I'll get started on cleaning up this mess."

"That can wait till morning, too. Most of it will dry on its own."

While the minister snored in comfort, Tim, his eyes opened, lay stretched out on the flimsy cot with his bare feet protruding a good foot beyond its edge. As island drums thumped in the distance, unsettling images of the cave crept through his mind.

****

The night in the Baptiste home had not passed smoothly. Their hut met the challenge of the pulverizing storm and remained reasonably intact. Its new white coating, on the other hand, washed away. It would require some minor patching of its mud walls and roof thatching. But these remained the least of the Baptistes' worries. A severe fever struck Ti Ti at the onset of the storm.

The toddler exhibited crankiness before the downpour and although most mothers would assume him to be cutting a new tooth, Marie Joseph instantly attributed his affliction to the revenge of the *loa*. As the storm crashed through the night, Ti Ti became progressively listless. Distraught over her infant son, Marie Joseph did not join her husband in search for the missing Bon Bon. In any event, Ti Bon quickly gave up on the hunt and told her the sow would have to fend for itself. She wiped her ailing child with a damp cloth most of the night, thankful, at least, that the storm provided her with an ample supply of water. Ti Ti, still ablaze at daybreak, emitted muted whimpers between bouts of shallow breaths.

"I will take Ti Ti to see *Soeur* Madeleine," Marie Joseph said with a forceful voice. "You must take the other children to my sister's and then go at once to see a *houngan*. Better yet, I want you to seek guidance from *La Reine* Memmene."

****

Ti Bon, with four children dutifully following him in single file, glanced at his dull, rain-washed home before turning onto the washboard dirt road leading toward the temple of the *Vodou* queen. If matters weren't bad enough, now that he'd ventured with the *blancs* inside the forbidden cave, his world had shattered further. Despite being hopelessly in debt to two hooligans, only one notion reverberated through his mind—*the loa of the cave must be appeased.*

Chapter 19

Revenge of the *Loa*

Madeleine slipped outside early Sunday morning to check for damage, greatly relieved to discover the cottage once again weathered a horrific storm. When Yvette did not arrive at six o'clock to prepare breakfast, she began to fret whether Yvette's family had safely ridden out the raging downpour. She paced about the screened porch, busying herself returning wind-blown objects to their proper places, until Tim and the minister finally stirred.

"Why don't we go check on the clinic?" Tim suggested after he joined her on the porch, his feet bare. "And everything else for that matter. We're not hungry, anyway, are we, Reverend Burkholder?"

"Uh, yeah, we can eat later. Is there any coffee around here?"

"I can fix some," she said.

"No, that's okay," the minister said. "Let's go see how the clinic fared."

The threesome quickly dressed for a hike and headed outside. A gully, gouged by the storm to nearly twice a man's height, obstructed the path in front of the cottage. The steep ravine continued alongside the road as far as they could see, but with only a trickle of water now passing.

"God Almighty." The minister gazed about. "I wonder how much rain we got last night."

"It's not unusual to receive half our annual rainfall in just a couple storms," she said.

Tim peered down into the gully. "At least the farmers should be happy."

"Just the opposite, Tom." His concern for those less fortunate once again surprised her. "Any crops already growing or seeds recently sown likely washed away. I've seen this happen over and over again. No rain, no rain, and then too much rain. Mother Nature can be so cruel."

Tim found a wooden plank stored next to her cottage, slid it over the gully, and crossed the improvised overpass before holding his hand out to her. She politely declined and proceeded on her own. The minister, left to fend for himself, nearly lost his balance halfway across.

They traveled downhill several hundred paces and came upon a group of villagers huddled together, murmuring. Madeleine spotted a woman she recognized. Upon making eye contact, the woman motioned her over. The two conversed in a hushed tone for several minutes before she returned to where Tim and the minister waited alongside the road.

"The gully has washed through the cemetery," she said. "We need to go there first."

"What about the clinic?" the minister asked.

"That can wait. Come, let's go."

The deep rut diverged sharply away from the road after one hundred yards or so. They followed the water-torn swath to the cemetery. Most of its coral-rubble wall had washed away. They soon discovered many of the stone gravesites had also proved powerless to the surge caused by the violent storm. Scores of skeletons escaped their tombs. Family members frantically raced about collecting bones to reconstruct their loved ones. Two women argued while tugging at a leg bone each needed to complete their assemblage.

Tim spotted Yvette wailing in the midst of the mayhem. "Madeleine. Over there. There's Yvette."

Madeleine's anxiety continued building as she crawled down into the gully. She sank to her knees in soggy earth the color of dried blood. Tim leapt down to lend a hand, but instead joined her in a quagmire of muck.

"Are you two okay?" the minister asked, watching in safety at the ledge. "It looks muddy down there."

Tim glanced at her. "The reverend has a penchant for stating the obvious."

She shook her head in agreement and would have chuckled over their predicament had she not been so pre-occupied with Yvette. Leaning on Tim's shoulder, she managed to free one of her legs and placed her liberated foot on a portion of the crumbled wall. She pushed down on solid footing while steadying herself on his shoulder, eased her other leg out of the mud, and then glanced back at her cohort, now hopelessly mired. "I'll be right back."

"Don't worry about me." Tim grinned. "I'm not going anywhere."

She climbed to the cemetery side of the gully and spoke to two boys. Both clearly found the sight of a *blanc* stuck fast in mud a source of high amusement. They agreed to be of assistance and, while she rushed to her panic-stricken housekeeper, they dropped into the ditch to pluck Tim out.

Tim thanked the boys and joined her and a sobbing Yvette a few gravesites away. "What happened?"

Madeleine took a deep swallow. "Yvette's older brother was buried last year in that washed-out grave over there." She wrapped an arm around the young, Haitian girl and pointed to an empty burial place. "They didn't find his bones."

"You mean his skeleton washed away?"

"No. I mean, there were no bones in the grave."

"I don't understand."

"I'll explain it to you later, Tom."

She attempted to console Yvette, but the distraught woman broke free of her hold and meandered away. Deeply troubled, Madeleine closed her eyes and shook her head. Long ago, she learned when

94

it comes to matters such as these, Haitians can only find comfort from their spiritual leaders.

The boys who helped Tim out of the mud built a path with fragments of the cemetery's wall so the two *blancs* could easily return to the other side. She rewarded each with several *gourdes.*

Reverend Burkholder stood with a puzzled look frozen upon his face. "What do these people do now? Re-bury their dead?"

"They'll bury those they find," she said, not wanting to go into any further explanations. "Let's go see how the clinic held up."

Within several hundred paces of the clinic, she thanked God she insisted her visitors ride out the tropical wave inside her cottage. The clinic's new metal roof had blown off and crumpled corrugated panels lay strewn everywhere, leaving the building's contents exposed to the full wrath of the storm. They poked their heads through an opened door now hanging by one hinge.

"Has it been looted?" the minister asked.

"I'd be surprised if it hasn't." she said, no longer able to conceal an outer shell of dejection. The clinic would likely be out of commission until another roof could be raised and lost medical supplies replaced, possibly at a cost more than she could afford.

"Haitians don't consider such opportunities as stealing." She shook her head at the devastation. "When you have basically nothing, it becomes a matter of survival to take advantage of any and all situations presenting themselves. To do otherwise would leave you at a disadvantage. It's survival of the fittest at its most basic level."

With her gaze now pointed to the ground, she felt Tim's firm hand touch her shoulder. "We better see what's left to salvage," she said.

She shrugged off his touch and proceeded to the clinic. They spent the better part of an hour gathering what remained of medical supplies. Marie Joseph appeared at the busted doorway, her young boy cradled in her arms. Madeleine raced over and, without exchanging a word, placed her hand on Ti Ti's forehead.

Tim followed behind. "What's the matter? Is he sick?"

"He has a fever. It could be bacterial, Dengue fever, or malaria."

"Can you help him?"

"If it's bacterial, antibiotics should work, but if it's Dengue or malaria, I'm limited to treating the symptoms and praying for a swift recovery."

She paused to consider another possibility she knew her visitors would not understand. "It could be the revenge of the *loa*. I'll give him antibiotics, for now. Marie Joseph says her husband is making arrangements for us to meet *La Reine* Memmene this evening. I hope it won't be too late."

"Aren't you taking this black magic stuff a little far, Madeleine?" Reverend Burkholder asked, shaking his head in disapproval. "You're a trained nurse practitioner, for heaven's sake."

Beyond caring what her two guests thought about native beliefs, she said, "I'll treat his body and the *mambo* will treat his soul. I'll also pray and hope you do, too. That's Ti Ti's best hope. There may be nothing more we can do without the *mambo's* intervention."

"What's a *mambo*?" Tim asked.

"A *mambo* is a *Vodou* priestess, in this case, *La Reine* Memmene. She's the queen of La Gonave."

"The queen?" the minister asked. "You must be joking. I think you've been on this island much too long, young lady. The only royalty in Haiti are vagabond Europeans."

Madeleine paused a moment to regain her calm. "*La Reine* Memmene is a queen to the natives of La Gonave. She is their spiritual leader. You don't have to wear a crown in Haiti to be a queen. We angered the *loa* of the cave. Now, Ti Ti has a fever…my clinic has been destroyed. I just hope we can get our souls cleansed before anything else happens."

"I'll pray to the one true God," Reverend Burkholder said. "I'm willing to go see this queen bee *mambo*, but at some point I may have to draw a religious line. The Catholics may fall for this garbage, but not the Methodists."

"I think it would be wise to follow Madeleine's advice on this, Reverend Burkholder," Tim said. He scanned the damage wreaked by the storm. "Look at what has happened so far. We could be next."

Chapter 20

Services

Madeleine saw no hope of restoring the shattered clinic. Where would she get the funds? Where would she find skilled labor with Port-au-Prince so decimated by an earthquake? Who outside of La Gonave would even give her clinic a second thought? She took a deep breath. The storm—the damage to the clinic—it could have been much worse. How many times had her mother said, "This too shall pass?" That comment had always seemed so ridiculous, but now, somehow, it brought a much needed measure of relief.

She returned to the cottage and prepared a late breakfast of buttermilk hotcakes. She garnished them with sliced bananas, mango preserves, and warmed honey.

The minister's glum expression disintegrated the instant he saw her arrive with the steaming platter. "Now this is my idea of how to get our souls cleansed."

"These really do look scrumptious," Tim agreed, his grin equal in warmth, but not in width, to the minister's. "It seems Yvette's not the only accomplished chef around here."

"I hope you like them." She placed the platter on the center of the dining room table.

The minister led them in a short prayer and with the ring of *amens* still filling the air, helped himself to a stack of three. Scarcely a word passed amongst the hungry threesome, who had eaten little since breakfast the previous day. After they polished off the platter, Tim helped with the dishes while the minister retired to the front porch where he soon dozed off in the comfortable rocking chair.

Tim took the opportunity to ask her about the *Vodou* ceremony they would attend. "When will we meet with this *mambo* lady?"

"There will be a ceremony tonight. It won't start until midnight."

"Midnight? I should have guessed. Where will it be?"

"*La Reine* Memmene's temple is halfway between here and Nan-Café, about ten miles away. We can drive part of the way, but we'll have at least a two-hour hike up into the mountains. It's a little off the beaten track."

"Boy, I'm not sure the minister will be up to it." Tim nodded toward Reverend Burkholder sleeping soundly with his mouth open. "He's not in very good shape, you know?"

"We'll just have to take it easy. Everyone who entered the cave must be cleansed. I know the minister doesn't believe in any of this. Maybe you don't either."

"I'm not sure what to believe, Madeleine. Everything in Haiti defies credibility." The haunting memory of being surrounded by eyes-opened corpses ensconced in a shadowy morgue flashed before him in its every grisly detail. "How do you stand it here?"

She placed the dish she was drying on the counter and gazed out the kitchen window. After a lengthy pause, she said, "As a young girl, I could never understand what enticed my father to drag my mother to this island. You know, his name was Tom, just like yours."

Tim sunk with guilt the instant she connected his assumed name to her father's. He yearned to tell her the truth, but the charade had gone too far. *How can I explain my lies?* Besides, the real Tim James was a despicable, drunken bum. At least, he could garner some respect as Tom Jamison, anthropologist.

"It wasn't until after my father died I figured out his motivation." She reached into the sink for another utensil to rinse. "He had everything he could possibly want back home in Illinois, but he never felt he made a real difference there."

"How could that be? Your father was a pediatrician. Surely, he knew he made a difference in the lives of the children he treated."

"Sure, Dad fully appreciated the importance of his profession, but he also knew another equally trained pediatrician could take his place. Here, on La Gonave, his presence made the difference between children living and dying. There would be no one else."

"What about your mother? Was she trained in medicine, too?"

She fell silent for a long moment before answering. "Mom wasn't formally trained in medicine, but she helped my father in every way she could and was equally devoted to the children. I guess you could say that's a family trait."

Tim placed the last of the cups and saucers in the wooden cupboard. "Is that why you remained?"

"I guess, in part, it is. One day, I knew this was what I had to do."

"Doesn't it get lonely?" Tim regretted his words almost as soon as they crossed his lips.

"Things don't always turn out like you plan. I didn't plan to be here alone."

"Ah, there was someone in your life who didn't want to join you? I think I'm getting the picture."

"Haiti's not for everyone. I have hundreds upon hundreds of needy, beautiful children to keep me company. We better get ready for church. Reverend Burkholder can finish his nap there."

****

Cleanup operations came to a standstill early Sunday afternoon throughout the whole of La Gonave. Church services had simply been delayed, not suspended. Mildred Sponheimer introduced Reverend Burkholder to the sardined congregants and invited him to share a few words. Rachelle translated the minister's short, touching sermon, in which he seamlessly strung together a number of familiar biblical passages. Despite the suffocating, midday heat, the service spanned its full two-hour allotment.

After the service, Mildred cornered the trio before they could make a speedy getaway. "I'm so pleased the three of you could attend our services today. We're quite honored."

"It's our honor, Miss Sponheimer," Reverend Burkholder said. "May I call you Mildred?"

She took a deep gulp. "Yes, please do. I don't like to stand on formality." Turning to Madeleine, she said, "I'm so sorry about your clinic, Miss McCoy. I wish there was something our mission could do, but our budget is hardly making ends meet as it is. Please be assured our prayers are with you."

"I appreciate your concern, Miss Sponheimer."

As soon as the last of the congregants filed out, the mission director changed the topic. "There's another matter I need to discuss with the three of you. It concerns *Vodou*."

"*Vodou*?" Reverend Burkholder asked. "What does *Vodou* have to do with us?"

"I've been endeavoring for over thirty years to abolish this satanic cult from La Gonave. I'm sure you've heard the drums at night."

"I've heard them, that's for sure," Tim said.

Mildred ignored Tim's effort to join the conversation. "This devil worship is getting out of hand. That's why God has seen fit to punish these people so severely. Until they totally forsake the devil, they'll never find redemption."

"You don't mean to say the misery these innocent people are suffering is a punishment from God, do you?" Madeleine asked.

"I most certainly do. How else do you think an uneducated band of slaves defeated Napoleon's army and won their freedom? They made a pact with the devil, that's how, and God has been punishing them ever since. We Christians are their only hope. We must turn them away from the devil and toward the one true Savior. That's why I want to talk to the three of you. I heard from a reliable source there's going to be a big satanic ritual taking place tonight and I want you to help me find it."

"Just what are you planning?" Madeleine asked.

"It's simple," Mildred said, her eyes expanding to conform to her obese head. "The beating of their drums will lead us to their mountain hideout where they'll be performing their devil worshipping. Let them try to carry on with this Satanism while we come armed with the scriptures."

"Don't factor me in on this witch hunt," Tim said, shaking his head in disapproval. "These people have a right to practice their own religion. Who are we to meddle with their culture?"

"Culture? What culture? And religion? Ha. What do you know? I don't take kindly to being lectured by a handyman, I must say."

"Now just one minute, Miss Sponheimer," Madeleine said. "Mister Jamison is a graduate student at Syracuse University, studying anthropology. I suspect he knows a lot more about culture than all of us put together. You can count me out of this witch hunt, too."

Mildred raised her hands to her throat. "Reverend Burkholder, can't you talk some sense into these two? As a man of the cloth, I'm sure you agree these *Vodou* cults must be eradicated from my…uh…our island."

The minister re-buttoned his collar. "I abhor anything un-Christianlike, Miss Sponheimer, Mildred, but we can't expect those who have not dedicated their lives to Christ our Savior, as you and I have, to follow precisely in our footsteps. Madeleine and Tom are very good people. We each do our work for the Lord in different ways. I regret to say I, too, must bow out of this mission, not that I disagree with your sacrosanct aim, only in the manner in which it might best be achieved."

"You're absolutely correct, Reverend Burkholder," Mildred said, and released a thread-thin fissure between her lips that apparently served as the entirety of all the smile she could muster. "In my zeal to save souls, I sometimes forget the Lord's work can't be rushed. I hope to see all of you next week at our service." Without further word, she made a hasty retreat to the confines of her church, recently coated a gunboat gray.

Madeleine chuckled. "I don't think Mildred appreciated your opinion about religion and culture, Tom, although I thought what you said was absolutely on target."

"I simply believe these people have a right to their own religious beliefs, even if *Vodou* does scare the living, ah, bejeebers out of me."

Madeleine turned to the minister and said, "What do you think about all this, Reverend Burkholder?"

"All I know is we're going to a ceremony tonight to see a *Vodou* queen, supposedly to get our souls cleansed. The last person I want to encounter there is Mildred Sponheimer, banging on a pot with a wooden spoon while singing *Bringing in the Sheep*."

Madeleine and Tim chimed in with a resounding, "Amen."

Chapter 21

Undead

Yvette arrived shortly after the church service to prepare the Sunday evening meal. She grilled a tasty red snapper freshly caught by her father and accompanied it with yellow squash and rice mixed with black beans. She served dinner without uttering a word or displaying her effervescent smile, which previously brightened every meal. Her melancholy mood soon rubbed off on the others.

After they finished their dinner in virtual silence, Tim offered to do the dishes so Yvette could take the night off. Madeleine thanked him and explained work is therapy to Haitians. Yvette would feel punished if not allowed to cook and clean up after them. Madeleine promised to send her home early, as soon as she finished the dishes and straightened the kitchen.

The minister pulled away from the table, scraping his chair across the Mexican tiled floor. "Tom tells me this *séance* won't be starting until midnight. Is that true?"

"That's true," Madeleine said. "The ceremony can't begin on a Sunday or any other holy day for that matter."

"How long will it last?"

"All night…through much of the next morning."

"Goodness to God," the minister exclaimed. "Even revivals don't take that long."

"He's right," Tim added. "What are we getting ourselves into?"

Madeleine tightened her lips into a horizontal smile. "To be quite honest, your guess is as good as mine."

The minister slumped in his chair. "This is just great. We'll probably be sacrificed and burned at the stake."

"Maybe not in that order," Tim said with a chuckle.

Once Yvette finished the dishes, Madeleine sent her home, insisting she take the carefully wrapped leftovers to share with her family. She then joined Tim on the front porch. "Where's Reverend Burkholder?"

"He's on the sofa taking another nap. This midnight ceremony is a little past his bedtime, I do believe."

"Mine, too. That's probably not a bad idea."

"I don't think I could sleep right now. There's too much spinning through my head."

"You're not worried about this ceremony tonight, are you, Tom?"

"As a matter of fact, I am, a little. Aren't you the least bit alarmed by all this *Vodou* stuff?"

"Yes and no. If you think about *Vodou* as a religion, it's not so frightening. Up here in the mountains, in the dark with drums beating and stuff going on we don't understand, yeah, I find that a little unsettling."

Tim stole a glance at her, which triggered long-absent, inner stirrings. Guilt soon replaced these feelings as memories of Sarah surfaced. Overtaken by his customary sense of worthlessness, he sunk even further upon reflecting what Madeleine would think if she knew his real identity—Tim James, the drunken janitor.

"Would you like some coffee, Tom?"

"Sure." Tim responded in the affirmative more out of politeness than desire. "That sounds good."

"I'll be right back. You take cream and sugar, don't you?"

"Yeah, that would be great."

They sipped coffee and shared thoughts about the events of the day.

"I might as well tell you what's bothering Yvette so much, while the minister's asleep. He won't believe a word of this and I'm not sure you will either."

"Does it have anything to do with her brother's missing bones?" he asked.

"It has everything to do with them."

"How so?"

"There's a good chance Yvette's brother is among the walking dead. A zombie."

"Are you serious?" he tilted his head. "A zombie?"

"Yes, I'm serious. A zombie. It's not quite what it seems, not like in the movies. I thought you might be up on this. A scientist from Harvard shed considerable light on this subject. I have his book if you want to read it."

Tim repositioned himself on the wooden chair. "We Syracuse guys generally ignore the Ivy Leaguers, but sure, I'd like to read the book. Tell me, what's the story on these zombies?"

Madeleine explained how a witch doctor or, more correctly, a *bocor*, prepares a concoction that can place a person into a deep coma soon after he or she comes in contact with it. The victim's heartbeat and breathing become undetectable and when they are found in this condition they are invariably pronounced dead by whoever can pass as a physician. Since they don't embalm the deceased in Haiti, the law requires they be buried within twenty-four hours.

Tim vividly recalled his own near-death experience at the Port-au-Prince morgue. "Yeah, I know about that law. How do they poison their victims? Do they slip it into their food or drink?"

"Neither. The poison is a powder the *bocor* usually blows into the victim's face. Apparently, you don't have to inhale very much for it to take effect."

"What happens next?"

"The person is buried and that night the *bocor* sneaks into the graveyard and digs him up. In time, the victim comes out of the coma, but the *bocor* maintains him in a perpetual stupor by feeding him some type of mind-altering paste. It's all described in the book. The person everyone saw buried that day becomes the *bocor's* slave. Living dead to everyone else—a zombie."

"That's incredible. Do you think it's true?"

"You tell me. You're the one studying to become an anthropologist. I do know this. All Haitians believe in zombies. Yvette is convinced her brother is one and, for Haitians, there can be no worse fate."

He reflected upon the shocking tale Madeleine told. It sounded plausible if this scientist from Harvard was legitimate, unlike himself. "Can anything be done for her brother if they find him?"

"Haitians believe if a zombie tastes salt he'll come out of his stupor. Unfortunately, they also believe he's still dead, walking about without a soul. Dead, all the same. His family would never accept him back even if he did return. They've already buried him."

"This is horrible."

"That's why Yvette is so upset. Death they can deal with. The undead is another story."

"Now you really have me worried, Madeleine. I have been thinking or, at least hoping, most of this black magic hullabaloo was superstitious nonsense. Now it seems from what you're saying these *bocors* do have some scientific basis for their *Vodou* practice. I felt more comfortable thinking it was simply a magic show, mostly just smoke and mirrors."

"You better believe much of what they do is real, for good or for evil, Tom. These potions have been handed down from generation to generation, all the way back from Africa."

"How do you know which of these *Vodou* priests or priestesses can be trusted? Which ones know the good stuff?"

"Actually, they all know both," she said. "A good *houngan* or *mambo* needs to know what the bad ones are up to in order to be able to effectively counteract them. *La Reine* Memmene is as good and as powerful as they get. If Ti Ti's fever is due to a spirit's revenge or a *bocor's* bad intentions, she'll know what to do."

"Are you saying Ti Ti could have been poisoned by a *bocor*?"

"It's one possibility. It's also possible his illness is bacterial, viral, or even malaria. In any event, *La Reine* Memmene may be his best hope."

It all started to make sense. Why shouldn't Haitians fervently believe in *Vodou* teachings? Their religious leaders control life, death, and even undeath. A cadaverous chill fell over him as blocked memories emerged of his ghastly night in the Port-au-Prince morgue, the mysterious *Vodou* ceremony carried out in a tomb-filled graveyard and, most haunting of all, the ungodly Ebony Man, his penetrating eyes all afire.

Chapter 22

White Lace

When the ten o'clock hour arrived, the trio commenced the drive up a rock-littered, dirt road for the midnight, mountain ceremony. About forty-five minutes into the journey, they came upon Ti Bon, his wife Marie Joseph with Ti Ti cradled in her arms, and Colette, the younger of their two daughters.

Madeleine pulled her vehicle to the shoulder of the rudimentary road and turned off the engine. "We'll be on foot from here on," she said.

Pulsating *Vodou* drums resonated across the mountaintops. Tim and Reverend Burkholder slid out of the vehicle and stole glances at each other. The minister verbalized the question Tim had been thinking. "I thought this ceremony wasn't supposed to start till midnight?"

"It hasn't started yet," she said. "The drums are to guide us in. Don't take your flashlights. It's best if we leave modern-day magic behind."

Ti Bon lit a torch at the edge of the footpath, illuminating himself and his family. He would lead the troupe to *La Reine* Memmene's *Vodou* temple. They zigzagged in single file along the narrow cut in the side of the jagged mountain. With the night aglow by the light of a full moon, giant, ghostly shadows mirrored their every footstep. After nearly an hour of trudging across the steep, broken terrain and, with the pounding of drums growing more deafening, Ti Bon brought the group to a halt.

Panting, the minister patted his flabby chest and turned to Madeleine and Tim. "It's about time we took a breather. I tell you, I'm dying here."

After conferring with Marie Joseph, Madeleine said, "There's a problem up ahead. Apparently, a landslide has obstructed the path. Ti Bon is checking to see if there's another way."

"What will we do if we can't get across, Madeleine?" Tim asked, comforted by the thought of returning to her cottage.

"Not getting across isn't an option," she said.

Ti Bon returned about ten minutes later and motioned for the group to follow him. Tim caught a clear glimpse of the peasant farmer for the first time that night. He noted a face filled with sadness and wondered if Ti Ti's illness might be more serious than previously indicated.

Ti Bon led them at a rapid clip on a nearly indiscernible path above the landslide until the passageway rounding the steep mountainside narrowed to a width that would give even a sure-footed billy goat reason to pause. He gathered a pile of rocks to prop his torch, which illuminated their immediate surroundings. The depths of the gorge below remained a black hole. Ti Bon forged ahead, the toes of his bare feet being all that fit on the narrow ledge. Dislodged pebbles echoed off the cliff's wall before falling into the dark silence.

The minister peered into the abyss. "That ledge is mighty narrow. How far down do you think this goes?"

Tim shook his head. "If we fall, we're goners."

Marie Joseph, Ti Ti strapped to her back, glided across the ledge with the equally agile Colette not far behind. Madeleine suggested she should cross next, followed by the minister, and then Tom. They each held their breath, faced the rock wall as Ti Bon had before them, and then negotiated the toe-size ridge together, maintaining an arm's reach of the person closest to them.

The minister panicked halfway across. "I can't go any further. I'm scared shitless. Excuse me, I mean I'm too scared to—"

The rock the minister clawed in his right hand broke free and cascaded down the bottomless gorge. Tim snatched the minister's arm with his leading hand and clung with his other one to a gnarled tree root. Fortunately, it held fast.

"Madeleine, you go on ahead," Tim gasped. "The minister and I will back off. He'll never make it."

"You've got that straight," the minister said before she could respond.

Unhindered by Reverend Burkholder, she swiftly negotiated the ledge and caught up with the Baptistes. Tim and the minister slid their way back to where the torch marked the point of safety. A few minutes later, her voice rang out over the pounding drums. "Tom. Reverend Burkholder. Are you two okay?"

"We're fine," Tim said. "What do we do now?"

"Ti Bon says he'll get some help to clear the landslide. The reverend should wait, but you should come with us now."

Tim felt perplexed as to what to do, but the minister wasted little time in resolving his quandary. "Go ahead. I'll be fine right here. It won't bother me one blessed bit if I miss this whole dang ceremony. Just leave me with the torch."

"You're sure?"

"I'm sure. You go and put in a good word for me with that *mambo* lady."

The minister hugged the torch and lumbered his way back to the main path. Tim inched across the ledge and quickly caught up with the others. The hike, thereafter, consisted of a dizzying succession of jagged, hairpin turns. About the time Tim found himself gulping at the thin air, they arrived at a flat parcel overshadowed by an enormous kapok tree adorned with numerous beads and nondescript colorful objects, along with a black-and-white speckled hen, recently beheaded. Hundreds of candles, each melted tight into spent *clairin* bottles, flickered amongst the maze of the tree's supporting buttresses. The flames weaved snake-like in all directions.

Tim made eye contact with Madeleine. "I can't believe there's such a massive tree on this island. How did it escape the ax?"

"This is a sacred tree. It is a home to the *loa*. Haitians would never cut down such a tree. I'm surprised the missionaries haven't found it, though. They would surely cut it down."

"Why would missionaries cut down such a magnificent tree?"

"They'd do it in a vain attempt to stamp out *Vodou*. The Catholic Church made a concerted effort back in the nineteen thirties and forties to wipe out anything associated with *Vodou*. They cut down every sacred tree they could locate, burned *Vodou* temples, you name it. Ultimately, they gave up. The Protestants are now on the same kick, zero tolerance for *Vodou*. You heard Mildred Sponheimer. They call it devil worship."

"I'm sure glad this tree was spared. There can't be more than a handful of trees this size left anywhere in Haiti."

"You're probably right."

"Are we almost there?" he asked, hopeful their grueling trek would soon come to an end.

"We'll be coming up on the *houmfort* any time now."

"*Houmfort*? What's a *houmfort*?"

"A *houmfort* is a mystery house or what most people might call a temple. I don't know if we'll be allowed to enter it. Next to the *houmfort* will be a *péristyle*, a thatch-roof temple with no walls and a center post called a *poteau-mitan*. That's where the main ceremony will take place. Make sure we stay close to Ti Bon so I can ask him to explain everything that's happening."

They soon arrived at a plateau where a swarm of well over two hundred Haitians amassed outside a *Vodou* complex matching her description. Ti Bon approached a man within the assembly, who by his demeanor and those around him exuded high stature. The dignitary barked a command and four strapping, male youth sped down the path to where the minister had been left.

"Those young men were sent to clear the path for Reverend Burkholder," she whispered to Tim. "It will take a while. He'll probably miss the ceremony."

"I don't think he'll be terribly upset about that."

A woman in a long, white, cotton dress led them to the front of the *péristyle* and motioned for them to sit on the grassless ground. Ti Bon and Marie Joseph, Ti Ti still held in her arms, soon joined them.

Tim nudged Madeleine. "Where's Colette?"

The swelling throng took places on the ground, starting at about an arm's length behind them. Madeline caught Ti Bon's attention and asked him a question in *Créole.*

She translated Ti Bon's response. "Colette's inside the *houmfort*, but Ti Bon wouldn't say why."

The beating drums came to an abrupt halt, along with the murmuring of the congregation. A decrepit, old woman wearing a tattered and grungy dress entered the *péristyle* and lit three candles resting on a wooden altar. The candles illuminated a wooden crucifix and a faded black-and-white photograph propped up by small shells. Three ceramic bowls sat at the base of the crucifix, while a bowl made from a dried calabash sliced in half rested at the foundation of the altar.

A bonfire exploded in front of the altar, apparently signaling the drummers to recommence their rhythmic beat. Only three drums, each made from a hollowed-out log, were in use. One stood about five-foot high, another half that size, and the third, smaller yet. The largest drum, painted royal blue with a white cross emblazoned across its base, displayed remnants of fur along its sides where twine fastened the rawhide head. The drummer stood on a stool and beat the immense instrument with a stick held in his left hand. He alternated the beats with the heel of his right palm. The two other drummers struck their instruments only with their hands. Streams of sweat glided down the three shirtless drummers as they pounded out a frantic beat. A woman periodically wiped their brows with a dingy rag.

A procession of celebrants, led by a bare-footed elder with a red turban on his head, emerged from the *houmfort*. The man, wrinkled in face and body, vigorously shook a gourd rattle with a tiny bell at its tip. Behind him, two young women clad in white waved red flags emblazoned with yellow serpentine symbols. The man Ti Bon spoke to earlier about clearing the path appeared next. Garbed only in ragged shorts barely held up by his narrow hips, he cupped a sword with both hands, stopped at the bonfire, lowered the blade into the flames, and then positioned the reddened steel sideways in his mouth, which he clenched with his teeth.

"How can he do that?" Tim asked Madeleine. "How can he not burn?"

"I have no idea. I've often seen Yvette pick up hot pots off the stove with her bare hands, but nothing like this."

Next, a rotund woman dressed in a scarlet robe and adorned with a feathered headdress stepped out of the *houmfort.* She slithered toward the fire. Everyone's eyes, including those of the *blancs*, remained fixed on the brightly clad figure casting a ghoulish shadow.

Saucer-eyed, Madeleine grasped Tim's arm. "That's *La Reine* Memmene. Isn't she spectacular?"

"Spectacular wouldn't be my choice of words, but yes, she's something else."

About twenty barefoot girls wearing white robes and matching scarves wrapped around their heads formed a two-by-two line. They danced with dizzying repetitiveness around the bonfire and the *Vodou* celebrants, all the while chanting, *"Damballah Queddo, Nous p'vini."*

"What's going on?" Tim asked.

"The young girls in the white robes are called *hounsis*. They're informing *Damballah*, the serpent god, that they're coming."

As the *hounsis* continued their dancing and droning chant, *La Reine* Memmene pivoted in place and then fell prostrate. The drums ceased. The girls stopped dancing. Only the crackling fire emitted sound.

The old man resumed rattling his seed-containing gourd for a brief moment. The sword bearer, the blade now removed from his mouth, made a pronouncement. *"Legba, Damballah, et tous les loas, nous offrons des mercis."*

"The man with the sword is a *houngan*," Madeleine whispered to Tim. "He's thanking the *loa* for making their presence. *La Reine* Memmene is now possessed."

The scarlet-robed *mambo* seemingly floated to her feet. Her contorted face appeared more animal than human. After the drummers resumed at a softer beat, she motioned toward the *houmfort,* where an emotionless Colette appeared at the single door. She wore a white, lace dress with a white veil covering her face, looking much as if about to make her first communion. At her side, restrained by a leather leash, stood a quivering young goat cloaked in identical white lace. Together, they stepped forward, although the goat struggled to break free.

The drumming intensified once Colette and the goat became encircled by the *hounsis*. Colette knelt before the imposing *mambo*. The old man rattled his gourd with a fervor that would have exhausted most men half his age. The sword-bearing *houngan* jabbed a wooden stake into the ground with his free hand, tethered the goat to it, and forced the terrified animal to its knees.

Tim sensed the shadowy presence of on-lookers behind him—something was about to happen—something sinister. "I don't like the looks of this," he muttered under his breath.

Madeleine did not respond.

The *houngan* knelt behind Colette and the tethered goat, again holding his sword like a chalice. *La Reine* Memmene raised her right hand over the young girl and animal as if to consecrate them. The *houngan* stood up and pointed his sword above his head. The drumming increased in intensity, metering the pulse of the congregation.

Tim vaulted to his feet, but before he could make another move Ti Bon grabbed him. Others in the crowd helped Ti Bon wrestle the sacrilegious *blanc* to the ground.

Although Madeleine had not budged, two men seized her by the arms.

"They're going to kill her," Tim cried out. "They're going to sacrifice her." Restrained or not, he could see Madeleine had become incapacitated by shock.

The *houngan's* sword swiftly found its mark. The white-laced goat died without a sound.

The mob turned jubilant, dancing, singing, and embracing one another. Ti Bon and the others released Tim and Madeleine. Ti Bon engulfed his wife in a full-body embrace. Tears streamed down their cheeks.

Overwhelmed with joy, Tim took Madeleine into his arms and kissed her lips. The drummers stopped, bringing the entire congregation to a standstill.

La Reine Memmene raised above her head a calabash bowl from which a viscous, red liquid dripped. She lowered it to her lips, took a drink, and passed it to the *houngan*. He, too, drank the liquid, placed his right index finger inside the bowl, and smeared a red sign of the cross on Colette's forehead. Only then did Tim realize the red liquid to be the blood of the slain goat.

After the congregants repositioned themselves on the ground, *La Reine* Memmene motioned for Madeleine, Tim, and the Baptistes to approach and kneel before her. The *mambo* handed the blood-filled, calabash bowl to Marie Joseph, which she readily drank. The young mother scooped some of the blood on her fingers and dripped scarlet droplets into Ti Ti's open mouth before passing the bowl to Ti Bon, who swallowed a measurable amount before handing it to Madeleine.

She sipped from the bowl and then turned to Tim. "Just take a little. This is very important."

He took a deep gulp of his own saliva before placing the warm liquid to his mouth. The taste proved not to be as unpleasant as the thought.

Tim sensed *La Reine* Memmene's stare long before returning eye contact. His shirt had ripped open in the scuffle with Ti Bon and the others, exposing his silver cross. She sauntered up to him, placed her hand on the cross, and said in English, "This is indeed a sacred night. I speak in the tongue this holy one understands. Just as the Almighty God of all gods, all peoples, tested Abraham, so have the spirits tested Ti Bon and Marie Joseph. Their faith and devotion did not prove to be wanting. The spirits have been merciful."

La Reine Memmene took Ti Ti from Marie Joseph's arms. The *houngan* handed the *mambo* a small knife, which she used to make small incisions in the child's scalp. The old woman, who earlier lit the candles, brought out a wooden bowl containing a steaming herbal potion and poured it onto a white bandanna. The *mambo* wrapped the dampened cloth around Ti Ti's head before returning the still feverish boy to his mother.

"The young boy will be fine," *La Reine* Memmene said, still speaking in English. "The spirits remain angry their cave has been violated, but no harm will come to any of you this night."

The *mambo* cupped Tim's chin in her right hand. "I have been awaiting your return. The spirits foretold it. No harm will ever come to the one who wears the Spanish sea-god's cross." She then returned, followed by her court, to the mystery house.

Tim's gaze snapped to Madeleine. She shrugged, only adding to his bewilderment. He clutched the cross in his right fist. "What in the world is she talking about? The Spanish sea-god's cross?" A familiar fear overcame him. He frantically scanned the crowd, experiencing what he couldn't see—the piercing stare of the Ebony Man.

The drummers resumed their ear-shattering beat.

****

Madeleine meandered to the altar and picked up a creased, black-and-white photograph of a white soldier seated in a chair lifted by four Haitian men, somewhat reminiscent of an ancient pharaoh transported by slaves. Even with dying candles and, despite the fading of decades long past, she instantly noted the uncanny resemblance of the man in the picture and the blond-haired anthropologist who had just kissed her.

Chapter 23

Le Roi Blanc

The frenzied jubilation of the congregation played out into the deep hours of the night, although *La Reine* Memmene and the other *Vodou* celebrants had long before sequestered themselves in the silence of the *houmfort*. Tim and Madeleine sat shoulder-to-shoulder against a velvety-flowered tree, engrossed by the marvelous spectacle of primal dances and songs they surmised had origins in darkest Africa. Mired in the gesticulating throng of worshippers, the Baptiste family paid its homage to the merciful *loa*.

Despite the commotion surrounding them, Madeleine couldn't take her mind off the faded black-and-white photograph of a young soldier, the spitting image of the anthropologist sitting next to her. She glanced at him and thought of their kiss. *Did I return it?* He caught her totally by surprise.

The celebration waned as the sun arrived and the bottles of *clairin* emptied. Although the drummers stopped drumming, the dancers stopped dancing, and the singers stopped singing, the lovers kept loving. Some may have called this an orgy, but it did not seem that way to Madeleine and Tim. Most of the assemblage brought their own straw mats and spread themselves out wherever space allowed.

"I want to apologize for what happened tonight," Tim said, interrupting the silence between them. "I was out of order. I guess I got caught up in the celebration."

"There is no need to apologize, Tom."

****

Tim rapidly fell into slumber, while Madeleine remained awake, re-living tucked-away memories of Dr. Bruce Thorton, the man she almost married. She met Bruce in college and recalled how they spent many a sultry, Illinois summer evening planning their future lives together. They planned to spend three months out of the year on La Gonave before starting a family of their own, an event not to occur, they both agreed, for at least four years. Bruce initially shared her excitement to work alongside her father in Haiti, but as the wedding date drew near, he began to espouse a growing list of concerns. Ultimately, the newly minted physician chose a residency at a prestigious Chicago hospital, along with a shiny sports car, over her, Haiti, and La Gonave's needy children.

She glanced at the handsome, blond-haired anthropologist sleeping comfortably against the tree. She recalled the words she spoke the day before when Tom asked how she could stand it here all alone. "Haiti is not for everyone."

****

A swift kick to his boot-covered left foot startled Tim into consciousness. He opened his eyes to a grinning Methodist minister. "*Voilá*, 'tis me," the reverend said. "Looks like I missed a great party. You two seem to be getting a little cozy."

"You don't have to worry about that," Madeleine said with a tone of finality no one could help but notice.

An uncomfortable moment passed.

"Where's a fella supposed to get breakfast around here?" the minister asked, glancing about with a concerned look.

"Don't worry, Reverend Burkholder," Madeleine said. "We'll be eating all day long. I hope you like goat meat."

"Goat meat sounds great to me. I worked up quite an appetite watching those young, Haitian bucks clearing rocks off the path. Mildred Sponheimer may think the French lost their colony due to witchcraft or something, but it's clear to me these people are simply stronger than any soldiers Napoleon could possibly muster up. I'll bet every man, woman, and child on this island can easily lift his or her own weight."

"I can't argue with you on that," Tim said.

"I'm sure you and Madeleine could hold your own, but let's face it, most of us *blancs* are absolute wimps."

"Strength is measured in many ways," *La Reine* Memmene said, having quietly strolled up from behind. "Welcome, Reverend Burkholder, we have been expecting you."

"I…ah…it's a pleasure to meet you, *mambo*, I mean Memmene, *La Reine* Memmene."

The portly *mambo* chuckled. She spoke in *Créole* to her young ladies-in-waiting gathered behind her. They chuckled, as did Madeleine.

"I'm getting the feeling I'm the butt of a joke," the minister said, a wry smile crossing his face.

"Actually, what *La Reine* Memmene had to say about you was quite flattering," Madeleine said.

"That's okay. All I need to know is if our souls are cleansed, or at least yours and Tom's."

"There is much left to do before your souls will be cleansed," *La Reine* Memmene said, her cheerful demeanor dissipated. "That is, except for the one of you whose soul needs no cleansing."

Reverend Burkholder burst into a beaming grin. "As a minister of the Christian faith, it's often assumed my soul is beyond reproach. However, let me say, I, too, have on occasion, very few occasions, been guilty of sin."

The *mambo* looked the minister squarely in the eyes. "Your soul is very much in need of cleansing, Reverend Burkholder. The only pure one among you is the one with blond hair."

Dumbfounded, Tim concluded this *mambo* lady might know *Vodou*, but she sure as hell didn't know jack-shit about him. He assumed she was going to say Madeleine, the sensuously attractive nurse practitioner. She radiated a pureness more than anyone he'd ever met. He realized she intimidated him. *If she's not perfect, then who the hell is?*

"Well, Saint Thomas," the minister said. "I guess you can head back to Anse-à-Galets now."

"He who is to come must stay," the *mambo* said. "I will conduct a ceremony later this morning, in my *houmfort*, where I will decree all you must do. Be aware, if it were not for *le Roi Blanc de La Gonave,* you would all be dead. Come, follow me. The feast is ready."

A dozen or so women scurried about preparing the feast, some baking cakes and breads in adobe ovens, while others stirred cast-iron caldrons steaming with rice, millet, yams, or beans. Several goats and chickens, recently slain and butchered, joined the sacrificial offering, all of them grilling over charcoal fires on bamboo rotisseries of various shapes and sizes.

The minister wandered over to where the food cooked. Tim and Madeleine tagged along. "Smell that aroma," he said. "There's enough food here to feed an army."

"Look around you, Reverend Burkholder," Madeleine said. "There is an army to feed." Scores of Haitians silently congregated a respectful distance away, all exhibiting the bright-eyed look of festive anticipation.

"Looks like we must be the guests of honor," the minister said. "I'll bet they're waiting for us to start before they dig in."

La Reine Memmene motioned for her *blanc* guests to wait and then sashayed amongst the fires to inspect the food, sampling it here and there. After a short while she backtracked to the waiting *blancs.* She gazed about until she spotted the Baptiste family in the crowd and signaled them to join the honorary party for the feast. Ti Bon, beaming, held one arm around Colette and the other around Marie Joseph. Ti Ti fervently nursed at one of her breasts.

Madeleine raced over to greet them. "Look at Ti Ti," she hollered. "His fever is gone."

"I can't believe it," Tim said to the minister. "That kid was boiling last night. The *mambo* put some sort of herbal potion on his head and, take a look at him now, he's sucking away like there's no tomorrow."

Once the Baptistes and *blancs* joined together, *La Reine* Memmene directed them toward a table of rough-sawn wood set with faded, mismatched china and mixed patterns of stainless steel tableware. "Please be seated," she said. "No one else may feast until you have first been satiated."

Tim shook his head. "I can't sit here eating while all these hungry people are waiting for us to finish."

"We're the guests of honor," the minister said. "The sooner we eat, the sooner they eat. Besides, who are we to question their customs?"

"The reverend is right," Madeleine added. "It would be considered rude of us not to dine first."

A line of women, clad in their traditional long, white cotton dresses, served the feast. Each brought out separate bowls of the various prepared foods, along with an assortment of fresh fruits. To accompany the food, Madeleine explained, they served a brownish-colored liquid made from the root of a sacred plant. The Baptistes enjoyed the strong brew, but the *blancs* mostly sipped out of politeness. *La Reine* Memmene sat with them, but did not eat or drink. Younger girls, also dressed in white, rapidly cleared the table after the guests of honor finished their meals. This signaled to the crowd their time to feast had arrived.

The hungry horde descended upon the food with abandon, yet equitably distributed it amongst themselves. They ate with their hands or used small, tin cups. *La Reine* Memmene joined the crowd and ate as they ate. The cooks replenished the ovens, caldrons, and rotisseries as rapidly as they emptied. No one would go home hungry this day.

Marie Joseph departed to take Colette and a healthy Ti Ti to Anse-à-Galets, where her other children stayed under the watchful care of her sister. Ti Bon remained behind with the *blancs*.

The atmosphere turned suffocating from a combination of torching heat and thin mountain air. The minister stole a modicum of relief in the shade of the tree where he earlier found Madeleine and Tim. He fell soundly asleep despite the ruckus of a gathering of children giggling and poking each other whenever flies dotted his sun-reddened face.

Tim and Madeleine strolled through the temple complex and exchanged a few words now and again. He suddenly felt the need to clear the air. "I want to apologize again for last night, Madeleine."

"There is no need to apologize, Tom. We are two adults who shared a kiss. That's all. I've already forgotten about it."

Madeleine's off-hand remark caught him off guard, almost as much as the inner stirrings he felt the moment he kissed her. She obviously didn't share these feelings. *Maybe this is for the best.* "So, we're still friends?"

Madeleine cocked her head to the side with a sparkle in her eyes and a smile that would melt any man. "Of course we're still friends. Very good friends."

They rounded a corner of the *houmfort* and came upon a naked, pot-bellied boy with hair tinged orange. "What's with this kid's hair?" Tim asked. "He's the second kid I've seen like this."

"It's a sign of severe vitamin deficiency, Tom. He's extremely malnourished. I need to find his parents so I can get him to the clinic, or at least what's left of the clinic."

Madeleine knelt to the level of the boy's eyes, held his hands, and spoke soothingly in *Créole*. He bolted away in midsentence.

"What happened, Madeleine? Why did he run away like that?"

"He told me his parents are dead." She stood up and shook her head forlornly. "As are his brothers and sisters. He's all alone. I told him he could live with me, but that was a mistake. He apparently heard the ridiculous rumors of *blancs* eating Haitian children. It's so sad."

Tim placed his right, index finger on Madeleine's cheek to capture a tear rolling out of her eye. He left his finger there and fought his urge to kiss her again. "Madeleine, you can't continue to carry the weight of all these children on your shoulders. You're just one person. You can only do so much."

She removed his hand from her cheek, but did not let it go. "You're right, Tom, I know. Sometimes I feel so helpless. I should be able to do more. I guess I'm still my father's little girl, striving to live up to all his expectations."

"I'm sure if your father was alive today, he would be very proud of you and the work you're doing, Madeleine."

The minister interrupted the warm interlude. "There you two are. I've been looking all over for you. The *mambo* lady is ready to see us in her big house. What did you call it? A house fort?"

"It's called a *houmfort*," Madeleine said, dropping Tim's hand. "It means *mystery house*. This is exciting. I've never stepped inside of one of these before."

"Tom, I have got a question for you," the minister said. "Were you ever in the army and stationed on this island or something?"

He returned a puzzled look before responding. "The army? Not me. No way. No how."

The minister presented him with the faded, black-and-white photograph Madeleine viewed earlier on the altar of the *péristyle*. "Then how do you explain this picture?"

He stared at the photo a long moment before answering. "Gosh, this looks just like me, but believe me, it's not. Take a look at this uniform. It looks like something out of World War I. This photograph was obviously taken long before I was ever born."

"Tom," Madeleine said. "There's something else I've been waiting for the right moment to bring up."

"What's that?"

"*La Reine* Memmene referred to you earlier as *le Roi Blanc de la Gonave.*"

"What on earth does that mean?"

"The literal translation—*the White King of La Gonave.*"

Chapter 24

Houmfort

An old lady, the one who lit the candles the previous night, led Madeleine, Tim, Ti Bon and, lagging a few paces behind, the minister, inside the darkened *houmfort*. She directed them toward a candle-lit altar at the far side before passing from their sight, never uttering a sound. The knee-high altar, a thick slab of wood about three feet wide and twice that in length, rested on columns of loose stones and overflowed with an odd assortment of offerings, candles, and crucifixes. The offerings—coins, bars of soap, strings of beads, dried grains in wooden bowls or plastic containers, old photographs, and other nondescript items—lay haphazardly strewn about. Only the foot-high, tarnished, silver crucifix at the center of the altar appeared to be in an arranged position. Several smaller crucifixes, mostly made of wood, occupied whatever space remained. Lit candles placed in the mouths of empty *clairin* bottles added an eerie illumination to the surroundings. Two red-painted serpents decorated the whitewashed mud wall behind the altar. They looked to be slithering in the flickering light.

"Now I know why they call this place the mystery house," the minister said, his eyes wider than usual. "Nothing here makes any sense."

"There is much here making sense for those who can see through the eyes of their souls," *La Reine* Memmene said, her voice rising softly from the direction of the altar. "Please, join me."

With their eyes now adjusted to the darkness, the foursome spotted *La Reine* Memmene sitting cross-legged on a straw mat, an arm's length in front of the altar. Between the altar and mats, ground corn poured on the dirt floor formed a multiplicity of geometric figures. The *mambo* motioned to four straw mats arranged in a semi-circle around her. They each picked one and sat down, with all but the minister crossing his or her legs in the same manner as the *mambo*. Reverend Burkholder stretched spread-eagle and leaned backward on the palms of his hands.

"Welcome to the house of the spirits," *La Reine* Memmene said. "It is good you have come for the spirits are in a merciful mood. They are pleased the one who is to come has come." She stared directly at Tim, a stare he could not return.

"My mother told me what her mother was told by hers," *La Reine* Memmene said. "The covenant has now come to pass. The White King has come to reclaim his throne."

Mystified, Tim nudged Madeleine, but received no verbal or visual response.

The minister held up the photograph he snatched from the *péristyle's* altar. "Are you saying Tom Jamison and the person in this picture are one and the same?"

"You of all people should know better than to desecrate an altar, Reverend Burkholder," *La Reine* Memmene said, her stare even more scolding than her tone.

The candle-lighting lady mysteriously reappeared and plucked the photograph from the minister's hand. She bowed to the queen and left to return it to its holy place.

"To answer your question, Reverend Burkholder, pictures are but pictures and flesh is but flesh. It is the soul that endures. Mister Jamison is not who he says he is."

The minister and Tim shot glances at each other. Tim lowered his head. *Is the jig up? Does she know my true identity*?

The *mambo* continued her discourse. "It is up to the spirits to decide when the one who is to come will be. For now, he is safe under the protection of the Spanish sea-god's cross. We will speak no more of this. There are other matters we must attend to first." She spoke in *Créole* to Ti Bon, who periodically nodded his head in respectful reply.

Reverting back to English, she said to the *blancs*, "Ti Bon will lead you on your pilgrimage to salvation. I trust *Soeur* Madeleine to translate that which you must all know. Go, now, there is still much feasting to be done."

They exited the *houmfort*, the brilliance of daylight momentarily blinding. Bottles of *clairin* passed freely amongst the celebrants, serving notice the festival would continue to build steam, along with the heat of the day. Much food remained to be consumed.

"Let's get ourselves another bite to eat," the minister said. "Madeleine, I hope you're going to give us the skinny on what we have to do to get our souls cleansed. That is, all of us but the White King of La Gonave."

"I have a news bulletin for all of you," Tim said. "I'm not a king. I've never been a king. I don't ever want to be a king, particularly of La Gonave."

"What are you complaining about?" the minister asked. "You don't even need to have your soul cleansed. I sure wish I could be the king. How about you, Madeleine? Don't you wish you were getting some royalty out of all of this?"

"Me thinks he protests too much," Madeleine said with a chuckle. "I'm quite satisfied being in the presence of His Majesty."

Everyone except Tim laughed, including Ti Bon, who apparently didn't need to understand English to appreciate her humor.

"I have another question for you, Tom," the minister said between guffaws. "What's the deal with this silver cross around your neck? Where did you get it, anyway?"

"I found it in Port-au-Prince," Tim said, opting not to mention he awakened one morning and discovered it fastened around his neck, or that he first saw it on the Ebony Man.

Madeleine positioned her head only inches away in an attempt to read the worn inscription. "Let me have a look at this, Tom. There's writing on here, but it doesn't appear to be Spanish. I think it's Italian."

"Who or what would be the Spanish sea-god, anyway?" Tim asked.

"I can only think of one thing," Madeleine said. "*La Reine Memmene* must believe your cross previously graced the neck of none other than Christopher Columbus."

Chapter 25

Les Arcadins

Ti Bon arrived at Madeleine's before daybreak on Tuesday, squatted against the outside wall of the screened porch, and silently waited for the others to arise. Madeleine, being the first to stir, spotted him when she strolled out into the kitchen. "*Bonjour*, Ti Bon."

His face radiated a rare warm glow. "*Bonjou', Soeur* Madeleine."

Although asked several times, he refused to join them for breakfast and remained squatted on the porch while the others ate. The conversation around the table turned to the soul-cleansing odyssey about to begin.

"Exactly where are we going for this baptism by fire?" the minister asked Madeleine.

"The only thing I know for sure is we're heading over to the main island and we'll be gone for at least two days."

"Two days?"

"I'm afraid so, Reverend Burkholder. *La Reine* Memmene said Ti Bon will lead us. He's not very talkative, as I'm sure you've noticed. He'll tell us what we need to know when we need to know it."

"What should we bring along?" Tim asked.

"I suggest you pack as light as possible. There's no telling how much walking we might be doing. We need to be down to the dock in thirty minutes."

"We better get a move on, Reverend Burkholder," Tim said. He picked up his dishes to take to the kitchen.

The minister rose to his feet and flattened his lips, producing neither a smile nor a frown.

****

They sailed across the La Gonave Channel aboard the Nazarene's sloop with Cristophe again at its helm. They landed at the same concrete dock where Tim and the minister first embarked to the outer island.

Tim held the line attached to the bow, jumped to the pier, and secured it to a corner post. He raced to the opposite post, caught the stern line thrown by the captain, pulled the vessel tight against the dock, and fastened the line.

Madeleine took his hand and leapt to the pier. "You certainly seem to know your way around boats, Tom."

"I've been on a few. How about you, reverend, can I give you a hand?"

"I think I can handle it this time. This dock may not be as big and fancy as the one on La Gonave, but it sure seems more practical, considering the size of most Haitian boats."

Tim hopped back in the sloop to assist Ti Bon with gathering their belongings. To his surprise, Ti Bon had not brought anything except the tattered, grimy clothes he wore. The Haitian farmer quietly waited for him to jump to the pier before disembarking himself.

"Hey, take a look at that beauty of a car," Madeleine said. She pointed at the minister's luxury vehicle. "I wonder who the rich, fat-cat is that it belongs to."

"It probably belongs to some high-level, governmental official," the minister said, "or, perhaps some hot-shot administrator working for a development agency."

Tim lowered his head.

"We *peóns* won't get to ride in the lap of such luxury," Madeleine said. "We'll be taking a *tap tap* to Magazin-Carrier."

Tim strolled closer. "When are you going to tell the reverend and me what's in store for us?"

"I'm afraid I don't know any more than what I told you. It's up to Ti Bon, not me. He only told me where we're heading and what to bring. We're in his hands from here on."

Ti Bon motioned to the *blancs* to gather their backpacks. He led them by foot to *la Route Nationale Numbre Une.* He hailed one of the ubiquitous *tap taps* already hauling its obligatory overload of passengers. The *tap tap* rolled to a gravel-spewing stop. They tossed their backpacks on top of its brightly painted, metal roof. Madeleine and Tim quickly joined their gear, but the minister remained firmly planted on the ground. Ti Bon argued with several of the passengers sitting on the open-air bench seats until one eventually relented, freeing up a few inches in the middle. Creating considerable upheaval, the minister squeezed into his allotted sliver. Once assured he was settled, Ti Bon joined Madeleine and Tim above. He banged on the roof to signal the driver to depart.

"There's always room for more when you're in Haiti," Madeleine said.

"I'd rather be up here in the fresh air than packed in that sardine can down below," Tim said. "How far is it to Magazin-Carrier?"

"It shouldn't take more than thirty minutes or so, assuming no accidents along the way."

He wished she had not mentioned that particular possibility. *Could it be my accident happened just a week ago?* Given all that occurred in the past week, his prior miserable existence seemed more distant. As mournful thoughts of Sarah began to surface, he forced himself to concentrate on the barren sights passing by as they bounced along the pot-hole road.

They arrived at Magazin-Carrier forty-five minutes later, suffering only one minor delay along the way when an old, blind man wandered into the middle of the road, stopping traffic in both directions. Rather than helping him to the side, the drivers blasted their horns, confusing the poor soul all the more. After several minutes of this dueling-horn stalemate, Tim jumped off the *tap tap* and guided the confused man to the shoulder of the road. Madeleine applauded. He hopped back onto the *tap tap.* The traffic recommenced, barreling past the blind peasant as if he did not exist.

Along the shore of the small, fishing village, women cleaned fish and naked boys splashed about in the turquoise sea. A wooden sailboat, similar to the Nazarene's, but absent any trace of a motor, bobbed a short distance offshore.

"Ti Bon says we'll be taking that boat to Les Arcadins," Madeleine said.

"Les Arcadins, where's that?" he asked.

"It's a small group of islands about a mile or so offshore. There, all of us, except *Your Highness*, will start our cleansing."

"I'm never going to live this down, am I?"

"Nope."

"How are we supposed to get aboard the boat?" the minister asked. "I'm not swimming out there, I can tell you that."

"That won't be a problem," Madeleine said. "We'll be carried to it."

Four chisel-chested men in cutoffs gathered before them. As the minister previously surmised, lifting weights equal to or even in excess of their own proved to be effortless tasks. Each of them, the *blancs* and Ti Bon, arrived at the small sailboat absolutely dry. Other passengers, all Haitian, were transported to the sloop in the same manner. One lady carried two oil-stained packages. Two other women brought bowls of assorted fruits, vegetables, and cooked rice. One man pranced about the sloop like a caged, black panther and, every so often, swung a machete in the air. Another man, dressed totally in black, sat in silence on the gunwale and made no attempt to acknowledge anyone's existence.

The captain untethered the boat from the buoy and raised the sails. As if by divine command, a brisk breeze swooshed the vessel out to sea. Les Arcadins, small and low-lying, did not become visible until they nearly sailed on top of them. The captain guided the sailboat through a narrow passage of the reef-ringed cays and dropped anchor in waist-deep water. No porters awaited the passengers. In fact, excluding a flock of laughing seagulls, the islands appeared deserted.

No one moved. The Haitian with the machete slid off the boat, waded to shore, and commenced to dart about the island, brandishing his weapon like a warrior armed with a saber. After vanquishing his invisible enemies and securing the beachhead, he motioned to the rest of the passengers to come ashore.

"It looks like we're going to get wet, after all," the minister said, shaking his head while watching the passengers wade to the shore.

Madeleine pulled off her sneakers, slid into the clear water, and gestured for Tim and the minister to join her. "It's refreshing. We'll dry in minutes once we're on shore."

Tim removed his boots and socks and then hopped overboard. Reluctantly, the minister followed suit. Only then did Ti Bon make a move to depart the boat.

By the time they reached the shore, a five-foot wooden cross had been inserted into the sand and a charcoal fire lit at its base. The woman with the oil-stained packages pulled out two roasted chickens, complete with tail feathers, which she placed with cooked rice and assorted vegetables into an oversized, cast-iron skillet so the meal could be warmed.

The machete man continued racing about chasing invisible images. A woman waving a red flag on the end of a stick not much thinner than she soon joined in his crusade.

"What in heaven's name is going on here?" the minister asked Madeleine.

"According to Ti Bon, we're here to pay homage to *Agoué Royo*, the sea god, and his wife, *Hersulie*. This meal is prepared for them. The man with the machete and the woman with the flag are chasing evil spirits away."

"You mean this meal isn't for us?"

"I'm afraid not," Madeleine said. "It's all for the gods."

"What if they don't show up?" the minister asked.

"That won't be a problem. The meal will be delivered to them."

"Delivered to them? What do you mean?"

"Just wait. You'll see."

After the meal was prepared, one of the women returned from the boat with a large wooden tray, set it on a makeshift stand, and covered it with a spotless white tablecloth. Madeleine waded back to the boat, returned with her backpack, and carefully pulled out two place settings of gleaming bone china, crystal goblets, and sterling silverware. She arranged them on the tray in a proper setting for two.

"Boy, it looks like you're pulling out all the stops," Tim said. "Where did you get this stuff?"

"Ti Bon informed me we would need a service for two and that it was an absolute requirement it had never been used. These were in the hope chest I began collecting in high school. This seems like as good of use for them as any."

The warmed chicken, rice, and yams, along with some fresh fruits, had been equally apportioned on the dishes. A generous measure of *clairin* bubbled in the crystal goblets. The man dressed in black, a highly renowned *houngan* according to what Ti Bon told Madeleine, came forward and lit a candle on the tray. All the Haitians, including Ti Bon, broke into a droning chant. When they finished, Ti Bon whispered something to Madeleine.

She turned to Tim and the minister. "We each need to hold a corner of the tray. We have to walk it out into the water as far as we can."

"It figures," the minister said. "I was just getting dry."

"We'll get wet going back to the boat, anyway," Tim said.

They carried the tray into about four feet of water, taking great care to keep it steady, released it, and then watched it unerringly float into the reef passage, eventually bobbing out of sight.

While wading back to shore, the minister asked Madeleine if the spirits had finally been appeased.

She conferred with Ti Bon before making a reply. "*Agoué Royo* and *Hersulie* are hopefully enjoying their meal even as we speak. Ti Bon informs me this is but the first step in our journey."

Chapter 26

Friendship

As the sailboat returned to Magazin-Carrier, a half-dozen porters waded out into waist-deep water in anticipation of carrying the passengers ashore. After everyone except Tim and Ti Bon were carted to dry land, Tim motioned for the peasant farmer to depart, but the Haitian refused and made a like gesture. Tim also refused, sat on the transom, and then folded his arms to indicate he intended to be the last passenger to go ashore. Not to be out-done, Ti Bon sat on the deck and folded his arms, as well. Neither man spoke, which hardly mattered since neither understood the other's language.

The boat captain, clearly amused by the standoff, indicated with a nod of his bald head that the time for Tim and Ti Bon to disembark had arrived. Neither man budged. The captain shrugged and departed.

"Where are Tom and Ti Bon?" the minister asked, looking around the shoreline. "I thought they were right behind us."

"I think they're still on the boat," Madeleine said. "What could they be up to out there? It looks like they're just sitting."

"Why on earth would they just be sitting there?"

Madeleine shook her head. "I have no idea. I think I'll go back and see."

Without the assistance of porters, she waded back to the sloop and discovered two grown men sitting, arms folded, not speaking, nor looking at one another. "Why are you two just sitting here?"

"Don't ask me," Tim said. "Ask Ti Bon."

Getting a similar response from Ti Bon, Madeleine said, "You know, Tom, Ti Bon feels it's his place to be last. He's just trying to be respectful."

"I know he is, Madeleine. I want to go last this time out of respect for him."

"I'll tell him what you said, but don't be surprised if he still insists on departing last."

After a brief exchange with the spindly Haitian, Madeleine said, "Ti Bon appreciates your offer, Tom, but insists he go last."

"Nothing doing." He reversed his crossed arms.

Madeleine glanced at Ti Bon, who also made a show of repositioning his arms. "I have an idea. Why don't I go last?" She repeated her suggestion in *Créole* to Ti Bon.

Neither man agreed.

Madeleine plopped herself onto the deck and crossed her arms to mimic the two stubborn men. All forced back grins a brief moment later.

"Okay, I have another idea," Madeleine said. "I'll get off first and the two of you can get off simultaneously. I'll watch to make sure neither of you cheats."

Tim accepted the suggestion, as did Ti Bon, once it was translated to him.

They departed the vessel in unison, arrived ashore together, and warmly shook hands. Two proud men from different worlds shared a ritual of mutual respect. From that moment on, they were more than acquaintances on a journey—they had become friends.

Chapter 27

Saut d'Eau

After a late afternoon lunch of grilled fish and rice at one of Magazin-Carrier's many open-air stands, Ti Bon located a *tap tap* heading in the direction of Saint-Marc. All four of the La Gonave delegation managed to commandeer a seat in the passenger compartment, sharing the space with a half-dozen peasants and a variety of livestock.

Along the way, Madeleine pointed out a complex quite familiar to Tim and the minister. "Hey look, there's the famous beach club. I've always wondered what that place is like inside."

"It's best you never lay eyes on the inside of those sinful walls," the minister replied with an all-knowing nod.

"It can't be that bad," Madeleine responded. "What do you think, Tom? Is it tantamount to Sodom and Gomorra?"

Tim swallowed. *When you're on the edge of hell, it's only a matter of time before the devil creeps in.* "I suspect it's just another resort where the rich and famous go to have a good time. There's probably no more sinning going on there than anywhere else."

He stared at the concrete walls surrounding the resort. It seemed like a lifetime ago when he worked there. Guilt permeated him like vinegar to a sponge when he realized he never notified Sir John he would not return. He wished they could make a stop so he could personally thank the man for keeping him employed through his two-year drunken stupor, but that would be difficult under the circumstances. The staff would recognize him and his cover would be blown. Worse, Bertram DuMarche might spot him. Other memories, painful ones, stood as greater barriers to him ever stepping foot inside the club again.

"I'm sure we couldn't even afford to eat there," Madeleine said, "let alone spend the night."

"Which brings us to my next question," the minister said. "Where are we spending the night?"

"We're on our way to Saut d'Eau," Madeleine said. "This place should appeal to you, Reverend Burkholder."

"Why's that?"

"It's a sacred waterfall where the Virgin Mary was believed to have been seen atop a palm tree."

"Hmm…sounds like some sort of Catholic propaganda to me, but I'd like to see a waterfall."

"You'll get to do more than just see it," Madeleine said with a wry grin.

"I'm afraid to ask what you mean by that. You still haven't answered my question. Where are we staying tonight?"

"Ti Bon hasn't clued me in on that yet. He simply says the spirits will provide."

Tim put his arm around Ti Bon. "I, for one, trust our good buddy here. He got us to Les Arcadins and back without a hitch. I'm sure he knows what he's doing."

A slight grin crossed Ti Bon's lips.

"I hope you're right," the reverend said.

They turned off *la Route Nationale Numbre Une* about thirty minutes later. A number of United Nations military and emergency vehicles streamed toward Port-au-Prince. They agreed their current plight paled in comparison to the sufferings cast by the devastating earthquake. They twisted their way up an unnamed road littered with potholes threatening to become craters, joining a convoy of *tap taps* heading to the holy falls. In addition to *tap taps* stuffed with Haitians of all ages, the massive pilgrimage included wiry peasants making their way on foot or riding equally bony burros along the roadside. The pedestrians, carrying their possessions on their heads, maintained perfectly erect postures over the mountainous terrain.

"It looks like we're not the only ones going to get our souls cleansed," the minister mused.

"Tomorrow is the *Fete de Vyèj Mirak*, the Festival of the Virgin of Miracles," Madeleine said. "It's one of the holiest days on the *Vodou* calendar. Not even an earthquake would cancel this ceremony. We're fortunate to experience it."

The minister glanced at Tim and shook his head.

Darkness preceded their arrival to Ville Bonheur, a normally peaceful hamlet near the sacred falls. Multitudes of men, women, and children swarmed the streets. Although every square inch of space appeared occupied, the crowd continued swelling in numbers as a steady stream of packed *tap taps* rolled into the village. The single Catholic Church spilled over with worshippers at every doorway and window.

Ti Bon motioned for the *blancs* to follow. He weaved them through the amorphous mass to a back street leading directly into the surrounding jungle. The rock-littered road narrowed to a footpath lighted by candles every ten feet or so. Shadowy figures flickered amongst the thick undergrowth a short distance away.

"Where's he taking us, Madeleine?" Tim asked.

"I have no idea."

Her answer provided little comfort. Tim glanced at the minister trailing not far behind. His facial expression didn't indicate much comfort either.

They continued along the serpentine path, through the thick foliage, for several hundred yards. It ended at the entrance of a small, mud hut, its door slightly ajar. Inside, a one-foot-high, silver crucifix reflected the flickering light of candles burning atop a wooden altar. Ti Bon genuflected at the door and entered. Madeleine repeated his religious entry into the shadowy space. Tim glanced at the minister, shrugged, and followed suit. The minister, standing outside for only the brief moment it took to realize he was alone, made a half-hearted genuflection and joined the others.

Five straw mats lay across the dirt floor. Ti Bon had already situated himself atop one of them.

From a dark corner *La Reine* Memmene's familiar voice broke the silence. "Welcome, my dear ones. I have been expecting you."

Despite pounding drums, voracious mosquitoes, and bedding offering only a hint of cushioning, the weary travelers fell asleep under *La Reine* Memmene's watchful eyes. With a pointed knife, she cut small locks of hair from Tim and Madeleine, placed the strands in a leather pouch, slipped out of the hut, and ambled in the direction of the drums.

****

Dawn arrived quickly. Madeleine, the first of the travelers to stir, stretched and opened her eyes to the soothing aroma of brewed coffee. Through the slightly opened door she spotted *La Reine* Memmene sitting outside on a wooden stool by a charcoal fire.

Roosters in the village crowed, signaling time to arise. Ti Bon jumped to his feet and joined the *mambo* outside. Madeleine followed.

La Reine Memmene poured coffee into tin cups for each of them. Speaking in *Créole*, she asked them to tell her of the events of the previous day. They told of their journey to Les Arcadins and the strange ceremony in which they provided a feast to the sea spirits.

A few minutes later, Tim and the minister dragged themselves outside. They both required several sips of the thickened brew to become fully awake.

"Boy, this sure hits the spot," Tim said. "The last thing I remember was curling up on a straw mat."

"The spirits wanted each of you rested for this day," the *mambo* said. "It is also important for you to eat." Holding a crumpled paper bag, she pulled out several small cakes topped with grated coconut and distributed them.

"Hey, these are pretty good," the minister said, his mouth half full. "Don't tell me you were up all night baking."

The *mambo* broke into a belly laugh and almost fell off her stool. Wiping a tear from her eye, she said, "I have met many white ministers over the years, but none like you, Reverend Burkholder. You almost seem human."

"The reverend is definitely one of a kind," Tim said. He wanted to blurt out the minister's other profession, but knew better.

He spotted an object hanging around Madeleine's neck. "What's that leather thing you're wearing?"

Madeleine peered at the small leather pouch dangling an inch or two below her breasts. She placed the object into her left hand and gazed up.

"The *ouanga* is a gift from me," *La Reine* Memmene said. "It is a charm that will bring you good fortune."

"Good fortune? We could all use some of that," the minister said.

"You will have your fortune, my dear Reverend Burkholder. Keeping it will be the difficulty."

The minister's smile vanished.

"Come, it is time for us to go." For this holy journey, *La Reine* Memmene made it clear she would lead the way.

They hiked up a jagged path to an improvised corral. A man tending several burros saddled one and offered it to the *mambo*. Despite her considerable bulk, *La Reine* Memmene deftly positioned herself on top of the scrawny animal. It faltered only momentarily.

"What about us?" the minister asked.

"You have offended the spirits, Reverend Burkholder, not I. The climb up the mountain is but a small penance."

The ascent up the steep mountainside proved grueling for those on foot. They trudged to the precipice and headed down the opposite side, coming to a promontory overlooking the falls, the Tombé River cascading down in three tiers.

"Magnificent," Madeleine said. "It's breathtaking…almost surreal. I had no idea such a place existed on this island."

"Neither did I," Tim said. "Neither did I."

Innumerable pilgrims had already made their way to the falls, some standing along the water's edge while others waded in pools. The vast majority of worshippers immersed themselves within the falls, water pounding over them as they laughed, sang, and prayed. Some remained fully clothed. Unashamed, others frolicked in the nude—all in their own world—the world of the *loa.*

All but *La Reine* Memmene rushed down and joined the other penitents. Ti Bon stripped off his clothes and found a place under the falls. The *blancs* took off only their footwear and joined him. Crystal clear water showered upon them, its force massaging their bodies as it cleansed their souls.

****

Tim positioned himself along the edge of a rocky pool and marveled at the pageantry surrounding him. Haitians from all walks of life— rich and poor, young and old, healthy and infirm—experienced soothing spirituality in the cascading waters of Saut d'Eau. Interspersed within the mass of devoted pilgrims, *mambos* and *houngans* performed their mysterious rituals.

His gaze was drawn to where Madeleine relaxed on a nearby rock, gently combing out the knots in her hair while also experiencing the serenity of the falls. Her dripping wet dress clung against her body, accentuating her femininity.

Sensing the intensity of his gaze, Madeleine said, "It's not polite to stare."

"I'm sorry. I didn't mean to." He quickly concocted an excuse. "I was wondering what was in the pouch *La Reine* Memmene gave you. What did she call it?"

"It's called an *ouanga.* She instructed me to never open it, except in a moment of total despair."

"What did she mean by that?"

"That's a good question. I wish I knew."

He squatted beside her and tenderly clasped the leather charm in his right hand. His heart raced as he lost himself in her emerald eyes. "Are you supposed to wear this all the time?"

She returned an extended gaze. "*La Reine* Memmene said I would know when it was time to remove it."

The young *blancs* waded into the shallow pool and chatted about nothing in particular, as budding lovers often do. His mind spun with euphoria, but he could not utter any words to profess his true feelings. Even if she did share his feelings, he doubted they would remain once she learned what a dishonest excuse of a human being he really was. He had to tell her the truth. He had to tell her everything, and soon. *But how?*

The minister, having fallen asleep while sunning himself on a rock, missed the romantic interlude unfolding in the pool. On the other hand, *La Reine* Memmene missed nothing. She directed a knowing nod to Ti Bon, who returned an equally knowing expression.

When the sun reached its zenith, *La Reine* Memmene gathered the three *blancs* and Ti Bon, positioned them in a circle around her, and spoke in English, and then in *Créole.* She explained that at Les Arcadins they gained the blessing of *Agoué Royo* and *Hersulie.*

Although the sea gods were not the most powerful of spirits, no one could leave or return to La Gonave without them knowing; therefore, they must never be offended. Here at Saut d'Eau, the group made peace with *Damballah Wedo* and his wife, *Aida*, having joined them in the sacred waters. *Damballah*, the serpent god, possessed much influence over the other spirits, and any bad intentions by offended spirits of the cave would now be withdrawn. She ended her discourse by informing them that *Erzulie Freda*, the spirit of love, placed a special gift inside each of them. She bowed her head in silence.

The minister, unable to contain himself any longer, asked, "Have the spirits cleansed our souls?"

The *mambo* lifted her head slowly. "The Almighty has cleansed your souls."

The group continued to experience the sacredness of the falls till nearly dusk, whereupon *La Reine* Memmene remounted her burro and ushered them back up the steep, rocky ridge. They paused on the promontory overlooking the cascading waters and peered across the placid panorama where the angle of the late afternoon sun provided a brilliant rainbow inside the spray. Another gift from the *loa*.

Chapter 28

Erzulie's Night

The La Gonave pilgrims enjoyed a dinner of roasted chicken, rice, and fried plantains. The meal mysteriously materialized at the hut upon their return from the falls. Afterward, they sat around a small campfire reminiscing about the colorful events of the past two days. To Reverend Burkholder, the past forty-eight hours seemed like an eternity—an eternity that could have been better spent searching for gold. This caper far exceeded the time he planned to devote and he would have long ago made excuses to forego this soul-cleansing excursion and return to Port-au-Prince if he was not so certain a fortune in *Taíno* gold waited to be discovered in that creepy cave on La Gonave. On the other hand, if he didn't hit paydirt soon, he would resort to putting a serious squeeze on the wallets of Richy Richardson and Sir John Winston. He calculated the bill he would send to the attention of Richy and concluded he would send the same bill to Sir John. After all, each client represented an entirely separate case. Ministers might work for some higher cause, but G. Vincent Bennett, attorney at law, worked solely for material gain.

Fortunately, the group would head back to La Gonave tomorrow morning. With today being Wednesday, he decided to give it until Sunday, gold or no gold. He remained confused as to what to do about Tim. He had grown fond of him and hoped he could actually be of some help. Maybe it would be best if he convinced him to stay on La Gonave until the dust settled. He figured the young man would not object, considering the pretty nurse practitioner who would keep him company. He would find a way to get him out of Haiti, later. *Squeezing another couple grand out of Sir John should be a snap.*

After settling upon his back-up plan, he yawned and said, "I don't know about anyone else, but I'm beat. I think I'll get some shuteye. I assume we'll be getting an early start tomorrow?"

"We will leave shortly after breakfast," *La Reine* Memmene said. "You are all invited to a celebration tonight. I hope you will attend."

"I'll go," Madeleine responded. "I wouldn't miss it for the world."

"Yeah, I'd like to go, too," Tim said.

The minister took a deep breath and exhaled with considerable emphasis. Adding another cultural experience to his resume would never be high on his bucket list. "I guess that means I'm going, too. I assume Ti Bon wants to go and as sure as…ah…heaven, I am not gonna stay in this hut alone."

"Ti Bon is also very tired," the *mambo* said. "He prefers to stay. So it is settled. The two young ones and I will go to the celebration."

The *mambo's* tone left no room for debate, not that the minister had any notion to do so. He held up the palms of his hands as if making a peace offering. "Sounds like a splendid plan to me. Now, don't you two kids stay up too late. We have a big trip ahead of us tomorrow."

****

La Reine Memmene led Tim and Madeleine down a moonlit path on the outskirts of the village. Along the way, they encountered numerous pilgrims jostling about. Nearly everyone recognized and acknowledged the La Gonave queen. About twenty minutes later, they came upon scores of Haitians huddled together in a large clearing. *La Reine* Memmene took the young couple by their hands and weaved to a central location close to a wooden altar set in a similar fashion as the ones they had previously seen. The *mambo* motioned for them to sit, excused herself, and then withdrew into the crowd.

A hush fell over the growing throng of worshippers as an opening in the congregation materialized directly across from them. Three men carrying drums came forward, stopped near the altar, and commenced a soothing, sensual beat.

A procession of young women dressed in white seductively danced a circle around the altar and drummers until, without anyone providing a signal, the drumming ceased. The dancers then led the crowd in a jubilant chant. *"Viv la Vyèj…Viv la Vyèj…Viv la Vyèj…"*

Everyone chanted all the louder when four men appeared, carrying on their shoulders a flower-decorated float with a statue of the Virgin Mary at its center. Moments later, the dancers raised their hands into the air to signal the crowd to be silent. They performed a sensuous song as their slender bodies pulsated in primal synchrony.

"What are they singing?" Tim asked Madeleine.

"Whatever it is, it's not *Créole* or French," she said. "It must be an African dialect. Haitians often don't even know the meaning of the words themselves. They call it *langage.*"

The crowd consisted solely of couples, nearly all affectionately holding their arms around each other. Tim gazed at Madeleine and felt compelled to do the same. She scooted closer to him and gently placed her head on his shoulder. He squeezed her tighter, but immediately experienced a cocktail of emotions, some good and some not so good.

The singing and dancing continued for nearly an hour. The four men lifted the float after the performance ended. The crowd jumped to its feet and roared, *"Erzulie. Merci…Erzulie. Merci…Erzulie. Merci…"*

Couples began embracing and kissing. Tim felt a little awkward and at first pretended not to notice. Emboldened upon further reflection, he softly said to Madeleine, "I suppose it would be rude of us to not properly share in this celebration?"

"It would be very rude…very rude indeed."

They kissed lightly and then kissed deeply and passionately.

The Haitian celebrants, two-by-two, leisurely departed. Eventually, a bank of clouds enshrouded the moon, leaving the two *blancs* alone in total darkness. In a state of mutual, delirious arousal, those all-encompassing words escaped Madeleine's lips. "I think I'm falling in love with you, Tom."

Whether it was her declaration of love, or her profession to another namesake, he jerked back and covered his face with his hands. "Madeleine, I don't know what to say."

She pulled him to her chest and held him like a frightened child. "You don't have to say anything. I'm not asking for a commitment. I don't need you to say anything."

He would never have hesitated to take advantage of such a situation in his more youthful days, but things were different now. He knew what love was. He found it with Sarah and, to his utter confusion, had now found it with Madeleine. *If only I were not living such a horrendous lie.* He became further ensconced in a fog of self-worthlessness. "I have feelings for you, Madeleine, but I doubt things can ever work out between us. I'm not the man you think I am."

"I know the kind of man you are, Tom. You're warm, sensitive, and very loving, even if reluctantly so. Are you trying to tell me there's someone else? It never even occurred to me there might be someone waiting for you back home. I've been so self-centered. Please, forgive me."

"Forgive you? I'm the one needing forgiveness." The impulse to spill out his guts and all the lies pressed toward a breaking point. He recalled the minister's cautions and, although nothing about this ruse felt right anymore, he couldn't bring himself to divulge the full truth. "Let me tell you, there's no one else, at least not anymore."

"What is it? Has someone hurt you? Is that why you're not able to share your feelings toward me? Are you afraid I might hurt you, too? Believe me, I know those emotions all too well."

"Someone did hurt me, but it's not like you think." The time had come, although he still wavered, for some truths to be disclosed. At least those unrelated to his recent deceptions. "I was married a couple years back. Her name was Sarah."

She positioned her hand on his shoulder. "Tom, I know it must be devastating to have a marriage fall apart, particularly if you're the one still in love. But, that doesn't mean you can't love again. I can't believe someone could ever abandon you."

Tears streamed from his eyes. He was thankful she could not see his face. "It didn't happen that way. Sarah didn't just leave me. She left this world."

Her right hand reflexed to her open mouth. She pulled him toward her, hugged him tightly as tears rolled from her eyes, and whispered, "I'm so sorry. I'm so sorry."

After a few minutes of shared tears, she asked, "Would it help to talk about it? I have a feeling you've been holding this in way too long."

"I'm not sure I can."

"Try. I know it will help. How did she die?"

He spoke the words he managed to sidestep for nearly two years. "She drowned." It sounded even worse to say them. The irrevocability of just two words, but having finally set them free, the incessant anchor tugging at his heart lightened.

She squeezed him tighter and fought to retain her composure. "My God, how awful. I can't imagine experiencing something so terrible."

He dropped his head. "I can't imagine it either, but it happened, and it was my fault."

"Your fault? Don't blame an accident on yourself. You're not to blame, Tom."

That damn name again. "I was responsible for Sarah's death. It shouldn't have happened. I failed her."

Her tears flowed in torrents. "Tell me what happened. You shouldn't be blaming yourself, Tom."

He mulled confessing his name was not Tom, but thought better of it. He would tell her the truth, soon. He just wasn't ready to let her know what sort of lowlife she had fallen in love with, but he was ready at last to talk about Sarah. "I used to be a dive instructor during the summers to help pay for my education. I trained Sarah. She was an excellent diver, but I still never let her out of my sight, until that night nearly two years ago."

"You were diving at night?"

"Yeah. I was taking a group out for a night dive. Sarah had been on several with me before. We had three novice divers, so I made Sarah buddy up with my assistant, Marcos. He was a damn good diver. I would have trusted my life with him. Instead, I entrusted my wife's. That was a mistake I'll never forgive myself for."

"Did they both drown?"

"No, just Sarah. I led the dive and kept a close watch on the beginners. Marcos and Sarah followed behind the group. One of us always led while the other followed. That way we could keep track of everyone. When we got back on the boat, we did our usual head count. We kept coming up one short. At first, I didn't even realize it was Sarah who was missing."

He paused a moment while she comforted him by rubbing a hand through his hair. "I screamed at Marcos, 'Where's Sarah?' He stared back at me with a blank look on his face. I grabbed him by the throat. The other divers had to pull me off. He said he thought she swam up to be with me…he was busy watching all the paying customers."

"So, it wasn't your fault. It was your assistant's."

"It was my fault. I was the dive leader. I was her husband. It was my fault she drowned."

She tightened her eyes shut and rocked him against her like a helpless infant. "It's not your fault. It's not your fault. It's not your fault."

Chapter 29

Lost Soul

The thatched-roof mud hut did little to muffle the drumbeats throbbing from every hillside. The minister lay wide-awake, fear and annoyance competing for his attention. A few feet away, Ti Bon slept as if dead to this world. *When will these damnable drums stop? When will the others return?* There was safety in numbers. To make matters worse, each and every drumbeat thumped through his full bladder. He would have to pay a visit to a nearby tree.

The minister poked his head out the doorway and bemoaned the absence of the damn moon. He spotted the last remnant of a candle flickering near the pathway, tiptoed out, and carefully secured the wax stub between his left thumb and index finger, thereby keeping his right hand free to take care of business.

He chose a tree not far off the path and relieved himself. Fumbling to zip his pants, molten wax dripped onto his hand, causing him to drop the candle. "Shit."

The sting soon subsided, but now he couldn't see a damn thing. He shuffled in the direction he thought led to the path, figuring once there he could easily find his way back to the hut. He only ventured a short distance away, but to his dismay, no barren walkway appeared where he thought it should be.

"Damn, where the hell am I?"

Certain he had to be in the vicinity, he paced the number of steps he calculated it would take to reach the hut. It was not there. He took another ten steps for good measure. Nothing. He hollered for Ti Bon, but stopped upon realizing the futility of trying to be heard over the pounding drums. Panic seeped through his bones. The drums ceased an instant before he was about to bolt into the darkness.

He heard footsteps at a distance. "Tom? Madeleine? Is that you?"

No one answered.

"Okay, okay, the joke's on me. I got lost out here when Mother Nature called."

Silence.

"Is that you, Ti Bon? I know you can't speak English, but keep walking toward my voice."

The sound of footsteps shuffled in his direction.

"Thank God you found me. I was about to have a little panic attack here."

The cloud shrouding the moon passed. A male Haitian, nearly twice Ti Bon's size, stood before him. Only ragged shorts covered his massive body. His skin glistened in the darkness of night.

"Who…who are you?"

The ivory whites of the Haitian's eyes widened and narrowed. A gold-capped tooth accentuated his evil smile.

"Look, I don't want any trouble here." His voice reached a higher pitch than intended. "I just got a little lost. I'll be on my way now."

The Haitian clamped his over-sized right hand onto the minister's saggy left shoulder. "You are not lost, Reverend Burkholder. Come with me."

He wondered how the behemoth knew his name. "We're going back to the hut, right?"

"Come with me."

With the Haitian's giant hand still attached to his shoulder, the minister had little choice but to comply. They meandered deep into the jungle. Moonlight sneaking around the trees bestowed the leaves and branches with a ghostly effervescence. After a time, the moon could no longer penetrate the dense jungle and, although blackness overtook them, the colossus continued to lead the way. They stopped at a clearing about an hour or so later.

"Damballah," the Haitian roared. *"Nous p'vini."*

Flames exploded into the night's still air. Drummers, now visible, commenced a pulsating beat. The pressure of the Haitian's hand built upon the minister's shoulder and forced him to his knees.

"Now, my good minister, it is time for your faith to be put to the test."

"I'm…I'm not really a minister. You have to believe me."

"Your faith fails you so soon? I'm disappointed."

Terror heightened as a sneer crossed the huge Haitian's face. "Okay, I am a minister, but I have recently fallen from God's grace."

"Then I shall see to it that God's grace never returns." He placed a black, top hat on his equally black head. "I am *Baron Samedi* and on this night I shall possess your soul."

The *bocor* slithered to the fire and became engulfed in flames. He beckoned for one of the young women, now dancing near the drummers, to join him. Fearlessly, she slid out of her white dress and entered the inferno. Her ebony skin, matching his, sparkled in the blazing fire. She withdrew a few minutes later. The sweat oozing from her nude body served as the only visible effect of the flames. She approached the terror-stricken *blanc*, knelt before him, and unleashed a glare so piercing it burned his eyes. She soon diverted her attention to a white-feathered creature in her hands and soothingly talked to it till the dove cooed in return.

The instant the minister's panic began to abate, she bit off the bird's head and spat it to the ground. She held the lifeless form above her and dripped its blood into her open mouth. Once satiated, she tossed the bird's remains in the direction of its severed head. She cradled her hands around the minister's neck and, with crimson liquid sliding down her chin, joined her lips with his.

The minister awoke the next morning with a whirlwind of disjointed thoughts bouncing off the walls of his skull. When the spinning began to clear, he realized he lay in the safety of the hut prepared for him and the others by *La Reine* Memmene. Streaks of sunlight sliced through the cracked, wooden door. Familiar voices emanated from just outside. About to chalk up the previous night to an overly imaginative dream, he sensed something crusty on his lower lip, squeezed his eyes shut, and slowly extended his tongue. The distinctive taste of blood shot chills through what he prayed was still his soul.

Chapter 30

Witch Doctor

The minister pulled himself off the straw mat, departed the hut, and faced wide-eyed stares from his companions. "What's the matter with you all? Never seen an unshaven minister before?"

Madeleine raced over to him. "What happened to you, Reverend Burkholder? You have purple blotches all over your face. Look, they're on your hands, too. You're covered with them."

He looked at his hands in bafflement. "What in God's good name has happened to me?"

"Reverend Burkholder, you have been poisoned," *La Reine* Memmene said, the calmness in her voice at odds with her words. "The purple markings are but the first sign. If we do not act quickly, by tomorrow, you will join the unliving."

"Poisoned? Unliving? What in heaven's sake are you talking about? I may look like I have some sort of jungle rot, but I feel absolutely fine."

"If you are not treated soon, my dear reverend, you will not see many more days," the *mambo* said. "Tomorrow, these blotches will erupt into pustules. You were correct to call it jungle rot. This poison will cause you to rot as surely as if you were already dead and buried."

He grew more frantic as the conversation continued, but couldn't bring himself to mention anything about his bizarre encounters of the previous night. "Has someone got a mirror? I have to see myself."

"I have a small one," Madeleine said. "I'll get it." She handed him a small makeup mirror from her backpack. He stared into the mirror. His expression grew more dumbfounded with each passing second.

Madeleine squeezed *La Reine* Memmene's arm. "Is there a treatment you can give him?"

"The potions needed to counter this poison are not in my possession. There is not time to return to my *houmfort* on La Gonave. We must go at once to Cap-Haïtien. A *houngan* there, his name is Jacques LeFrance, will be capable of treating him."

"Now wait one minute. This Jack France guy sounds like some sort of witch doctor to me. I want to go to Port-au-Prince and see a real doctor."

"Do so and you will rot to death in a hospital bed," *La Reine* Memmene countered. "Your Western doctors have no remedies for jungle poisons."

"She's right, Reverend Burkholder," Madeleine said. "In all my medical training, I have never seen or heard of anything like this. What you're calling witch doctors are actually herbalists. It makes sense. If someone can poison you with a potion then someone else can cure you with another. It's your best chance."

"It sounds like this might be your only chance, Reverend Burkholder," Tim said. "Besides, the Port-au-Prince hospitals must be overwhelmed by earthquake casualties. We might not even be able to drive there."

He contemplated his dismal options. "Okay, I'll let this herbal remedy guy treat me, but he better not be wearing a top hat and call himself Baron something-or-other."

The *mambo's* eyes widened. "Is it *Baron Samedi* to whom you refer? What do you know of him?"

"Nothing. Those blasted drums gave me nightmares last night, that's all."

"Nightmares are the reality in which dark spirits reside, my dear minister. There is more danger here than your physical being."

"I'm rotting to death. You said so yourself. What could be worse than that?"

La Reine Memmene paused before answering. "As a minister, you are as well aware as I the body travels with us for only a short journey, while the soul travels for eternity. I fear, Reverend Burkholder, your soul has been stolen."

The *mambo's* words both baffled and terrorized him. For once, he found himself speechless.

"Everyone, collect your things," *La Reine* Memmene said. "We must hurry. The poisoning of the minister is a *bocor's* proclamation he is challenging my powers."

A bocor. He questioned how he let himself get so entangled in this *Vodou* crap. How unfair would it be to have stealthily escaped the wrath of the New York mob, create a new life for himself, only to later die in the jungles of Haiti? *Surely I have never done anything so bad as to deserve this.*

The group gathered their belongings and headed to Ville Bonheur. Once there, Ti Bon located a *tap tap* destined for Cap-Haïtien. The occupants, patiently waiting for the *tap tap* to reach its compulsory over-allotment of passengers, became squeamish the instant they spotted the purple-blotched *blanc* board. A hysterical mother holding a small child jumped off the back of the corroded vehicle, causing the others to bolt in chain reaction, some crawling out the side of the *tap tap* rather than risk coming in contact with the hideous creature. Hearing the ruckus, the driver hopped out and ordered the La Gonave contingent to exit his vehicle.

Despite *La Reine* Memmene's assertion the blotched *blanc* carried nothing contagious, the driver relinquished his demand only when told he would be paid in advance for a full load—a Haitian load. Madeleine explained the situation to the minister and he reluctantly forked over the dough.

The driver clunked the *tap tap* into gear and they pulled away, but not before Tim caught a glimpse of a towering figure standing at the edge of the crowd. He wrapped his arm around Madeleine, pulled her closer, and maintained his protective grasp long after losing sight of Ville Bonheur and the Ebony Man.

They made excellent time going downhill from Ville Bonheur and across the flats of *la Vallée de l'Artibonite*. The pace slackened as they headed north and traveled over and around several mountain ranges. Small villages dotted the steep, rolling countryside.

Apparently, only Madeleine paid any attention to their unique designs. "Has anyone else noticed how the mud huts look nothing at all alike in each village?"

"That's because each village reflects ancestry to different parts of Africa," *La Reine* Memmene said. "The European colonists thought they could prevent alliances from forming among slaves if each plantation owned Africans speaking a different language."

"I'm surprised the Europeans had any plans at all," Reverend Burkholder said, speaking for the first time since entering the *tap tap*. "It seems they have botched up everything on this island."

La Reine Memmene nodded her head in agreement. "What the white man failed to realize…still fails to realize…is that it is not language that binds Africans together. It is our culture. It is *Vodou*."

They arrived at the outskirts of Cap-Haïtien after a bumpy and dusty, six-hour journey. The driver dropped them off at a small, wooden shanty with bright blue walls and a blood-red roof. The crosses affixed at the precipice of each gable were painted white. Tropical plants of every imaginable variety covered the grounds. Some plants showed signs of being cultivated, but most of the vegetation appeared to be growing wild.

"This is the home of Jacques LeFrance," *La Reine* Memmene said. She rapped on the carved, mahogany door.

It creaked open. A sliver of a lady poked her wrinkled face through the sliver of the doorway. She opened it further upon recognizing *La Reine* Memmene. She invited them to enter. They instantly became engulfed in the fumes of burning herbs. Several haphazardly arranged wooden shelves in what would normally serve as a living room held a mishmash of cans, wooden bowls, and jars. The latter contained liquids of various colors and viscosity. Two imposing glass carboys rested on the top shelf of the rack closest to them. One contained live scorpions and the other held tarantulas.

The minister's eyes bulged. "Where in God's good name have you brought me?"

"I have brought you to your cure," the *mambo* said.

"I knew we should have gone to Port-au-Prince. Let's go. I'm not letting some quack witch doctor lock me up with a bunch of scorpions and giant spiders."

The *mambo* marched straight to where a diminutive old man sat in the far corner smoking a pipe. The herbalist made no attempt to stand as they spoke in hushed tones for several minutes. Meanwhile, Tim and Madeleine attempted to relieve the minister's apprehensions, his blotches having now turned a deeper hue, by explaining how many modern-day drugs originate in tropical jungles.

La Reine Memmene gestured for the minister to join her. Tim and Madeleine prodded him along.

"*Monsieur* LeFrance wishes to examine you," the *mambo* said.

The hairless, shiny-headed herbalist rose in painstaking motion to his feet. A soiled, bluish-gray robe covered his five-foot, frail frame. His hunched posture made him appear even smaller. He slid his spindly fingers over the blotches on the minister's face and undid the buttons of the minster's shirt, one of which was missing. The blotches on his chest appeared even deeper in color against his otherwise chalky skin.

"I'm not letting him pull down my pants," the minister said to the others gathered around him.

The rickety old man sat down on his rickety chair, rested his jaw on his right wrist and, after an excruciating pause, announced a diagnosis.

Madeleine exhaled a sigh of relief and patted the minister on the back. "The herbalist says he can cure you."

"Are you sure about this, Madeleine? I trust you because of your medical training. Should I go through with this?"

"My advice to you isn't medical, but if I were you, I'd let him treat me."

"That's good enough for me." He sighed deeply, although he wished he could be treated by a real doctor, if such a person even existed in Haiti.

"Before he can begin the treatment," the *mambo* said, "you must agree to the terms of payment."

He rolled his eyes and prepared himself for the big squeeze. He hated it when the shoe was on the other foot. "Okay, okay, how much money does this guy want?"

"He does not require money," the *mambo* said. "For treatment, he wants one coconut custard pie, a six-pack of Pepsi, and a live chicken proven to lay eggs."

"Well, if I give him some money he can go out and buy those things himself."

The *mambo* shook her head. "He only accepts payment in goods and services. He has no use for money."

"I'll be dead by the time we can hustle up a pie, a live chicken, and a six-pack of beer."

"Pepsi," the *mambo* said.

"Pepsi, that's right. Where am I supposed to come up with this pie?"

"I can make the pie," Madeleine volunteered. "I'm sure we can find the ingredients in Cap-Haïtien."

"Well," the minister said in a huff, "don't forget time is of the essence here."

"No payment is required until you are cured," the *mambo* said. "You must now only agree to the terms of payment."

He paused to reflect upon the absurdity of the situation and leaned over to Tim. "If I don't make it through this," he whispered, "I want you to find this old codger a pie and stuff it in his face."

"That's your dying wish?"

"That's my dying wish."

Chapter 31

Interrogation

Mildred Sponheimer gestured for Marie Joseph to take the seat across from her spacious desk. Mildred's assistant, Rachelle, entered the office holding a wooden tray with a plastic pitcher of ice water and two matching tumblers. She set it on a wicker stand and, without being acknowledged, stood to the side.

"I am so pleased you could find the time to visit us this Thursday afternoon, Misses Baptiste."

Rachelle translated.

She then offered Marie Joseph a glass of water.

More filled with fear than thirst, the young mother politely refused, remaining stiff as a chair stacked upon another. Feeling certain Premíse and Colette would be expelled from school because the damage caused by the big storm had precluded her from working at the children's clinic, her heart raced. Despite the air conditioning set to a subterranean temperature, sweat beaded upon her brow.

"I understand, Misses Baptiste, your husband left La Gonave for the main island with Miss McCoy, Reverend Burkholder, and that handyman. Do you know what business they're attending to there?"

Trapped, Marie Joseph could not admit Ti Bon had been possessed and he and the three *blancs* had gone to the main island in order to have their souls cleansed to appease the *loa* for their cave transgression. Any hint a member of her family still practiced *Vodou* would surely result in expulsion for all her children. "I am but a woman. My husband does not share his business dealings with me."

"Surely, Misses Baptiste, your husband must have given you some indication as to where he and the others were going."

"He only told me he was going to the main island. I do not question his motives. I am but a simple woman. I do not understand worldly things."

"Did you, by chance, overhear conversations between your husband and Miss McCoy?"

Realizing she simply wanted information about *Soeur* Madeleine, Marie Joseph couldn't figure out a way to divulge anything without incriminating her husband. "I do not concern myself with the dealings of my husband. He forbids it."

"Yes, I understand that. The bible teaches a woman should be submissive to her husband, but isn't it possible you accidentally observed things or overheard certain conversations as you were going about your household chores?"

Marie Joseph felt the noose tightening. She would have to disclose some information, and carefully. "Yes, I may have seen things or heard things, totally by accident, of course."

"Of course, please continue."

"My husband showed the *blancs* to a cave on our property. They have interest in the cave. I know not why."

Mildred paused before continuing her interrogation. "I take it this blond-haired ruffian who calls himself an anthropologist has some academic interest in this cave?"

"Yes."

"Did they all go inside the cave?"

"Everyone but Ti Bon," Marie Joseph said, electing to be less than truthful.

"Did they take anything out of the cave?"

Finally, a question she could answer truthfully. "No, they came out with nothing."

Mildred motioned to Rachelle to turn the air conditioner to a lower setting before continuing her questioning. "Have you noticed, purely by happenstance, if Miss McCoy and the blond-haired young man have been spending time together?"

She did not see any harm in answering this question. "Yes, they spend time together."

"Have you heard, perhaps from someone else in Anse-à-Galets, if they have been spending time at night with each other?"

"I only hear rumors."

"These rumors…what is the talk in the village?"

"*Soeur* Madeleine is in need of a man. It is only natural."

Mildred gulped, thanked Marie Joseph for stopping by, and excused her, but then tendered another request. "Misses Baptiste, I would appreciate if you would determine the full nature of the relationship between Miss McCoy and the young man who has so recently joined us here on La Gonave. I also feel Miss McCoy is very much in need of a man. It's my hope I might be of some assistance in this matter. Good day, Misses Baptiste."

"Good day, *Madame* Sponheimer."

****

Mildred Sponheimer stared at the blank wall directly across from her desk. Wasn't it bad enough these heathen blacks mire themselves in promiscuity of the likes only Satan can comprehend? Now a tawdry situation had developed with a white woman. She could not allow her thirty-plus years of evangelism on La Gonave to be sullied by such an abominable affair. *Steps will have to be taken.*

****

Marie Joseph headed home in a state of relief, having survived the ordeal without divulging any information that might get her children expelled from school. Obviously, the mission director was mostly interested in discovering what was transpiring between *Soeur* Madeleine and the handsome man who recently arrived. This also interested her and, in fact, nearly all gossip amongst the women at the Nan-Café market the previous day centered upon this subject. Mildred Sponheimer simply displayed normal womanly curiosity. She smiled with content. All the other women in the village were being nosy, whereas the director of the Greater Evangelical Mission had given her a directive to keep an eye on this evolving relationship.

She eyed two men on blue motorcycles waiting by the door of her home. "What business do you have here?" she asked.

A burly man, a gold chain dangling around his neck, spoke. "Where is your husband?"

"I do not know."

"We know he left La Gonave a few days ago," the man said. The other man, spindly, remained silent, although she sensed his steely eyes examining her from head to toe.

"My husband has business to conduct on the main island. I know not what."

The silent man swung himself off his motorcycle, swaggered over, circled around her, and unleashed a lewd stare even a street whore would find revolting. Terror overtook her like warm, stagnant air. She forced herself to maintain eye contact with the man wearing the gold chain.

"Your husband owes us much money," the gold-chain man said, his eyes as menacing as his tone. "He cannot hide from us."

"I know of no such money owed by my husband. We owe no one anything."

He repositioned himself upon his motorcycle. "We wouldn't have slaughtered your precious pig had nothing been owed us."

"Our pig was lost in the big storm."

"We killed your pig in front of your husband's very eyes. Does your husband tell you nothing, woman?"

Startled by this revelation, she fought to retain her composure. "My husband tells me that which I need to know."

"Your husband owes us fifty thousand *gourde*s for stealing our white powder."

"I know nothing about any white powder."

"Maybe we can help your memory." He turned to his partner and nodded a command.

The steely-eyed man made a slow circumference around her, stopped, placed his hand on the collar of her dress, and ripped it down to her waist. Both men leered at her milk-swollen breasts. The man with the gold chain said, "You could fetch a fair price in Port-au-Prince."

The silent man clamped a grimy hand on her right breast and a smug grin crossed his otherwise blank face. Repulsed, she spat into his eyes. He released his hold to wipe himself. His partner smirked. The silent man, his blank face turning uglier, smacked her across the cheek with the back of his hand, knocking her to the ground. He unbuttoned his trousers and let them fall, exposing his intent to force himself upon her, stopping with overt reluctance only when the spokesman barked, "Let her be."

The gold-chain man squatted and scrunched her chin with his powerful hand. "Pray your husband has not fled for good. If he doesn't return shortly, my partner and I will have our way with you and your daughters."

He further tightened his grip on her chin, forcing her lips to part. "Do you understand, woman?"

Terrified and weeping, she squealed an affirmative reply.

He released his grip, stood, and stormed to his motorcycle. The other man, still fully aroused, remained standing above her. He paused for her to make eye contact before covering himself and joining his partner. They sped away, kicking up pebbles within a cloud of red dust.

Chapter 32

Contact

Two blue motorcycles rested on kickstands outside a lone, thatched-roof hut in the Nan-Café highlands. An antenna extending at least fifty feet into the cloudless sky served notice to anyone who dared approach that this mud-covered shelter was no ordinary home.

Marcel tugged at the gold chain fastened around his thick neck. "Things are not working out as planned, Delmar." He spoke in perfect English this time. "The boss isn't going to be happy about this."

His steely-eyed partner broke his customary silence. He also spoke in English. "Shit, Marcel, you should have let me fuck the truth out of that skinny-ass bitch."

"Shut your foul mouth, Delmar. Maybe that's how you conduct business in Miami, but you're in Haiti now. You'll do things my way here. Is that understood?"

"The only damn thing your way has gotten us so far is one fuckin' shit-ass pig."

He grabbed Delmar by the throat. "That fuckin' shit-ass pig was about the only thing those poor slobs owned. Their meager possessions are not what we're after."

Delmar reached into his back pocket for his knife, but thought better of it when Marcel tightened his grip and his face turned vicious.

"Make no mistake about it, one more move and I'll break your noodle of a neck. Do you understand me now?"

Delmar gasped for air. "Okay, okay, I'll do as you say."

"See to it you do." He released his hold. "I'm in charge. You would be wise not to forget that."

"I said I'll do as you say." Delmar rubbed his bruised throat. "What do we do now?"

"I'll call for instructions." He slipped over to the table with a ham radio set hooked to a twelve-volt battery and picked up the receiver. "Calling royal flush. Calling royal flush. This is pair of aces. Do you read me? Over."

The radio sputtered static in return.

"Calling royal flush. Calling royal flush. This is pair of aces. Do you read me? Over."

After several calls, a British-accented voice came on the line. "This is royal flush. I copy. Over."

"We made contact with that Baptiste woman. She knows nothing of any use to us. Over."

"You're absolutely certain? Over."

"Absolutely. We await instructions. Over."

"I need something to tell the boss. Over."

He paused before answering. "Inform boss subjects left La Gonave two days ago to purchase supplies on the main island and will return tomorrow or the day after. Over."

"Are you certain? Over."

"We're certain. Over."

"Let me know as soon as they return. Prepare for plan B. Do you copy? Over."

"We copy. Over."

"Don't fail me on this. Over."

"We copy. Out."

Sweat streamed down Marcel's burly neck.

Delmar glared at his partner. "You don't have a fuckin' idea when or if they're coming back."

"If they don't return soon, we'll meet the same fate as that shit-ass pig. You heard our instructions. We prepare for plan B."

Chapter 33

Cormier Plage

La Reine Memmene insisted Tim and Madeleine take a *tap tap* to Cormier Plage, a small resort village within an hour's drive. After all, the *mambo* explained, she and Ti Bon would be busy assisting the herbalist. Besides, as the reverend added, there simply would not be enough room for all of them to spend the night in a home packed with any number of dried plants, live critters, and jars filled with bubbling, multi-tinged potions.

"I'm not sure that's a good idea," Madeleine said.

"I agree," Tim added. "There's plenty of floor space."

"Please," the minister said, "get yourselves a good night's rest. Waiting around for my purple blotches to disappear is nerve racking enough without you two pacing about. I'll be fine. I'm already figuring I'm better off here with this herbalist than I would be with some quack doctor in Port-au-Prince. Those guys' diplomas aren't worth the paper they're written on. At least I know this fellow is the real thing, whatever that might be."

"Are you sure you'll be okay?" Madeleine asked.

"As sure as I'm a Methodist minister."

****

The French West Indies-style resort at Cormier Plage rested at the foot of the coastal range along the shore of *la Baie de L'Acul* amidst an array of lush, tropical plantings. Two fully-plumed peacocks strutted the grounds and met them at the entranceway. The quaint complex consisted of a handful of wooden bungalows and a larger colonial-era building housing the front office and dining room.

Stationed at the front desk, a plump, Haitian woman smiled and greeted them in perfect English. "Good afternoon. How may I help you?"

"We need a place to stay tonight," Tim said, purposely being vague so as not to appear presumptuous to Madeleine. He hoped she wouldn't request a separate room.

"You are in luck. We have one vacancy. How many nights will you be staying? Cormier Plage is a perfect hideaway for honeymooners."

He and Madeleine blushed and stole glances at each other. "We just need a room for one night," he said, more than a little delighted with his good fortune.

"Excellent. You will be in bungalow number six. It is the one at the far end. Will you be joining us for dinner this evening? We will be featuring a West Indies buffet."

Although they had eaten little the last couple days, food remained low on his priority list. Before he could answer, Madeleine said, "That sounds wonderful."

"Please sir, sign our register. We are proud to have guests from all over the world."

He took the pen tied by a string to the leather-bound register book and boldly wrote, Madeleine and Tom Jamison, Syracuse, New York, U.S.A.

The woman turned the register around, read the inscription aloud, and released a broad smile. "Welcome to Cormier Plage, Mister and Misses Jamison."

He and Madeleine blushed again. Grabbing the key, he asked, "What time do you begin serving dinner?"

"The buffet starts at eight. Enjoy your stay."

"Thank you," Madeleine said as they bounded, hand-in-hand, out the entryway.

A ceiling fan cooled the charming bungalow decorated with vibrant, primitive artworks and a full ensemble of matching rattan furniture that could benefit from a fresh coat of varnish.

The sun-filled bathroom particularly pleased Madeleine. "A shower with hot water. I can't believe it."

He stood on the balcony overlooking the secluded beach. "If you think hot water is inviting, take a gander at this."

She joined him on the balcony to share a postcard vista of a white-sand beach partially shaded by a fringe of rustling palm trees. With each ripple reflecting the late afternoon sun, the blue and turquoise water glistened like a sea of jewels. "My God, this is absolutely breathtaking."

He maintained his focus upon the beach, although sensing more than his heart rate rising. "I don't suppose you brought a bathing suit along?"

"Unfortunately, the answer is no. Who would have thought? Don't tell me you brought one."

"No. It never crossed my mind, either."

Madeleine cocked her head to the side and, with her melting smile glowing, offered a suggestion sounding nothing short of fabulous to his ears. "It's not like bathing suits would cover any more than our underwear. What do you think?"

He didn't need to think. "Let's grab a couple towels from the bathroom shelf and high-tail it to the beach."

They strolled to a far corner of the white, powdery beach where they found a rope-braided hammock tied between two palm trees. It was the perfect repository for the outer garments they swiftly shed. They momentarily paused to admire one another before darting into the beckoning sea. Madeleine's leather charm still dangled about her neck. They spent the remainder of the afternoon frolicking in the rejuvenating waters of *la Baie de L'Acul*. After swimming, they placed their towels together and dried in the palm-frond, defused rays of the baking Haitian sun.

After a long interlude of balmy silence, Madeleine said, "I'm feeling a little guilty enjoying this time on the beach with you while the minister may be dying."

"As a minister, I'm sure he's got the good Lord on his side. He also has the *loa*. That's a powerful one-two combination, I have to admit."

"It sounds like you're starting to come around with *Vodou*, Tom. What changed your mind?"

"The mystical pageantry we experienced at the falls would give anyone cause to reconsider *Vodou*. Before then, I always thought of *Vodou* as being black magic and evil."

"There's good and evil in everything, Tom. To the people of Haiti, *Vodou* is the spiritual glue holding them together. Without a religion having roots in their African ancestry they could never survive the squalor and torment existing in their lives."

He rolled to his side to face her and gently touched his hand on her smooth, high cheek. "Without you, Madeleine, I couldn't survive the squalor and torment in my life."

They exchanged a meaningful and passionate kiss. They remained on the beach, waves gently rolling, until the sun disappeared behind puffed clouds and the horizon gradually transformed into a patchwork of multi-hued pastels.

****

The sun had been up for over two hours Friday morning when Tim gradually awoke. He glanced to his side, expecting to find Madeleine. To his chagrin, he found only a dented pillow where her head had recently been. He sat up. He smiled contentedly at the pattering sounds of the shower and her soft voice singing a *Créole* tune. He spotted Madeleine's leather charm draped over the wicker end table and considered peeking inside. His gaze inexplicably

177

shifted to a series of old books on a crooked shelf above a table. The title of a particular hardback caught his attention—*The White King of La Gonave*.

He slipped out of bed and yanked the volume off the shelf. Spellbound, he turned yellowed page after yellowed page until he came upon a collage of black-and-white photographs. In their midst, he spotted a picture identical to the one he saw adorning the *péristyle* at *La Reine* Memmene's compound. Its caption read: *Coronation ceremonies and procession for the White King of La Gonave.*

Baffled by his resemblance to the man in the picture, he failed to notice Madeleine standing in the doorway of the bathroom, a towel wrapped around her slender frame and another forming a turban upon her head. "My, my, aren't we being modest today?" she said.

Startled, he realized he was nude, but made no effort to cover himself. "Madeleine, come here. You won't believe this."

She unwound the turban, shook her moist hair free, and strolled over. She placed an arm around his waist. "What is it, sailor?"

He pointed to a dog-eared page. "There's the picture we saw at *La Reine* Memmene's temple. It says it's the coronation of the White King of La Gonave."

"You have to be kidding. Let me see this." She took the book from him, stared at the photograph, and then turned to the front jacket cover. The book, authored by Faustin Wirkus and Taney Dudley, had a bottom caption which read: *The true story of the sergeant of marines who was crowned king on a voodoo island.*

Peering over her shoulder, his shock grew upon further examination of the front cover. "Holy shit. I don't believe this. I never knew."

"You never knew what?"

"Wirkus is my mother's maiden name. My middle name is actually Faustin."

"Are you saying you're related to Faustin Wirkus…the real White King of La Gonave?"

"That appears to be the case."

"How could you not know about a relative who was the White King of La Gonave, of all things?"

"My parents died in a car accident when I was nine. I moved from Pennsylvania to Florida to live with an aunt on my father's side. I never got to know anyone on my mother's side of the family. My only connection to Haiti is the carved mask that was theirs. Damn, it must have been passed down from…well…the White King of La Gonave." He stood by the side of the bed and shook his head. "To think I always wondered where my parents came up with Faustin as a middle name. When was this book written?"

Madeleine flipped pages until she found the copyright date. Pointing to it, she said, "1931."

"This is amazing. Faustin Wirkus must be…let's see…he could be my great-grandfather."

"That would make you the great-grandson of the White King of La Gonave. You're the heir to the throne."

He turned back to the page with the picture of the marine sergeant. "He sure was a handsome fellow."

Madeleine knelt beside him and squeezed her arms around his solid hips. "Good looks must run in your family."

Her compliment, followed by a strategically placed kiss, jolted him to full arousal. He reached down and undraped the towel concealing her supple figure. He lifted her up and, while cradling her in his arms, flooded her burgundy nipples with crazed attention until her breathing turned shallow. He toppled her onto the bed where they continued to seize upon their mutual passion for the second, delirious time.

They showered together later that morning, expending the last drop of hot water before retreating from each other's embrace. They dried themselves off and reluctantly dressed. As Madeleine placed the leather charm around her neck, he released a contented sigh. True to *La Reine* Memmene's words, she certainly knew when to remove the *ouanga*.

He grabbed the orange book off the shelf. "Gosh, I wish I could keep this."

"Why don't you just ask the woman at the front desk if you can borrow it? You can probably find a copy back in the States at one of those stores specializing in old books. You could get the address from her and mail this copy back."

"Do you think she'll let me?"

"It doesn't hurt to ask."

They checked out of the small resort, paying with the money Reverend Burkholder gave them. The woman at the front desk allowed him to borrow the book and seemed pleased a *blanc* actually wanted to read an old book about Haiti.

Chapter 34

Cap-Haïtien Market

Ti Bon, standing vigil outside the herbalist's house Friday morning, lit up with a grin when Tim and Madeleine arrived. The usually reticent farmer spat out detail after detail about the minister's miraculous healing. Madeleine asked him to slow down so she could understand everything he said. When he finished, she translated the fabulous news to Tim. The minister had been cured. The purple blotches had totally vanished.

"Now, this day is perfect," Tim said, still wallowing in the euphoria of their blossoming romance. "Let's go see our buddy."

They entered the house and found the minister and the herbalist sitting next to each other on identical rickety chairs, both smoking pipes. The minister pulled his pipe to the side. "I believe we owe the good doctor here a laying chicken, a coconut custard pie, and a six-pack of beer."

"Pepsi," Tim and Madeleine blurted simultaneously.

"That's right, Pepsi. What are you two waiting for? You have some shopping to do."

"Don't you want to come along?" Madeleine asked.

"Not really. I'm content just to sit here and smoke this pipe."

"What was the treatment like?" Tim asked.

"Beats me. He gave me a lot of things to drink. It all tasted like *clairin* to me. I think I'm acquiring a taste for that, uh, island moonshine."

"Where's *La Reine* Memmene?" Madeleine asked.

The minister took a long puff on his pipe. "She said something about having some affairs to handle. She'll be back anytime now.

Will you two hurry up? The sooner my debt is paid, the sooner we can head back to La Gonave."

"That sounds good to me," Madeleine said.

Tim's own reaction came as a surprise to him. Returning to La Gonave didn't sound bad at all. He gazed at Madeleine standing by an open window. The sunlight dancing across her long, auburn hair, added even more radiance to her natural beauty.

****

Tim and Madeleine caught a *tap tap* and twenty minutes later arrived at Cap-Haïtien, a coastal city aflutter with activity. Still outrageously congested by American standards, Cap-Haïtien exhibited a vibrancy lacking in Port-au-Prince, the earthquake notwithstanding. Beggars abounded, but seemed less desperate than those at the capital. A smile and a "*non, merci*" proved sufficient to send most on their way.

A young boy calling himself Eldin sidled up to them to serve as their unsolicited guide. He led them to the central, open-air market, where an assemblage of plump women, all holding brightly-colored clothes, pleaded for Madeleine to buy something. One woman raced over with a lime-colored dress with flowers embroidered in reds and yellows across its front. "Twenty-five dollars for the beautiful lady." Her tooth-filled grin proved nearly impossible not to return.

The woman held the dress up to Madeleine, turned her head to Tim, and gave her best sales pitch. "Won't you buy your beautiful lady this beautiful dress? Look at her dress. It is old and worn. Your beautiful lady needs a dress as beautiful as she. Twenty-five dollars. It's a bargain."

"Sold," Tim said, unable to control himself.

"Tom, we don't have money for this. I don't even know if it will fit."

"One size fits all," the seamstress swiftly interjected.

Tim could see in Madeleine's eyes she loved the dress. Besides, he wanted to see her wearing something other than her usual drab garb. "You heard her. One size fits all. Don't worry about the money. I'll pay the minister back when we return to La Gonave." He knew he couldn't repay the minister, but figured with having already fallen into insurmountable debt, another twenty-five bucks didn't make much difference.

Madeleine beamed. "Is there somewhere I can try it on?"

The delighted seamstress summoned several friends. They surrounded Madeleine and held up bolts of cloth, beginning at the level of her neck and dropping to the cobblestone street, which essentially formed a changing room on the spot.

Madeleine, her head poking above the cloth walls, smiled at Tim. "Well, I guess I'll try it on."

She unbuttoned her old dress, let it drop, and donned the new one. "I think it fits."

The women holding the cloth walls backed away and admired Madeleine in the new dress. Tim gawked and said nothing as he reached for the money in his front trouser pocket.

"Fifty dollars…only fifty dollars," the seamstress said.

Tim countered with a grin intended to disarm. "No, we agreed to twenty-five."

"Okay, thirty-five dollars. This beautiful dress for your beautiful lady, only thirty-five dollars."

Madeleine began speaking in perfect *Créole*, which brought everyone in the vicinity to stunned silence.

Turning to Tim, the astonished woman said, "Twenty-five dollars it is. A good price."

Tim paid the woman in U.S. greenbacks. The watchful eyes of her companions tabulated each bill as he placed them in her hand. "What did you say to her, Madeleine?"

"I simply told her we can buy the same dress in Port-au-Prince for ten dollars."

"I would have paid one hundred. You look absolutely stunning."

In her excitement, Madeleine forgot about her old dress. She belatedly turned, only to find another woman walking away with it.

"Do you want me to go get it?" Tim asked.

"No. I have a new dress. I want her to have my old one. Thank you, Tom. I love it." They exchanged a kiss. The market women hooted and hollered. Three other women ran up with dresses they also tried to sell. Tim and Madeleine cheerfully declined.

They found the Pepsi, pie ingredients, and a laying hen at different stalls in the market. Tim carried the hen in his right arm, a hood placed over its head to keep it motionless. He held the six-pack at his left side. Madeleine carted four coconuts, six eggs, and other pie ingredients in a straw bag. They paid their guide a handful of *gourde*s and caught a *tap tap* back to the herbalist's home.

Tim pulled up a stool and provided company to the minister and the old man. Ti Bon brought out a bottle of *clairin* and squatted on the floor next to them. The men shared the liquid spirits in silent camaraderie. Madeleine and *La Reine* Memmene remained in the kitchen where they prepared the coconut custard pie.

After an exchange of small talk, the *mambo* asked, "Did *Soeur* Madeleine find reason to remove the *ouanga?*"

Madeleine's blushing smile returned all the answer *La Reine* Memmene required.

Chapter 35

Shallow Grave

Madeleine slid the coconut custard pie out of the kitchen's coal-fired oven and placed the steaming dessert on a wooden crate to cool. *La Reine* Memmene nodded her head in tacit approval. The two women returned to the living room and found four glassy-eyed men sharing a nearly empty bottle of *clairin*.

"Is it pie yet?" the minister asked, his voice slurred.

"The pie is made," *La Reine* Memmene said, her accompanying glower dampening the minister's celebratory mood. "We go now. There is still much to be done before we return to La Gonave."

With the festivity prematurely ended, at least as far as the men were concerned, the La Gonave contingent extended a warm round of gratitude to the herbalist for saving Reverend Burkholder's life.

The minister, now a staunch believer in herbalism, if not *Vodou* itself, shook the elderly man's gnarled hand. "May God bless you, my dear doctor. I owe you my life. I'll be forever in your debt."

Madeleine translated the reverend's words into *Créole*. The herbalist's dour demeanor remained throughout the exchange.

Turning to *La Reine* Memmene, the minister asked, "Is there something else I can do or give him to better show how appreciative I am?"

"You displayed your gratitude in the material world and in the spiritual world. You can do no more."

****

The sun settled for the evening by the time they crossed *les Montagnes du Nord* and descended into the low-lying *le Plate au Central.* Soon thereafter, the *tap tap* came to a standstill in the middle of the road.

"Why are we stopping?" Tim asked. "There's nothing here."

The minister glanced about in puzzlement, the *clairin* having worn off an hour earlier, and concluded only two speeds existed in this miserable country—slow and stop. "This place looks totally deserted."

"Looks can be deceiving," *La Reine* Memmene said. "No space in Haiti remains unoccupied for long."

True to her words, a line of at least three dozen men, women, and children became visible in the light of the partial moon, all wobbling and swaying like drunkards as they advanced toward the *tap tap.* An old man, shaking a gourd rattle, led the procession, while directly behind him four young men carried on their shoulders a small, white coffin. The full assemblage sang a song sounding like an Anglo-Saxon religious tune, although the *Créole* wording provided an island *patois*. The funeral procession drew near and their voices drowned out the humming of the idling *tap tap*. Once they approached within a few yards, the saddened eyes of the family and friends of the deceased became visible. They passed without paying any heed to the La Gonave pilgrims and slowly meandered out of sight.

"It seems odd no one was crying," Tim said. "It's obvious they're about to bury a child."

"In Haiti," *La Reine* Memmene said, "tear drops, like rain drops, are in limited supply. It is best for one to save tears for moments of joy."

A somber mood lingered aboard the *tap tap* for the remainder of the journey. They arrived about two hours later at Souvenance, a small village a few miles outside Gonaïves. "We will spend the night here," *La Reine* Memmene said.

The minister surveyed the grim surroundings, a grimness exceeded only by his facial expression. "I'm willing to pay for all of us to stay in a hotel tonight," he said, not wanting to waste any more time than absolutely necessary so he could get back to La Gonave, the cave and, most importantly, the gold. "Why don't we go on to Gonaïves and find ourselves a comfortable, clean place to stay there? We could even get something to eat at a real restaurant."

"Save your money, Reverend Burkholder," *La Reine* Memmene said. "Our accommodations are arranged. Your body is healed. Tonight, we will see if your soul can be saved. Please, everyone, follow me."

The minister exhaled into an extended frown. He had hoped the herbalist's curing of his blotches signified the end of his problems, at least those related to *Vodou* or other such matters. Now, it seemed, the *mambo* wanted to subject him to further indignities. He could not believe the crap hole he'd gotten himself into for a few lousy bucks—the pure absurdity of it all. But then, the image of the golden amulet Richy Richardson so foolishly let him see and touch sprang into his mind. An extra bounce came to his step.

La Reine Memmene led them through a maze of narrow, unlit streets until they arrived at a concrete block house, freshly coated with white paint. The structure glowed in the partial moonlight. A series of hand-size, black crosses formed borders around its front door and the two barred windows on either side. Before the *mambo* could knock, an occupant opened the door and peered out, only the whites of his eyes visible to those outside.

"*Bonsoir, Monsieur* Narcisse," *La Reine* Memmene said. "Everyone, this is Ambrose Narcisse, a very dear friend. Ambrose is the chief *houngan* of Souvenance. He will be our host for this evening."

Ambrose Narcisse looked like any other Haitian man of thirty-five— medium height, very slim, his complexion pure ebony. His clothing, all black and recently laundered, unmistakably set him apart as a *Vodou* priest.

He led them to the far side of Souvenance, to a *péristyle* surrounded by a six-foot-high, concrete wall. Broken bottles of *clairin*, their jagged ends pointed up, emerged from the rim of the wall along its full length. The minister wondered if the sharp glass served to discourage people from climbing in or climbing out.

The *péristyle* appeared larger and more prosperous than *La Reine* Memmene's, yet the *houngan's* deference to her made it overly clear the La Gonave *mambo* held a more elevated position in the *Vodou* hierarchy.

A meal of roasted pork, white rice, and sliced yams awaited them near the altar. Four women in traditional long, white cotton dresses held torches to illuminate the surroundings. The *houngan* gestured for his guests to eat, to which they quickly complied. They had nothing of substance since breakfast early that morning. Their host smiled upon witnessing their healthy appetites, particularly the minister's. After dinner, the Souvenance *houngan* and *La Reine* Memmene broke apart from the others and spoke in hushed tones. When their conversation ended, the *houngan* eyeballed the minister for some time and then lowered his head before departing the *Vodou* compound.

Reverend Burkholder wondered why he received such a rueful stare. "What's next? *Clairin* cocktails?"

"You will have your *clairin*, my dear minister," *La Reine* Memmene said, "but not in the manner to which you are accustomed. This night will not pass easily for the two of us. The time has come to pay a visit to the home of *Baron Samedi*."

The minister turned his head toward Tim and Madeleine. "What does she mean the two of us? You're coming, too, aren't you?"

"We'll be right there with you, Reverend Burkholder," Madeleine said.

The minister's apprehension continued to build as two torch-bearing women led the group from the *péristyle* into the rock-littered hillsides west of the village. After a short while they came upon a low-lying stone wall with a partially-opened wrought-iron gate. A familiar voice emanated from the darkness inside. "*Bonsoir, mes amis*."

La Reine Memmene responded for the group. "*Bonsoir, Monsieur* Narcisse."

After they slipped single file through the narrow passageway, the *houngan* swung the gate behind them. The creaking of rusty metal upon rusty metal provided an appropriate greeting to *le Cité du Morts*. Hundreds of exposed concrete slabs jutted out of the cemetery's rocky soil. Whitewash coatings rendered ghostly glows to the throng of tombs, most adorned with crosses and miniature edifices. Burnt-out candles and calabash bowls containing the traditional Haitian offerings of grains and other dried foods lay neatly arranged on nearly every grave.

Reverend Burkholder's apprehension turned to panic. Being purged of his purple blotches seemed like a picnic compared to what appeared to be in store for him.

The *houngan* led them to a far corner where a black, wooden cross stood in lonely watch over its silent domain. A pile of branches rested a few feet from its base. The two white-clad women who led them to the cemetery tossed their flaming rods into the pile, setting it ablaze. The bonfire illuminated three shirtless men carrying drums as they snaked out from the blackness. The men settled near the flames and commenced a pounding beat, breaking the dead silence. Their bodies soon became slick with copious layers of sweat.

The minister nudged Tim. "I'm out of here." He turned to make his retreat, only to face two half-naked, sculpted-bodied men who had silently slipped in behind him. They inserted their hands under the minister's flabby armpits, lifted him into the air and, with him still facing backward, carried him toward the fiery conclave. His feet kicked in a futile attempt to escape. "Tom. Madeleine. You're not going to let them hurt me, are you?"

Tim made a move toward the minister, but the glare in the *mambo's* eyes stopped him in his tracks. Madeleine clutched his hand and pulled him closer to her. "We'd better let *La Reine* Memmene perform these rites. Haitian's take soul snatching very seriously."

The two men released the terrified minister. He crumpled into a newly dug, shallow grave. The two white-clad women arranged around the edge of the burial cavity an assortment of colored bottles with lit candles inserted in their openings. The minister sat up in a daze and eyed the flickering flames that surrounded and imprisoned him. Incapacitated by fear, he could not rise to his feet, let alone bolt to freedom. In fact, he couldn't believe what in the name of holy shit was happening to him.

The *houngan* handed *La Reine* Memmene a small, clay bowl containing a yellowish, gelatinous substance. Using two fingers, the *mambo* extracted an eyeball-size clump and held the gooey mass within an inch of the minister's clenched lips.

The drums stopped.

"By thy will, good Lord, saints, and all the *loa*, I, *mambo* Memmene, beseech thee, *Baron Samedi*, Keeper and Lord of the Dead, give me back the soul of this good man."

The drummers began a beat so fervent their hands became a brownish blur. The *mambo* slapped her empty hand against the minister's forehead and stuffed the paste-covered fingers of her other hand into his open mouth. He gagged and grabbed at her hand, but could not dislodge her penetrating digits. When she pulled her hand away her fingers were free of paste. Gagging, the minister failed to disgorge the slick substance, which swiftly slid down his throat. His mind soon spun into a black fog. Scenes, beginning from his childhood and moving forward in time, flashed through his rattled skull. His entire sordid life—years in the orphanage, panhandling in Queens, jail time, cheating every sucker he came in contact with, his troubles with the mob, escaping to Haiti—all streaked by in disjointed images. His convoluted senses shaped a mystifying apperception of floating out of his physical being. He became a helpless and speechless spectator to ghostly rites where the focal figure was none other than himself.

The *mambo* unbuttoned the catatonic minister's partially opened shirt and rubbed *clairin* over the region of his heart. She grabbed a burning ember from the fire with her bare hand and positioned it near his chest. Flames exploded and disintegrated into a puff of smoke, leaving a reddened circle on his skin. The *houngan* handed *La Reine* Memmene a brightly-feathered fighting cock, which she released on top of his exposed chest. The cock pranced about, digging its sharpened talons into his soft, chalky skin. The bird glared one-by-one at the surrounding congregation, its eyes eventually fixating on Tim. It abruptly launched an aerial attack, but unlike his prior experience with a graveyard cock, Tim fended off this assault with a blow from his arm.

La Reine Memmene retrieved the agitated bird, clutched it with both her hands, and approached Tim, who now stood in frozen confusion. She positioned the cock's beak near his cheek and allowed it to unleash a vicious, blood-drawing jab.

"You must clear your mind of all thoughts, my holy white one," *La Reine* Memmene said. "Your spiritual powers, though well intentioned, provide much interference for me to contact the other world. *Legba*, the Keeper of the Gate, will only allow one of us to enter the realm of the dead this night. The *loa* possessing the cock has temporarily stripped you of your powers. These powers will return to you when your wound has healed."

Tim shook his head and turned to Madeleine. She returned a shrug.

The *mambo* knelt by the minister and commenced a melodious chant lasting far into the night. Her cadence rang in tandem with the pulsating beat of the drums. Finally, without making eye contact, the drummers and *mambo* came to a synchronized halt. Paradoxically, the silence of the graveyard now proved more deafening. The *houngan* reappeared, this time holding a black-and-white speckled hen. As he had with the fighting cock, he reverently presented the feathered creature to the *mambo*. She held the bird with both hands and passed it over the outstretched minister and then offered it some of the paste she previously forced down Reverend Burkholder's throat. The bird willingly ate and, shortly thereafter, collapsed.

La Reine Memmene placed the bird in the shallow grave alongside the minister. "*Baron Samedi*, I, *mambo* Memmene, your faithful servant, bestow to you this offering in exchange for this good man's soul."

The minister's eyes opened. He sat up in the shallow grave and stared about in bewilderment, all memories of his recent *Vodou* tribulations vanished.

Exhausted from the ordeal, *La Reine* Memmene slumped to the ground. The white-clad women hastily attended to her.

****

In another graveyard pocking the ravished countryside, a *bocor,* perspiration streaming down his smooth and shiny skin, stood before a wooden cross painted as deeply black as he. He dropped to his knees when his wobbly legs could no longer support his massive frame. He beseeched his patron spirit.

"My *Baron Samedi*, why have you forsaken me?"

From the pocket of his tattered shorts, Octave Polynice pulled out a small, mahogany box with a ring of crosses carved upon its lid. He removed the lid and turned its base upside down. A lock of the minister's hair and his shirt's missing button dropped to the barren ground.

"That which the others have said is true. Her powers are greater than mine."

Chapter 36

Descendants

Ambrose Narcisse led the La Gonave contingent back to his *péristyle*, bade them good evening, and left them to spend the remainder of the night within the confines of the white-painted walls of his *Vodou* temple. Ti Bon and the exhausted minister curled up on straw mats left by their host and instantly fell asleep. Tim and Madeleine, both wide awake after the harrowing cemetery experience, sat with *La Reine* Memmene beside a blazing bonfire set by one of the *houngan's* followers for their comfort. They spoke of the minister's recovery, his health and soul, and other matters pertaining to their recent travails. Later, and only after some nudging from Madeleine, Tim pulled from his backpack the orange-bound book he found in the bungalow at Cormier Plage and showed it to the *mambo*.

"Yes, I know of this book," she said. "It says in English things I have long known. These things have been passed down to me from my mother and from her mother."

"But, I'm not this person," he said. "The real White King of La Gonave could very well be my great-grandfather, but he would be over one-hundred-years-old now. He's long dead."

"I've known who you are, my dear one, from almost the first day you arrived to Haiti. The spirit of Faustin lives. It resides in you, his descendant."

"With all due respect, I'm not willing to be any kind of king."

"Then it shall be as you decree."

He shook his head in frustration. "I don't decree anything. I'm simply saying I'm not going to be the White King of La Gonave."

"As you say."

"That's right. As I say." Madeleine's accompanying giggle irritated him. "What's so funny?"

"Oh, nothing."

"What do you mean, nothing? You're laughing about something. Just because I don't like this king business is no reason for you to be making fun of me."

"I'm not making fun of you, Tom. It's just you sounded like you made a royal pronouncement abdicating the throne."

He gritted his teeth and stuffed the book in his backpack. "Then, by royal decree, I'm going to bed."

****

Madeleine and *La Reine* Memmene reverted to *Créole* as they chatted. *La Reine* Memmene kept her eyes fixed upon the blond-haired *blanc* curled up on a straw mat near Ti Bon and the minister. "I am not alone in recognizing this young man's powers."

Madeleine had not thought of her lover as having powers, although she wondered about the myriad of connections he had with Haiti, which by the same token were bewildering news flashes to him, as well. "What do you mean?"

"He did not come in possession of the Spanish sea-god's cross by chance. It must have been given to him as a gift."

"Who would have given it to him? What is its significance?"

"I can only answer your second question. The cross has been handed down within my line for as many generations as Africans have lived in Haiti. It was first given to an Indian queen in trade for an object made of gold. Its original owner was the first of many *blancs* to pillage this land."

"You mean the cross really did belong to Christopher Columbus?"

"His arrival was greeted as a visit from a deity. The original inhabitants of this land soon learned the Spanish sea-god and his followers had transformed themselves into emissaries of the devil."

Now even more confused, Madeleine asked, "Why is the cross viewed with such esteem?"

"The transformation from god to devil occurred at the moment the cross was exchanged for gold. The Indians soon began to die at the merciless hands of their European enslavers. We Africans were stolen from our homeland to replace the dying breed. A descendant of the Indian queen gave the cross to my ancestor with instructions to give it to a great *blanc* who was to come, Tom's ancestor, Faustin Wirkus, being the one so bestowed. After a few years, *Père* Faustin longed for his homeland, returned the cross, and left us, pledging to return one day."

La Reine Memmene released her gaze upon the young man sleeping a few human lengths away. She turned to Madeleine and said, "The covenant is now fulfilled."

"How do you think Tom came into possession of the cross?"

"This, I do not know. The cross was stolen from me more than twenty years ago. Whoever had it must have recognized its rightful owner."

"This is hard to believe." Madeleine said, embarrassed she'd spoken aloud what she meant to keep to herself.

"Is not everything in Haiti difficult to believe?"

She nodded in agreement.

"You and the handsome anthropologist make a lovely couple," *La Reine* Memmene said. "Might marriage be in your future?"

"I doubt that." She sensed the blood coursing to her cheeks. "We have feelings for each other, but it is confusing. Tom lost his wife in a tragic diving accident two years ago. He blames himself for it happening and I'm not sure he is ready to let anyone fill this void in his life. Plus, he made it quite clear Haiti is not in his future."

La Reine Memmene placed a hand upon Madeleine's shoulder. "You must be patient, my dear one. *Erzulie Freda* watches over those in love. When it is time, your young man will embrace you above all others. He will then see Haiti through your eyes."

Comforted by *La Reine* Memmene's words, she paused before posing a question of her own. "Have you ever been in love?"

La Reine Memmene gazed at the stars a moment and then dropped her eyes to the fire. "I was once married to a handsome Jamaican who came into my life many years ago. I thought he loved me, but he only loved that which I possessed—access to the spiritual world. I taught him that which I had been taught. Power that could be put to good—power that could be put to evil. He later abandoned me, taking with him our infant son."

Madeleine realized her dim circumstances paled in comparison to that of the grief-stricken queen. "I had no idea. No one in Anse-à-Galets has ever spoken a word to me about any of this. I'm so sorry for you. I can't imagine the pain you must have gone through. The pain you must still have. Do you have any idea what happened to your son?"

"I tried for years to find him. I was later told they might both be in Jamaica. I have heard no other word."

"What is your son's name?"

"He was christened Octave. Octave Polynice."

****

Only half asleep, Tim's eyes burst open the instant the name of the dreaded Ebony Man, the behemoth still haunting his very being, slipped across *La Reine* Memmene's lips.

Chapter 37

Plans

Full of excitement, a crowd of Souvenance inhabitants lined both sides of the road early Saturday morning as the La Gonave queen and her entourage departed. The villagers waved good-bye until the *tap tap* rolled out of sight. The trip aboard the *tap tap* to the coastal village of Montrouis, the port of embarkation for the public ferry to La Gonave, took two painful hours with UN relief vehicles still streaming to the shattered capital and refugees racing away. They arrived at the port and joined a throng of passengers packing a rickety, wooden craft gently bobbing offshore.

After boarding, Tim noted the absence of life vests. Aware most Haitians cannot swim and fear the ocean, he asked Madeleine, "Do you know if Ti Bon can swim? This banana boat doesn't look all that seaworthy to me."

Madeleine turned to Ti Bon and asked him a question in his native language. After a brief exchange, she turned back to Tim. "Ti Bon says we need not be concerned about our voyage to La Gonave for we have the blessing of *Agoué Royo* and *Hersulie*."

Countless passengers continued boarding and ultimately swarmed over every square inch of the deck. Tim wrapped an arm around Madeleine. "I guess it's fortunate for all these people we're blessed."

****

The combination of crowded conditions, sweltering heat, and open-sea swells approaching the heights of tall men made for an uncomfortable passage, particularly for the minister, who became seasick halfway across. With each nauseous turn of his stomach, he second guessed every aspect of the ridiculous venture he embarked upon. He vacillated between blaming Richy Richardson and Sir John Winston for roping him into this futile scheme, whereas his own accountability, fueled by excessive greed, never crossed his mind. The seas calmed, as did his stomach, within one mile of the shore of La Gonave. Weakened, but feeling better, his thoughts returned to the cave. With their souls now cleansed, all that remained was the small matter of exploring the cave and absconding with its *Taíno* treasure. The minister's lips curled into something akin to a smile.

****

Ti Bon, restless during the entire voyage, yearned for his wife and five children. He became overwrought with angst as his thoughts turned to the predicament into which he'd become hopelessly mired. *How am I to pay the motorcycle men who threatened me and my family? They'd already killed our pig.* Even though he'd simply tried to protect her, he wished he had told Marie Joseph the truth. Deciding he would tell her everything the moment he arrived back home, his thoughts returned to the fortune the menacing men had demanded. He gazed at each of the *blancs* for some time and eventually concluded they represented his only hope. After all, where else could he turn? He resolved to help the minister and his blond-haired friend find their worthless bits of clay. Afterward, he would plead his case to *Soeur* Madeleine, being certain she would be sympathetic to his plight and speak to the others on his behalf. *The sum of fifty thousand gourdes is but a pittance to any blanc.*

****

Thoughts of doom and gloom suffused Tim's mind. *What am I to do now?* He loved Madeleine and wanted to share the rest of his life with her, but certainly not in Haiti. *Will she be able to forgive me for my deceit? Will she still love me once she learns the truth?* He could not blame her if she never wanted to see him again. He began regretting ever kissing her, let alone having made love to her, twice no less. *Has this damned island robbed me of all sense of right and wrong?* No, he couldn't blame this quagmire on Haiti. He had to concede all his troubles this time were of his own making. His best hope would be to find the gold for the minister and get his debt paid. He would then tell Madeleine the truth about himself and beg for her understanding and forgiveness. If she would still have him, he would convince her to leave Haiti so they could start a new life together in the States. Periodically, they could return to Haiti to help the needy children. With her clinic essentially destroyed, surely she would see the wisdom of his plan.

****

Madeleine leaned against the side-rail of the ferry's gunwale in a state of confusion. She loved the blond-haired man next to her more than anyone she could ever imagine—more than she ever loved Bruce. *But how much does he really love me? Is he willing to forsake whatever life he had planned for himself and instead devote his life to me and Haiti?* She recalled the words the *mambo* had spoken. "When it is time, your young man will embrace you above all others. He will then see Haiti through your eyes." She settled on a plan. She would be loving and supportive and, just as importantly, patient. If Tom loved her then he would learn to love Haiti. They would rebuild the clinic and spend their life together. If not, she would continue alone, tending to the health of La Gonave's children, following in her father's footsteps, as she knew she must.

****

La Reine Memmene studied the *blanc* couple. Undoubtedly, the blond-haired man standing at Madeleine's side fulfilled the long-awaited covenant of the one who is to come. La Gonave desperately needed his energy, wisdom, and spirituality, even if he did not yet know of these things himself. As for the beautiful *Soeur* Madeleine, she already proved to be a gift from the *loa,* and her presence alone ensured this White King, unlike his predecessor, would remain on La Gonave for all his years. The *mambo* felt certain the *ouanga* had cast its spell—confident *Erzulie Freda* would not fail her or the people of La Gonave. These things *La Reine* Memmene had been told by her mother, who had also been told these things by hers.

Chapter 38

Homecoming

Ti Bon approached his home and spotted Marie Joseph leaning against the shaded wall of their hut. To his puzzlement, none of their children played outside. He instantly surmised his wife had sent the youngsters to her sister's so she could give him a proper welcoming. *This will be the perfect time to tell her the truth.* He quickened his pace, but much to his chagrin, saw no evidence in her eyes romance was anywhere in the offing.

"I am home," he said.

Her expression remained blank. "You tell me nothing of the money we owe. You tell me nothing about Bon Bon."

More than a little stunned his wife would have any inkling as to the absolute mess he had gotten them into, he asked, "How do you come to know of these things?"

"Two strangers on motorcycles tell me."

He didn't like the sound of this. "What else did these men tell you?"

"They tell me that which you already know."

"I know many things."

"They tell me what will happen to our children and to me if we do not pay the fortune we owe them. What are we to do, Ti Bon?"

He swallowed. "I have a plan. My white friends will help us."

"They agree to pay our debt?"

"When I ask…they will pay." He noticed a hint of a smile crossing her face after his minor embellishment. His home life would be back on track, at least for the time being. "Where are the children?"

"I sent them to my sister's. We can be alone for the remainder of the afternoon."

****

Mildred Sponheimer stood like a grotesque lawn ornament in front of Madeleine's home. "I've been worried to death about the three of you," she blurted as Madeleine, Tim, and the minister arrived. "No one knew of your whereabouts. I assume you had business on the main island?"

"Yes, we were seeking spiritual guidance at a Methodist church," the minister said.

"That's something we all can certainly use. Oh, Mister Jamison, I've been meaning to ask you how your research is going, what with the storm and the trip to the main island. I'm always fascinated by the history of this island. Perhaps all of you could join me for dinner tonight? I really must hear what this charming young man has to say about the previous inhabitants of La Gonave. Shall we say seven?"

"We just returned from a very arduous journey," the minister said. "We're all very fatigued. Perhaps we could make it some other night?"

"Nonsense. You have all afternoon to rest. You must eat dinner anyway, so you might as well dine with me. It's settled. I'll expect you at seven. I must be going now. Good day."

The dumbfounded expressions on the faces of Tim and the minister did not escape Mildred. She turned to Madeleine, who immediately said, "Seven it is. Good day, Mildred."

When Mildred reached the road, two men on blue motorcycles sped by and kicked up a cloud of dust in her reddened face. She hacked up dried dirt and then muttered, "And now we have heathens racing about on motorcycles. What's this island coming to?"

****

Mildred stood at the door as Madeleine, Tim, and the minister arrived at the appointed hour. "Welcome. I am so pleased you could honor me with your presence this evening." She noted Tim had shaved for a change and, after a brief exchange of pleasantries, escorted them into the living room.

Her residence appeared smaller than Madeleine's and lacked any semblance of feminine décor. Its one striking feature was the air conditioner cooling it to the point of discomfort to everyone except her. They sat upon uncomfortable, wooden furniture arranged around a small coffee table. A servant, whose plumpness mirrored Mildred's, brought out a plate of cheddar cheese and crackers. Next, she delivered a pitcher of iced tea and four glass tumblers arranged upon a wooden tray. The servant placed the tray on the coffee table and promptly retreated to the kitchen.

Mildred poured the tea and handed a glass to each of her guests. "Please, help yourselves to cheese and crackers. I've been saving them for a special occasion such as this."

The minister wasted no time in complying. "This really is a treat." Crumbs fell from his mouth. "Where were you able to purchase these, if you don't mind me asking?"

She beamed. "A minister from southern Indiana brought a group of high school students down a couple months ago. They were here for two weeks and helped us put a new roof on our church. They kindly brought me a few things they knew were not readily available in Haiti. Of course, most of what they brought I gave to our needy, Haitian brethren."

"How long have you lived on La Gonave, Miss Sponheimer?" Tim asked.

"It will be thirty-four years this coming November. Many missionaries have come and gone in that time, most of them unable to withstand the hardships we must endure here."

The conversation paused when her servant replenished the cheese and crackers.

"Madeleine, I pray so much you'll find it possible to stay," she continued. "You do know my offer for you to work at our mission hospital still stands."

"Thank you, Mildred. That's tempting, but I intend to rebuild the children's clinic. I'm committed to continuing my father's work."

She and Tim lowered their heads after hearing Madeleine's response. She hoped if Madeleine was not going to flee La Gonave she could at least be absorbed into the fold of the Greater Evangelical Mission. Not one to give up easily, she resolved to be even more proactive.

"Do you really think it will be possible to rebuild the clinic?" Tim asked.

The cook interrupted them before Madeleine could answer. "Dinner, it be ready."

The minister plucked a bite-size chunk of cheese and sandwiched it between two crackers as they moved into the dining room. The dinner entrée featured roasted pork with sides of mashed potatoes covered with gravy, canned corn, and chilled applesauce. A steaming loaf of baked bread added to the pleasant aroma. The minister ad-libbed his way through another bogus blessing.

"This pork is really tender," Tim remarked. Madeleine and the minister also chimed in with praise.

"Yes, the pork is especially tender." Mildred burst with pride. "Usually, the pork available on La Gonave is tough and stringy. However, this week my cook was able to purchase a cut from a well-fed sow."

"I'm surprised someone would butcher their sow," Madeleine said. "They're worth more as breeders."

"Someone else's loss is our gain," the minister said. He swiftly added, "All the same, I cannot help but feel remorse for any farmer whose sad plight forced him to sacrifice his breeding stock. I pray the money he made is sufficient to sustain him and his family for quite some time."

"Amen," Mildred added.

After dinner, the party returned to the living room where a lime custard pie and a pot of brewed coffee awaited them. Mildred wasted no time probing for information. "Tell me about your research, Mister Jamison."

He rattled off the spiel the minister had coached him to say.

"I see." Her eyes surveyed the other guests. "What do you do with these artifacts once you collect them?"

"First of all, I take detailed notes on their general condition and where I found them. I'll attach an identification code to each piece. Everything will be carefully packed and shipped back to Syracuse University where I'll analyze them."

"Tom will be writing his master's thesis based upon these artifacts," Madeleine said.

Unimpressed, Mildred nodded her head. "Do these artifacts have any value? I mean, in a monetary sense?"

"Collectors will pay for pre-Columbian artifacts, but everything I collect will be returned to a museum in Port-au-Prince."

It crossed her mind these bits of clay might be something from which the Greater Evangelical Mission could profit. The mission already made a tidy sum from seashells purchased from natives for pennies and sold to stateside visitors at a handsome profit. She would investigate this possibility as soon as this snippy student departed the island. "What's your interest in all of this, Reverend Burkholder?"

"I'm in Haiti in a purely ministerial capacity. I, of course, am more interested in the living than in the dead, but if I can give Mister Jamison a helping hand every now and then, I'm more than happy to do so."

The servant entered the room and collected the dirty dishes. Madeleine seized the opportunity to escape and stood. "Everything was excellent, Mildred. This really has been a splendid evening."

Tim and the minister rose to their feet and added their compliments.

"You're all quite welcome." She failed to acknowledge her cook. "I hope we'll be able to do this again. Shall I see you all in church tomorrow morning?"

"We plan to attend the early service with the Nazarenes," Madeleine said. "Afterward, we're going to do some spelunking."

"Spelunking?" Mildred's nose scrunched upon hearing of such gibberish.

"Cave exploring," the minister said. "We're not going to be doing any actual work, though, with tomorrow being the Lord's Day. Mister Jamison simply wants to reconnoiter a cave on some farmer's property. The real work will start on Monday."

"Where is this cave located, may I ask?"

"It's on the property of Ti Bon and Marie Joseph Baptiste," Madeleine said. "Just a short distance from Anse-à-Galets."

She found this snippet of information to be worthy of note. "Oh, yes, I know the Baptistes. Their children attend our mission's school. They're a lovely, Christian family."

Madeleine shuffled toward the door. Tim and the minister followed.

"I wish you luck in finding your artifacts, Mister Jamison," she said as they exited. "I'm sure you're eager to complete your work and get back to your schooling."

"Some things can't be rushed," Tim said. He glanced at Madeleine. "I'll take as much time as is needed."

She noted the exchange of eye contact between the couple. Disgusted at the thought of the array of immoralities that undoubtedly already transpired between them, she forced another smile. "It was certainly a pleasure to share this evening with such lovely people as yourselves. May God bless each and every one of you."

Chapter 39

Spelunkers

After an early breakfast and the Sunday church service lasting the obligatory two hours to the minute, the three *blancs* met Ti Bon at the entrance of the cave above his parched farm plot. Adhering to the script previously thrashed out with the minister, Tim took control of the group. "Okay, before we go inside, I want to go over some directions. Madeleine, you translate everything I say to Ti Bon."

Madeleine nodded her head.

"First, you each have two flashlights. I want everyone to double-check that both of them are in working order. I'll lead the way, followed by Reverend Burkholder, Ti Bon, and then Madeleine. We'll stay within touching distance of each other at all times. I'll be the only one who handles any artifacts we come across. Is that perfectly clear?"

Reverend Burkholder and Madeleine nodded their heads, as did Ti Bon once Madeleine translated the directions.

"Madeleine, you let me know if Ti Bon shows any signs of becoming possessed again."

"Not to worry. His soul is cleansed, remember?"

Tim fought back a grin. "Nevertheless, keep an eye on him. Are we ready?"

Much like fighter pilots about to embark on a dangerous mission, they gave each other the thumbs-up sign. They entered the cave and sped past the spot where, in what seemed like an eternity ago, Ti Bon had become possessed. After winding several hundred yards further, the tight passageway ballooned into a voluminous chamber sparkling with mottled stalactites suspended from a vaulted ceiling—a cathedral with inverted steeples. Dripping water echoed off the stone walls in piercing repetition. The damp, stagnant air conveyed an odor not unlike soiled laundry.

"My God, this is incredible," the minister said. His words eerily bounced off the inflexible walls. Bats in the cavern's upper reaches screeched at the disturbance. The spelunkers clumped together.

Tim said softly to the minister, "I think it would be a good idea if we kept our voices down. Let's see if we can find the source of the dripping sounds."

They discovered water percolating out of the wall at a far corner. It formed a small pool below and the overflow streamed down another dark passageway. Tim aimed his flashlight at a pile of narrow, chalky objects. He picked one up and reckoned it to be a human bone broken in half, its marrow removed, and depictions of deities engraved on its outer surface. Next to the bones, he spotted a handful of marble-size stones. "Does anyone have any idea what these might be?"

Madeleine knelt to take a closer look. "I'm guessing they're gallstones."

The minister snatched an object at the edge of the pool, but dropped it the instant he realized his discovery to be a human skull. It bounced on the sandstone floor with a clapping echo. This newest disturbance prompted the bats to screech another chorus.

Tim shined his light at the skull and then to the minister's eyes. "I believe I gave instructions no one except me was to touch anything."

The minister covered his eyes from the blinding light. "Don't worry, I learned my lesson. I won't slip up again."

Ti Bon drew Tim's attention by pointing his light to another corner of the chamber. There, on top of a rock ledge, several intact clay vessels lay neatly arranged.

"I think you've hit a gold mine," Madeleine said.

"Gold?" the minister said. "Did someone say gold?"

"A gold mine of pottery is what I believe Madeleine meant," Tim said, surprised the minister rather than himself had difficulty keeping a lid on his excitement.

"What do you make of all of this, Tom?" Madeleine asked.

Tim flashed his light around the cavern's walls. He recalled reading about the Mayans in National Geographic and figured pagan rituals performed by *Taínos* could be every bit as morbid. "I suspect this was a site for human sacrifices. Maybe even cannibalism."

"Couldn't it just be a ceremonial burial ground?" Madeleine asked, her eyes dancing about.

"That's a possibility, but why are these bones broken in half with their marrow removed? How many other skulls are in that pool? My guess is this wasn't the final resting place of choice."

Madeleine took a deep swallow and then looked about with her flashlight. "I wonder where the water leads. It sure is a shame it doesn't flow in the direction of Ti Bon's property. I can't even imagine what this water would mean to him."

"Actually, it wouldn't be too difficult to set up a siphon and run some water to his property," Tim said. "We're still well above his land."

"That's a fabulous idea," Madeleine said. "Could you really do it?"

"I don't see why not. There's plenty of water here for Ti Bon's farm and these skulls."

"That's a dandy idea, Tom," the minister said. "I'll be happy to pay for the piping. Let's follow this stream and see where it leads. Who knows what else we might find around here."

The corridor receiving the stream of water looked to be slightly larger than the one originating from Ti Bon's farm. Eroded, jagged edges on either side suggested the trickling stream had once been a gushing torrent. Broken terra cotta lay strewn about the damp paths on either side of the shallow stream. Maintaining the ruse of a scholarly expedition, Tim periodically knelt down to examine clay fragments. No sign of gold, so far. He surprised and dismayed himself for being so adept at running this con. These and other self-deprecating thoughts spun through his mind as he stooped over to examine yet another smashed piece of pottery. His eyes widened when the artifact in his hand weighed too much to be clay. With only the minister hovering over him, he scratched the mud covering to reveal a metallic, yellowish color.

"Bingo," the minister said.

Tim turned off his flashlight to lessen the chances Ti Bon or Madeleine would see him place the gold artifact in his pocket. "It looks to me that everything in this cave is pretty well smashed. I'll wait until tomorrow to examine them closer and take samples, along with detailed notes. I want to pick up the pace now so we can see how far this cave goes. As soon as our lights begin to dim, we'll head back. We won't use our back-up lights unless absolutely necessary. Let's go."

A spot of illumination became visible ahead of them after they traveled another several hundred paces. The light grew in size and brightness as they continued in its direction.

Tim stopped. "Listen."

"What is it?" the minister asked.

"Listen. That's the sound of a waterfall. The light up ahead must be where the stream exits the cave."

Their flashlights were no longer needed once they came within one hundred yards of the opening. Just as he surmised, the cave led out to a mountainside where the stream cascaded down at least one hundred feet to a large pool. A towering mountain rose directly across from the cave opening. The gorge below reached a dead end on one side where the mountain converged with another. An immense wall of rocky rubble, too steep to be climbed without special gear, blocked the other end, making the pool inaccessible from the ground below.

"Incredible," Madeleine said. "Look at all this water. It is such a shame there's no way for anyone to get to it."

"It may not have always been that way," Tim said.

"What do you mean?"

"The gorge could have been accessible prior to a landslide or, more likely, human intervention."

"What do you mean, human intervention?" the minister asked.

"What I mean is humans, probably *Taíno* Indians, could have purposely blocked the gorge to keep the Spaniards out."

"Why would they do that?" Madeleine asked.

"That's what I intend to find out." The adrenaline rush Tim felt had little to do with gold. Searching for pre-Colombian artifacts proved to be as exciting as diving an uncharted coral reef. "I think it's time to unwind some of this rope we've been lugging around all morning. I'm going to climb down and check the area out below."

"Are you sure about this, Tom?" Madeleine asked. "It's a sheer drop. There's nothing for you to hold onto."

"Piece of cake. I used to go rappelling all the time when I was growing up. I'll just tie off the rope on this rock and wrap it around this other one over here. Going down is the easy part. Coming back up takes a little more energy. It can't be more than one hundred feet. It's no big deal."

"It would be a big deal to me," the minister said. "There's no way I could do it."

"Don't worry, I'll be fine."

He secured the rope to two rocks and tossed the free end over the side of the cliff. He borrowed the minister's belt, made two loops around the rope, and fastened it around his own belt. Without hesitation, he swung out over the side, took three large hops against the rock wall, and landed at the bottom of the gorge.

Madeleine placed a hand on Reverend Burkholder's shoulder. "Impressive."

The minister nodded in agreement, while Ti Bon's eyes remained widened from the moment Tim had hurtled himself over the edge.

Tim approached the pool and stood on a large boulder along the bank. With the early-afternoon sun still high, he peered through the crystalline water and surmised the shallow shoreline dropped steeply. He stripped off his clothes, stacked them in a bundle, and dove into a deep section. The cool water further energized him.

The minister glanced at Madeleine and caught her attention by coughing. She blushed and backed away. "I'll just wait back here. Let me know when he's dressed."

Tim plunged to the bottom of the pool—about twenty-five feet. After a nearly two-minute reconnaissance, he rose to the surface for air and then surface-dived again. He lost half his breath upon making an eye-popping discovery. Scattered along the bed as far as he could see, gold artifacts of every imaginable shape and size glistened, even in the subdued sunlight. He seized a nearby crescent-shaped object, wiped off its silt coating, and admired the engravings decorating both sides. Ecstasy filled his mind. The glittering gold meant freedom—freedom from debt—freedom from deceit. *I only have to pull off this charade for a few more days.*

Numbness from oxygen deprivation set in. He swam to the surface with the precious *Taíno* artifact clasped in his tightened fist. He slid up to the shoreline and effortlessly hoisted himself onto the flat boulder he originally used as a diving platform. He held the artifact to his side, returned to his clothes, and placed them over his dripping skin. While scaling the cliff, he heard a slapping splash over the rumbling of the cascading falls. He peered below and spotted a large ripple in the middle of the pool. He figured a loose rock must have fallen from above.

Chapter 40

Counselor

Madeleine retired early Sunday night, providing Tim and Reverend Burkholder the opportunity to discuss the cache of gold at the bottom of the pool.

In perpetual motion on Madeleine's rocking chair, the minister asked, "How many gold artifacts would you estimate you saw down there?"

"Too many to count. There were hundreds."

The minister continued admiring the crescent-shaped artifact in the flickering light of the oil lamp and repeated the same line of questions they briefly went over earlier when Madeleine and Yvette had been out of the room. "You're sure you can dive down there without any SCUBA gear?"

"Like I said, it can't be any deeper than twenty-five feet. I could free-dive that in my sleep. Don't worry. Getting the artifacts out of the pool will be the easy part. Getting them up to the cave and back here is the part I'm worried about. How do you suppose we pull that off without Madeleine or Ti Bon becoming any the wiser?"

The minister stopped rocking and rested his chin on his left wrist. After a brief pause, he said, "I think I have an idea. Madeleine said she wouldn't be able to go with us tomorrow because she'll be taking an inventory of what's left at the clinic. I'll pay Ti Bon a few *gourdes* to help her clean up the debris. That will leave just you and me to return to the cave."

"What will we carry the gold artifacts in?"

"We can use the metal tool box I brought along. We'll empty it somewhere along the way and fill it with the gold."

"That's not a bad idea," Tim said, protruding his lower lip and nodding his head. "We can just go back and forth each day with the tool box."

"Exactly. It'll look like we're using some tools for excavations or something. How many loads do you think it'll take?"

Tim paused to consider the dimensions of the toolbox and the staggering number of gold artifacts he spotted scattered along the bottom of the clear pool. "I guess it'll take five or six loads."

"Five or six loads?" The minister's eyes brightened.

"At least. I'm not sure the two of us will even be able to carry a full box at a time. We're talking gold here, you know."

"Yes, we're talking gold."

A cloud of guilt fell over Tim as he contemplated the layers of lies mounting between himself and the one he loved. "Tell me, Reverend Burkholder, why can't we say anything about this to Madeleine? I'm sure she'd understand the need for secrecy. It's not like we're planning on keeping the gold for ourselves or anything."

"Of course not."

"Why can't we just tell her, then?"

"Because there's no need for her to be endangered by any of this. Gold has the nasty habit of attracting a bad element, if you know what I mean. We should move as quickly and quietly as possible before the word gets out. Besides, what possible reason can there be for her to know anything about why we're really here?"

Tim desperately wished to unburden himself of some of his lies. "There is one reason."

"What would that be?"

He took a deep breath and extended his exhale before answering. "I guess it's time you knew. Madeleine and I are in love."

Reverend Burkholder's jaw fell to the level of his second chin. "Love? When did this happen?"

"It just did. It wasn't something either of us planned on happening."

"Are you sure she feels the same way about you?"

"As sure as I can be." He turned his head to gaze into the darkness of the night.

"Your life is in serious danger until your debt is paid in full." The minister's voice had turned stern. "I suggest we continue everything as planned. By the end of the week, I can leave with the artifacts and take them directly to the museum."

"What am I supposed to do?"

"You wait here and help Madeleine the best you can. I'll collect your finder's fee and pay off your debt to this Bertram DuMarche thug. Once this matter is resolved, you can tell your sweet pea as much or as little of the truth as you dare, but don't be surprised if she dumps you."

"Believe me, I've thought of little else."

"You agree it's best to leave everything *status quo* until your debt is squared away, don't you?"

"Yeah, that makes the most sense. At least, then I'll just be a liar…a penniless liar, but at least I won't be in debt way over my head and worrying about someone putting a bullet in it."

"If it's true love then everything will work out fine. Now, let's get some sleep. We have a lot of work ahead of us. The sooner we get these artifacts to the museum the sooner you two love birds can start a new life together."

They crawled into their respective berths, Tim on the cot and the minister on the sofa. Tim turned out the lantern. "I appreciate your counsel, Reverend Burkholder. I'm beginning to see the connection between your ministerial and legal careers. I can't imagine anyone being more suited to help people in trouble."

"Please, don't mention it, Tim. Our association is more rewarding to me than you'll ever know."

Chapter 41

Missing

The minister sipped at his second cup of coffee when Yvette arrived to prepare breakfast. "Good morning, Reverend Burkholder. You are up early this Monday morning, I see."

"Good morning to you, Yvette. Yes, I woke up before daybreak. Couldn't fall back to sleep for some reason."

"And *Soeur Ma-da-leen*…is she still asleep?"

"I suppose so. I haven't heard any movement back there yet."

"Would the reverend like muffins this morning?"

"The reverend would love Yvette's muffins this morning."

"Did I hear something about muffins?" Tim asked. Surprised he'd overslept, he sat up on the cot and stretched his arms.

"You heard correct," the minister said.

The muffins had been taken out of the oven and left to cool by the time a pale-faced Madeleine joined them.

"Is *Soeur Ma-da-leen* not feeling so well this morning?" Yvette asked.

"I'm fine, Yvette. Just feeling a little nauseous, that's all. I must have picked up a bug or something on the main island."

"Is there anything we can do for you?" Tim asked.

"I'll be fine. Why don't you two start breakfast without me? I don't think I can hold anything down at the moment."

After breakfast, Tim and the minister gathered their gear.

Color returned to Madeleine's face as she gently rocked on the front porch. "What are your plans for today, Tom?"

"I'm going to concentrate on collecting broken terra cotta for the next few days. I need to get special packing from Port-au-Prince for those intact vessels we saw."

The minister added, "Tom tells me it's the smallest artifacts that often have the greatest value from an archaeological sense. I guess that's big-time science for you."

"You two be careful," Madeleine said. "I'm sure Ti Bon is also excited about going back to the cave."

"I meant to tell you," the minister said. "I'm going to pay him to help you clean up the mess at your clinic."

"That's a nice offer, Reverend Burkholder, but I'd feel better knowing he's with you two."

"We'll be fine. Remember, these types of explorations are precisely the kind Tom has been professionally trained at the university to conduct."

"Be that as it may, if the two of you aren't back promptly by three this afternoon, Ti Bon and I will be marching in there to pull you out."

"No problem," Tim said. "We'll be back well before three."

Before Tim and the minister could slip out the door, Madeleine asked, "Why are you taking a tool box, Tom?"

Tim had hoped he wouldn't have to add to his mountain of lies. He reluctantly concocted another one. "Screw drivers, hammers, and such are essential tools of the trade. Not everything is conveniently lying about on the surface."

"Please be careful. Promise?"

"We'll be careful." Tim felt a rush of relief at finally saying something true.

Only when they reached Ti Bon's home did they realize they overlooked one minor complication. Ti Bon did not speak a word of English, while between the two of them their vocabulary in *Créole* could be counted on a single hand.

The minister gave him twenty *gourdes*, while repeatedly saying, "*Soeur* Madeleine," and then pointed down the road toward Anse-à-Galets.

Ti Bon apparently caught on as he pointed to himself and then to Anse-à-Galets, before saying, "Ti Bon…*Soeur* Madeleine…*oui, oui.*" He then traipsed down the road toward town, a man obviously on a mission.

****

The cave cast a darker, eerier atmosphere with only two explorers wandering inside. When they arrived at the large chamber, which Madeleine had christened *the Basilica*, Tim said, "Gold or no gold, I'm never stepping foot inside this cave alone."

The minister's eyes scanned the shadowy surroundings. "Those were exactly my thoughts, too."

They shined their lights at the same sights they saw the previous day. The pile of broken and engraved bones, along with their accompanying gallstones, lay where they had left them. Tim stepped over the dried body parts and directed his light at the terra cotta vessels resting on the rock ledge. The ornately engraved containers retained remnants of pigment from centuries long past.

The minister shined his light at the pool, kicked the skull he dropped the day before, and watched it roll to the edge of the water. "Do you suppose there could be gold artifacts in there? It sure would be easier than climbing down the cliff at the end of the cave."

Tim's beam of light joined the minister's. "If you want to stick your hand in there and root around, be my guest."

The minister continued to steady his light toward the murky water. The partly-submerged, empty-eyed skull returned a toothy grin. "Let's concentrate on where we're sure there are gold artifacts."

Tim pointed his light at the terra cotta vessels on the rock ledge. "Wouldn't the museum be just as happy with these?" he asked, impressed by their near perfect condition and unique shapes. "Maybe we should leave the gold where it is."

"The museum already has more clay pots than they can possibly display. Gold artifacts, on the other hand, are a rarity. Think of the tourists they'll attract. The international prominence the museum will receive."

"I guess you're right, but all the same, these vessels are extremely impressive."

"I'll inform the museum of their existence. They'll probably want to send a team of real anthropologists to conduct an intensive study."

"Why are we here, anyway?" What the minister just said puzzled him. "Why didn't they send real anthropologists here in the first place?"

"When you only have one team there's only so much terrain that can be explored," he said.

Tim thought he heard exasperation in the minister's voice.

"That's why you're going to be getting such a handsome finder's fee. Let's face it, you were lucky to hit the jackpot so quickly. You could have spent months out here and only have a cardboard box of broken pots to show for your efforts."

"Yeah, I guess you're right."

"Of course, I am. Now let's get to where we already know we're going to hit paydirt."

When they reached the end of the cave, Tim tied the rope off precisely as he had the day before, attached the toolbox to the rope, and carefully lowered it. He borrowed the minister's belt again, looped it around the rope before fastening it, and made his rapid descent. Once on the bottom, he dumped the tools, concealed them behind a few rocks, and placed the empty box near the water's edge. He looked up and gave the thumbs-up sign, which the minister promptly returned.

He climbed atop a boulder at the water's edge, undressed, dove into the cool, clear water, and quickly located the scattered treasure. He grabbed as many objects as he could hold in his hands, swam back to the surface, carefully laid the artifacts on a flat rock about the size of a manhole cover, and repeated the exercise until collecting what he calculated would be a full load.

Once out of the water, he arranged the artifacts to fit inside the toolbox as tightly as possible. With space still available, he checked the toolbox's weight and decided to return for another handful or two. He spotted a large swirl in the middle of the pool the instant he dove, made a somersault as he hit the water, and arrived back to the surface. With several powerful strokes, he reached the rock where he left the toolbox, pulled himself up, and spun around to face the water. Excluding the stream cascading down the wall from the cave above, the surface appeared perfectly still.

He narrowed his gaze to where he had been diving and noticed for the first time a sunken log he must have continually swum over while collecting the golden objects. He chuckled to himself. In his quest he made no other observations. Concluding he salvaged a sufficient number of artifacts for the day, he looked up and gave the minister the thumbs-up sign.

The minister returned it.

He wrapped the rope around the toolbox several times before securing it with several half-hitch knots. He climbed up to the cave and, with the minister's assistance, hoisted the gold-laden chest to the mouth of the cave. He couldn't remember the last time he felt so much in control of his life. Things had finally fallen into place.

Reverend Burkholder knelt beside the toolbox. "May I?"

Tim all but beamed. "Be my guest."

The minister unlatched the lid, paused to savor the moment, lifted it, and peered at the ungodly fortune inside. "Mother to Heaven, take a look at all this gold."

"It's a shame we have to turn it all over to the museum."

"Don't let the sight of all this gold cloud your judgment, my good man. From the time of Adam and Eve, greed has been the devil's single best means to lead men down the path to eternal damnation."

"I was just kidding, Reverend Burkholder. Believe me, I'm more than satisfied with simply having my debt covered. I'm also thrilled at being involved in this discovery. I think I may have missed my calling. I should have become an anthropologist."

The minister clenched several artifacts in his fist. "Yes, this is exciting. This discovery more than justifies all the volunteer time I've spent on the museum's board. You've done a great service for the Museum of Pre-Columbian Art and for the country of Haiti, my good man."

"I couldn't have done it without you, Reverend Burkholder. I think I've been remiss in not thanking you enough. Because of you, I'll soon be a free man."

"It's a pleasure working with you, Tim. I truly hope things work out for you and Madeleine. God knows you two deserve some breaks."

"I really owe you, Reverend Burkholder. I was a miserable mess before I met you."

The minister appeared uncomfortable at being on the receiving end of gratitude. "Why did you dive into the pool the second time only to pop right back up?"

Not wanting to admit being spooked by something he imagined in the water, he improvised a plausible answer, something he'd become adept at doing. "I guess I've been in Haiti way too long. I was actually going to try to stuff some more artifacts into the chest, but just as I dove, I realized with any more weight we might not be able to lift it."

"You think there are four or five more loads like this down there?"

"At least."

"At least? Hmm."

Each held an end of the toolbox and shuffled their way back through the cave. They set the box down to rest every hundred paces or so.

The exhausted minister winced with pain by the time they reached the chamber. "This isn't going to work. I'll never make it out of this cave with this box, let alone back to Madeleine's."

"What do you suggest?"

"Let's hide the chest somewhere in this chamber. We should be able to find one of those wooden handcarts somewhere in the village. I'm sure someone will either sell us one or, at least, rent one to us."

"So, we'll come back later this afternoon with a cart?" Tim asked. He didn't relish the thought of leaving the gold unguarded.

"Precisely. Have you got a better idea?"

Shrugging, he reluctantly agreed to the minister's plan. They hid the toolbox behind the rock ledge displaying the terra cotta vessels.

The noon hour had arrived when they returned to Madeleine's. They found Ti Bon in the backyard sweeping with a palm-tree frond small pebbles up against the fence. He apparently thought he had been paid to clean around Madeleine's cottage rather than the clinic.

"It looks like we got half the message across," the minister said.

"At least he's not sweeping off the road."

"Very true. Very true."

Tim glanced about Madeleine's yard in search of something they could use to carry the gold. He found nothing. "Let's go to the clinic and see how Madeleine's doing. We better enlist her aid in coming up with a cart or who knows what sort of worthless gizmo we'll wind up with."

The minister nodded his head. They left Ti Bon to complete his self-assigned tasks.

Madeleine was nowhere in sight when they arrived at the clinic. They found atop a wooden crate her clipboard with several items and numbers written down on a sheet of paper. The last entry stopped in the middle of a word, a broken piece of lead being the only remnant of her pencil.

Tim spotted Madeleine's leather charm on the floor. He held it out to the minister. "Something's terribly wrong. Madeleine never takes off this charm except to…she didn't voluntarily take off this charm."

"What are you saying?"

Shock waves swept through him with a shattering force he experienced only once before. That night…on the boat…Sarah missing…not again. He could hardly speak. "She's gone. Madeleine is gone. Something terrible has happened. I know it."

Reverend Burkholder placed his arms around Tim's trembling shoulders. "Now Tim, there must be a rational explanation for this. Madeleine could be back at the house even as we speak."

He grasped at this strand of hope. "You keep looking around here. I'm going to run back to the house. If she's there, I'll be right back. Either way, I'll be right back."

He darted off before the minister could respond, reached the cottage, tore inside, and raced through every room. Madeleine was nowhere to be found. Now even more frantic, he ran to the backyard where he found Ti Bon merrily sweeping away with his palm frond. Tim grabbed the Haitian by the arms and blurted out Madeleine's name.

Ti Bon's bewildered expression turned out to be all the answer he received.

He raced back to the clinic and found a rattled minister pacing about in a stupor. Out of breath and puffing between words, Tim asked, "What…what do we do?"

"Let's go over to the mission. Mildred Sponheimer seems to know everything that happens on this island. There must be a logical explanation for all of this. I'm sure Madeleine is fine."

For the very first time Tim detected a tone of dishonesty in Reverend Burkholder's voice.

Chapter 42

Ransom

Tim and the minister barged into Mildred Sponheimer's office. "We're looking for Madeleine," Tim said. "Something awful may have happened to her."

The mission director remained seated. Her lips tightened.

"There may or may not be a problem here, Miss Sponheimer," the minister said. "Madeleine appears to be missing. We thought perhaps you might know of her whereabouts."

"I assure you she's not here. Why on earth would you come to me?"

"We thought you might have heard something, anything," Tim said, although internal seeds of doubt that Mildred would be of the slightest help had already sprouted.

"How long has she been missing?"

"Since sometime between eight this morning and noon," the minister said. "We were doing some cave exploring while she was taking inventory at the clinic. When we returned she was gone."

"We found her clipboard," Tim said. "It appears she stopped writing midstream. I found her leather charm on the floor. She wouldn't have taken it off voluntarily."

"A leather charm? Why on earth—"

"That doesn't matter. The point is Madeleine has disappeared."

"My, my, this is indeed terrible. I'll alert everyone on my staff to be on the watch for her. I've been worried something like this might happen. A beautiful and single young woman has no place whatsoever being on this island. She's probably been kidnapped and will be forced into a life of white slavery."

Tim lurched forward. "White slavery? What in the hell are you saying?"

The minister placed a hand on Tim's shoulder. "Let's not jump to conclusions here, Mildred. We're all concerned about Madeleine. She's probably fine and, if she has been kidnapped, she can't be far away. She must still be on the island."

Mildred stood and put her right hand to her flabby cheek. An air of concern finally crossed her face. "I have noticed two strange men. They were riding motorcycles. No one seems to know who they are or where they came from."

"Where did you see these men?" Tim asked.

"I saw them pass by Madeleine's house the other day...Saturday...the day the three of you had dinner at my home."

"Do you have any idea where we might find these two men?" the minister asked.

"I had my assistant ask a few questions among our congregation after church. It seems these strangers are staying in a hut halfway between here and Nan-Café. I understand there's a large antenna attached to this hut."

His hand still resting on Tim's shoulder, the minister said, "I think we should pay these motorcycle men a little visit. Mildred, can you tell us how to get to this hut?"

"Ask my assistant on your way out. She can give you the precise directions."

Before they departed, Mildred reached into her front desk drawer, pulled out an object covered with a white handkerchief, unwrapped it, and displayed a shiny, snub-nosed revolver. "Here, take this."

"A gun?" Tim asked.

"Yes, a gun. As I said, a single, white woman can't be too careful on this island. I keep a gun in my office and one at home…for protection."

He took the gun and stuffed it in his back pocket.

"There's something else," Mildred said. "It has been reported a large yacht moored last night on the other side of the island, near Pointe-à-Raquettes. Maybe there's a connection."

They thanked Mildred and then got directions to the suspicious hut from Rachelle before hurrying off to Madeleine's to pick up her vehicle.

"Do you think these motorcycle guys could have kidnapped Madeleine?" Tim asked.

"Anything's possible," the minister said, "but in fourteen years in Haiti, I've never heard of a missionary, particularly a woman, being kidnapped. It's simply not a crime Haitians would find to be profitable and it is definitely not one that would be condoned by even the most ruthless of elements. On the other hand, if the situation appeared ripe for the picking, any other white, including you and me, would be fair game."

They came within sight of Madeleine's cottage and spotted two blue motorcycles parked outside her door. They darted into the house with Tim leading the way. A muscular Haitian, a gold chain draped around his neck, gently rocked in Madeleine's chair. Another man, a more typical spindly Haitian, sat on the chair across from him. His feet rested on the coffee table. Neither appeared surprised by their abrupt entrance.

"Where's Madeleine?" Tim asked with a glare. "What in the fuck have you done with her?"

The man wearing the gold chain smirked. His steely-eyed partner remained silent.

Tim pulled out the revolver and pointed the barrel within an inch of the larger man's face. "I repeat, what in the fuck have you done with Madeleine?"

The burly Haitian stopped smirking, but continued to rock.

The pistol shook in Tim's hand. "Are you going to answer me?"

A long pause passed. "We have your precious Madeleine. If you want to see her again, you best put that gun down and do exactly as I say."

"Why should we trust you?" the minister asked.

"What choice do you have?"

Tim glanced at Reverend Burkholder. Reluctantly, he put the gun on the coffee table. The silent man snatched it and examined every detail.

"Tell us," Tim said, his voice carrying considerably less clout without a gun in his hand. "What have you done with Madeleine?"

"We have your Madeleine in a safe place. She'll remain unharmed so long as you do exactly as I say."

"What do you want from us?" the minister asked.

"What do I want? I'll tell you exactly what I want. I want the gold."

"Gold? What gold?" The minister's charade of ignorance failed to meet his usual standard.

The steely-eyed man stood and placed the cold barrel of Mildred's gun on the minister's temple. His face turned uglier. "Let me waste him, Marcel."

Tim didn't wait for Marcel to answer. "We'll give you the gold."

"That's very wise of you," Marcel said. "Put the gun down, Delmar. These men want to cooperate."

Delmar sneered at the minister, sat down, and returned to idling his time with his new possession.

"You will deliver the gold to our hut at precisely ten o'clock tonight," Marcel said. "It's halfway between here and Nan-Café. You take—"

"We know where it is," Tim said.

"You do? Very clever. Delivering the gold to us shouldn't present a problem then."

The two men got up from their chairs. Marcel nodded to his partner. Delmar punched Tim in the stomach, doubling him over.

"That's for pointing a gun at me," Marcel said. His eyes turned darker than his skin. "As for you, Reverend Burkholder, my associate would never hit a man of the cloth. He would shoot one, though."

Both men snickered, swaggered out of the house, hopped on their motorcycles, and roared off in the direction of Nan-Café.

Chapter 43

Unveiling

Ti Bon rounded the corner of Madeleine's cottage as the two thugs sped away. He burst into the screened porch and found Tim bent over on the floor and the minister stooped over him. He lifted Tim to a chair, realizing these motorcycle men represented every much a danger to his white companions as to himself and family. He thanked the spirits for giving him the wisdom to send Marie Joseph and the children to her sister's. *They should be safe there. But, what about my friends? Were these motorcycle men out to harm them simply because they befriended me? Where is Madeleine?* He felt responsible for the harm spreading to all whom he became near.

****

Still doubled over, Tim said, "Those sons-of-bitches better not lay a single hand on Madeleine or I'll…or I'll—"

"Get a hold of yourself," the minister said. "They're not going to hurt Madeleine so long as we do exactly as they say. We'll give them the gold and that will be the end of it."

"I hope to hell you're right."

Opposite thoughts sprung through the minister's mind. He'd dealt with thugs like these in New York. Two-bit henchmen paid to carry out the dirty work. That's what made them dangerous. "I'm sure they just want the gold."

"Now that Ti Bon's here, let's head back to the cave," Tim said. "We can take Madeleine's Jeep. Ti Bon and I can carry the chest out."

"Good idea, but let's try to keep him in the dark about the gold. There's no sense getting him into danger over any of this."

"Agreed. Hopefully, he'll just think we've got some damn heavy tools or something."

"Right. Damn heavy tools."

****

With Tim at the wheel, they drove past Ti Bon's hut, straight through his parched cornfield, and stopped as close to the opening of the cave as four-wheel drive would permit. They hopped out and raced toward the cave. Tim and the minister carried flashlights. Ti Bon followed a few steps behind.

They reached the chamber and Tim ran directly to the rock ledge where he hid the chest. "It's gone." His raised voice echoed off the walls and the bats were none too happy about it.

He grabbed one of the terra cotta vessels and smashed it against the nearest wall. The continuous screeching of bats drowned out the echoes of the shattering pot. Once the bats settled down, a relaxed voice from a dark corner of the chamber rang out.

"Looking for a tool box, old chap?"

Tim recognized the British accent and shined his light at the voice. Perched on the toolbox, Sir John Winston held a semi-automatic rifle pointed directly at Tim's chest.

"Please don't make me fire this enormous gun. The bats do make such a racket."

Cloaked in darkness, Ti Bon's presence went unnoticed. He crept further into the recesses of the corridor connected to the chamber.

"So, you're the one behind this," the minister said. "Let me guess. Richy works for you."

The flash of a cigarette being lit in another corner of the chamber exposed Richy Richardson's face. "You've got it mostly right, Vinny, except Sir John works for me."

"What the hell is going on here?" Tim asked. "I thought you were my friend, Sir John."

"Nothing and no one are as they seem in Haiti. I thought you would have learned that lesson by now. Hasn't your new friend, Vinny, taught you anything?"

"Vinny? Who the hell is Vinny?"

"That's the name I used to go by," Vincent said, his gaze facing the ground.

"You mean before you became a lawyer?" Tim asked.

Sir John and Richy erupted into laughter. The bats joined them.

Richy lit an oil lantern to illuminate the chamber. He then moved closer to them. "Let me introduce you to Reverend Vince Burkholder. No, that's not it. I meant to say, G. Vincent Bennett, attorney at law. No, that's not right either. I know, let me introduce you to Vinny Berkowitz, concrete salesman extraordinaire."

Tim turned to the minister. "What the hell is going on here? Are you in on this?"

"Vinny's not in on this," Richy said. He sat on a boulder near Sir John. "Vinny Berkowitz is a freelancer, you see. That's what got him in trouble with the mob in the first place. Isn't that so, Vinny?"

"You tell me, Richy. You seem to know everything there is to know about me."

"I knew everything about you from the moment you stepped foot in Haiti. I control all the action on this island, Vinny. Unlike you, I always pay the family their percentage. Give unto Caesar that which is Caesar's."

"And leave everything else to us," Sir John added with a wink.

"Tell me, good ol' Vinny," Richy said, "were you planning on stiffing me, too?"

"Absolutely not. I was going to split the profits exactly as we agreed. I'm a legitimate businessman now."

"Legitimate?" Tim said. "It's obvious there isn't one ounce of legitimacy in your entire body."

Vinny placed his hand on Tim's shoulder. "You gotta believe me, Tim. I had every intention of paying off your debt."

Tim swiped his hand off. *How could I have allowed myself to be so duped by this slimy sack of shit?* "With the finder's fee you were going to get from the museum, Vinny?"

"You two can continue this spat later," Richy said, his accompanying smirk adding to the debacle. "We have more important things to discuss, now don't we?"

"Like what?" Vinny asked.

"Like exactly where we can find the rest of the gold."

"You have all the gold," Vinny said. "Everything we found is in the tool box. There isn't any more."

Richy tossed his cigarette to the cavern's floor. "Vinny, Vinny, the gig is up. Show us where to find the rest of the gold. We'll let the both of you go, the pretty lady, too. Then we'll be on our way."

"I'll show you," Tim said. "Just promise me no harm will come to Madeleine."

"You have my word," Richy said. "Sir John, you keep an eye on Vinny while our anthropologist here leads me to the mother lode."

Richy pulled a revolver from an ankle holster and shoved it into Tim's side. "Don't try to be a hero." He unleashed a sickening snicker. "Oh, by the way, my associate, Bertram DuMarche, sends his regards. You can thank him for alerting me of your special connection to La Gonave. Our mutual friend has an uncanny ability to get the lowdown on just about anybody. He thought this white king bullshit might come in handy someday. I have to admit, it has paid off in aces, sonny boy."

Tim's stomach dropped another foot. Bertram, Sir John, and the one man he thought he could absolutely trust, the attorney-cum-minister, had all conspired against him. How could he have been so naïve as to fall for every cock-and-bull story this Vinny asshole had thrown at him? *Who the hell goes by the name Vinny?* Under different circumstances he would have spiraled into a never-ending labyrinth of self-condescension. Now, only thoughts of saving Madeleine from the madness fired through every nerve ending of what remained of his frazzled brain.

Sucking in a deep breath to regain some level of composure, he led Richy down the corridor alongside the stream to the opening where the water cascaded into the clear pool. He pointed down without saying a word.

"It's underwater?" Richy asked.

"It's underwater…hundreds of pounds."

"How deep?"

"Twenty-five feet, max."

"You're sure?"

"I'm sure."

"Okay, let's head back inside."

They returned to the chamber. Richy ordered Sir John to tie Vinny and Tim together. "Keep a close eye on them. I'm going back to the hut to check on how our two Haitians and the pretty dame are getting along. I'll bring one of the gooks back to help us drag out the gold."

Sir John nodded.

Richy shined his light in the would-be attorney's, would-be minister's face. "I knew I could count on you, Vinny."

Chapter 44

Footsteps

Concealed in the unlit corridor, Ti Bon grasped the gravity of the situation unfolding only a few paces away, his incomprehension of English mattering little. The voices of two strangers, both filled with fury, had to be those of *blancs*. He thought this odd, for with the notable exception of the mission director, he only experienced kindness from those of light skin. He ventured closer to the lantern-lit chamber, housing its old, clay pots and a skull-infested pool, and spotted Tim and the minister bound together. He groped about for a rock suitable for use as a weapon, but reconsidered his options after he noticed the rifle held by one of the strangers.

Seconds later, a beam of light lunged through the corridor and missed him by a fingernail's width. The clapping of clumsy footsteps, the pace quickening, accompanied the source of light weaving toward him. Sweat coated Ti Bon's glistening skin, the coolness of the cave vaporized by his overshadowing fear. He slithered his way toward the corridor's opening above his farm and prayed to the *loa* to safely guide him through the blackness. The dancing beam of light and the echoing footsteps coming from behind made better time.

About to blindly bolt to avoid capture, he stumbled across a small crevice in the wall, no thicker than a skeleton, and squeezed himself inside by exhaling his lungs. The beam of light skimmed his partially exposed chest and miraculously passed him by. The footsteps, now sounding as if coming from a thick-booted soldier marching high-step in parade, advanced to within an arm's length. The footsteps stopped, although the corridor still resonated with the pants of a *blanc* not fully at ease.

Not breathing, Ti Bon feared his thumping heart would give him away and resolved to leap at the *blanc* the instant the light revealed his presence. The beam abruptly arched over him and across the ceiling to the opposite side. It then went back down the corridor toward the chamber, reversed itself, again eluding him. As it had previously, it tunneled its way through the corridor toward the exit. The claps of footsteps followed the light.

He crept after the footsteps, keeping a safe distance behind, and hoped the *blanc* would lead him to *Soeur* Madeleine. He felt certain she would be able to save their companions. When he neared the cave's opening, two blinding lights from outside momentarily flashed in his face.

He dropped to the floor of the cave and then realized the *blanc* had taken Madeleine's Jeep. He sprung to his feet and ran after the vehicle whipsawing down his rock-littered, corn plot. After eluding every rock, bush, and hole by pure memory, he latched on the spare tire fastened to the vehicle's rear end, much like a crab onto a piling. He summoned all his strength to retain his hold. His friends had fallen into serious peril because of him. He had to save them— or die trying.

Chapter 45

Delmar

Madeleine, her auburn locks unbraided and disheveled, stood erect with her back pressed against the center post of the dimly-lit mud hut. Her slender arms were looped around the post and her hands tightly bound. She glared at the two thugs sitting nearby on the earthen floor, her rising blood pressure adding streaks of color to her high cheeks. She had no clue as to what these foul men wanted with her, having been snatched at gunpoint with neither man uttering a word, and then hauled to this secluded mountain hut.

The spindly, steely-eyed man rose to his feet, inhaled the last remnants of his cigarette, flicked it to the ground, squashed it with his right foot, and approached her. His stare shifted from her face to her breasts, whereupon he maintained a lengthy pause, then to her lower waist, and down her legs. He raised his eyes and gradually repeated his lecherous surveillance. He pulled out a pocketknife, opened it with one hand, slid the blade against the top button of her Cap Haïtien dress, and sliced it off.

"What do you say, Marcel? Should we have a little fun while we're waiting?"

"Leave her be."

"I'm not going to hurt her. I only want to see what she's hiding underneath this dainty dress."

She retained her composure as a second button dropped to the dirt floor. *So they speak English.* She presumed them to be recently repatriated Haitians, their degenerate behavior undoubtedly honed in the barrios of Miami.

"My, my, aren't you the brave bitch," Delmar said.

Marcel rose to his feet and tossed his cigarette down. "Leave her be, I said."

Delmar swung around with his knife firmly in hand and faced his partner. "I'm getting sick of your fuckin' orders. What do you care what happens to her? She ain't one of our people."

"The boss told us to keep an eye on her. Nothing more."

"Keeping an eye on her, all of her, is exactly what I have in mind."

"You know what I mean. Leave her be."

Delmar raised his knife and took a step toward his burly partner. A vehicle bounced up the road, its headlights flashing through the partially opened doorway as it turned toward the hut. He folded the knife and tucked it into the back pocket of his skin-tight jeans.

The door swung open a moment later. A *blanc,* paunchy and old, strode inside and directed a sickening smile at Madeleine. "Looks like you two have everything under control here. There's a change of plans. Marcel, I want you to go back with me to the cave. Delmar, you stay here and watch over the pretty dame. I want you to take her to Pointe-à-Raquettes first thing tomorrow morning."

"Maybe it would be better if I stayed and you take Delmar," Marcel said.

"No. I need your strength. We got a lot of weight to drag out of that cave. Let's go. Time's wasting."

The *blanc* led the way out to the vehicle. When Marcel reached the door, he turned to Delmar and stared evilly. "Leave her be."

Delmar smiled.

Delmar waited until the lights faded into the night. He swaggered to where Madeleine remained helplessly bound. A look of pending triumph crossed his hostile face. "It looks like it's just you and me now." He pulled out his pocketknife and positioned the blade against the third button of her dress. "Now let's see, where were we?"

Madeleine squeezed her eyes shut as he removed button after button after button. She felt the cold blade slip between her breasts and underneath her brassiere. He sliced the undergarment in two and emitted a disgusting sneer—a sneer terminated by a swishing sound, followed by a thud.

Her eyes opened and her jaw dropped. An equally wide-eyed Ti Bon stood before her. He clenched a machete dripping with Delmar's blood.

Chapter 46

Truth Be Told

Madeleine dashed out of the hut in lockstep behind Ti Bon, the bloody machete still in his hand. The Haitian hopped onto one of the motorcycles, clueless as to how to start it, let alone drive it away. She hiked up her unbuttoned dress and straddled the seat of the other cycle. She backed the bike off its kickstand and kicked on the engine with her third try. Over the roar of the motor, she hollered for Ti Bon to sit behind her and to position the machete on the side of the seat. She nearly exhausted her skills of persuasion before he would hold his hands around her partially exposed waist. She shifted the motorcycle into first gear, where it remained while they puttered down the rocky road.

Her harrowing experience became a distant memory the moment Ti Bon told her two *blancs* had assaulted Tom and Reverend Burkholder at gunpoint inside the cave. He went on to say how he managed to escape and steal a ride to the hut where she'd been held.

"How will we overpower these white men, *Soeur* Madeleine? They have guns."

"I'm not sure. We could get help in the village, but I'm afraid we don't have enough time."

"We must save them ourselves," Ti Bon said, repeatedly nodding his head into her wind-blown hair.

They reached his farm about an hour later and parked behind his hut. He sprinted inside and returned with some kerosene-soaked rags. He handed the machete to her and then wrapped the rags around a wooden stake to use as a torch, which he lit when they reached the cave's entrance. They snaked their way toward the voluminous chamber, but froze the instant they heard voices.

Ti Bon rubbed out the torch with a bare hand, leaving only embers to provide sufficient illumination to avoid tripping on the various rocks scattered about. She edged closer and listened to the conversation of the two strangers, one being the old *blanc* who came to the hut and left with the larger of the two Haitian thugs. She did not recognize the second voice, although he clearly had a British accent.

"I'll take the first shift while you two get some shuteye," the older man said. "We won't be able to get to the rest of what we came for till sun-up."

"That sounds like a bloody good plan, mate."

She and Ti Bon listened to the shuffling noises of men spreading themselves out on the cave's floor. A paralyzing silence followed.

"Let's move closer to the lit chamber," she softly said to Ti Bon.

They positioned themselves at the edge of the shadows, where they spied the old *blanc* sitting on a boulder with a rifle slung across his shoulder. After two long hours, he sauntered over to his partner and gave him a swift kick. The rudely awakened *blanc* dragged himself to his feet, took the rifle, and exchanged places. The new guard, the one with the British accent, began to nod off about an hour later. He set the rifle down, sprawled out on the floor of the chamber, and soon joined his partners and their two captives in slumber.

She kept watch from the dark corridor as Ti Bon crept up to Tim and the minister. Ti Bon lightly tapped Tim on the shoulder. His eyes opened, but he didn't utter a sound. They glanced about to assure themselves the three hoodlums remained asleep. Marcel's snoring reverberated through the chamber.

Next, Ti Bon tapped the minister on the shoulder. He jerked. "Huh?"

The *blanc* sleeping by the rifle stirred, rolled to his side, and again became motionless.

Ti Bon paused several minutes before kneeling down to untie the ropes keeping his friends immobilized. Tim hopped to his feet and helped the minister to his. All but their eyes froze when Marcel's snoring ceased. An excruciating minute elapsed before his bellowing snorts recommenced.

From the shadowy corridor, Madeleine tightly gripped the handle of the machete and watched Tim, Ti Bon, and Reverend Burkholder shuffle toward her. The minister tripped on a rock and fell. An echoing clatter filled the chamber.

Richy sprung to his feet and pulled out his revolver. "Freeze."

The would-be escapees had no choice but to comply. The bats cheered.

Richy stuck the revolver back into his ankle holster and ordered Marcel to tie Ti Bon and their other two captives together. He then directed his ire at his partner. "Damn you, Sir John. Couldn't you keep your fuckin' eyes open for just two lousy hours?"

"It won't happen again, Richy."

"You're damn right it won't. You almost blew the whole deal."

Richy glanced at the corridor where Madeleine hid, walked over to Sir John, and spoke to him in a hushed tone before meandering out of her sight. An instant later, a light blinded her. The shiny machete shook in her quivering hands.

"What do we have here?" Richy asked. "I suggest you drop that machete, young lady. Someone might get hurt."

She released her hold on the machete and slowly rose to her feet. Richy motioned with his gun for her to move into the chamber and then triumphantly grinned. "Look who has decided to grace us with her lovely presence."

Sir John's eyes fixated on the bodice of her buttonless dress. "I would suppose Delmar simply lost his head over your feminine charms and let you go."

"Something like that," she said.

Marcel stood. "Should I check on Delmar?"

"To hell with Delmar," Richy said. "I never liked that skinny-ass runt. When we're through with this business, I want you to take care of that piss ant. Is that understood?"

Marcel nodded his muscular head. His lips curled to something short of a grin.

"Good," Richy said. "I won't tolerate any more fuck-ups. As for the three of you," he glared at Tim, Ti Bon, and the minister, "any more attempts to escape and the pretty dame with the nice cleavage will be accessorized with a lead slug."

"Why don't you let her go?" Tim said. "She doesn't have anything to do with this."

"If she keeps the three of you in line," Richy said, shoving her toward Marcel, "then she has everything to do with this. Tie her up with the others and tell this pea-brain farmer over here what I said about the lady being sent to the Promised Land if there's any more funny business."

Richy, Sir John, and Marcel, all signs of their previous drowsiness evaporated, sat on boulders positioned around their bound prisoners.

"Are you all right, Madeleine?" Tim asked. "They didn't hurt you, did they?"

"I'm fine. What do these thugs want with us?"

Before Tim could answer, Ti Bon, tears streaming out of his eyes, begged for her forgiveness for having gotten everyone into such grave danger. He rambled on about the white powder he found, what he'd done with it, and how the motorcycle men told him the powder was theirs and worth an unfathomable fortune.

Not waiting for Ti Bon to finish his saga, she said to their captors, "So this is all about drugs? I should have guessed. You're all despicable."

244

"What makes you think this is about drugs?" Richy asked with a smirk.

"Ti Bon told me everything. About the cocaine you mistakenly dropped on his farm. How he used it to whitewash his and his neighbors' homes. What do you expect to gain by this? The cocaine was washed away in the storm."

Richy slapped his hand across his face and peeked through his fingers. "Should I answer this or do Vinny and Tim want to help me out here a little?"

Her scowl intensified. "Vinny? Tim? Who in the world are you talking about?"

Tim strained to make eye contact. "It's a long story, Madeleine."

"We have lots of time for long stories," Richy said. "Where should we begin?"

"Let's start with the white powder," Sir John said. "That was my idea, if I dare say so myself."

"A fine idea, I must admit," Richy said. "Why don't you do us the honors?"

"Gladly. First of all, old chaps, the white powder certainly wasn't cocaine. Give us a little credit here. We wouldn't jeopardize a small bloody fortune for a big bloody fortune, not when any white powder would do. The white powder your peasant farmer used to whitewash half of La Gonave was arrowroot. Totally harmless, I might add."

"I don't understand," she said. "Why the ruse about drugs?"

"We needed access to this cave," Sir John said. "Mister Ti Bon here wasn't about to let anybody enter it because it was haunted by zombies or what have you. We thought we'd have him thrown in prison for possessing coke, but his little whitewashing business required us to take another tack."

"And what was that?"

"Hey, that part was Marcel's idea," Richy said. "You tell her, Marcel."

"Yes sir, Mister Richy. You see, ma'am, we simply demanded that Mister Baptiste pay us fifty thousand *gourde*s for the powder he stole from us. We knew he couldn't pay such a sum and would be desperate for money, even if it meant letting white men enter his cave."

"If this isn't about drugs then it must be about broken terra cotta," she said. "Instead of being drug dealers you're grave robbers. Don't you realize these pre-Columbian artifacts have scientific value far exceeding their monetary worth? Tom is an anthropologist doing important research here."

Their three captors broke into another round of laughter. The bats joined them.

Eyes watering, Richy said, "Maybe it's time for me to introduce you to your anthropologist and the holy minister. Your two confidants are not what and who they purport to be. Let's start with your so-called anthropologist, who you seem to have taken quite a shine to. Meet Mister Tim James. He's not an anthropologist. In fact, for the past two years he's been none other than the head maintenance man at the beach club in Saint-Marc. Most of that time, he was too drunk from cheap booze to carry out his important duties."

Richy paused so his partners' smirks could rub salt into the wound. "And, to add to his illustrious résumé, the lad gambled away about everything he owned and then some. In fact, your distinguished anthropologist is, by my count, over fifty thousand dollars American in debt. You picked a real winner, sweetheart."

She turned to Tim. "Is this true?"

"I can explain." His voice crackled.

"What's there to explain? You lied to me. Everything between you and me has been a lie."

"No, it hasn't. I love you, Madeleine. That's all that matters."

"Don't talk to me about love. You don't know the first meaning. To think that I…that we…I can't believe this."

"You needn't feel so bad, little lady" Richy interjected. "More than a few Haitians in these parts think there's something special about this guy. I don't buy in to that crap, but I sure as hell took advantage of those that do. He has been quite the calling card for smoothing things out with the voodoo witchdoctors 'round here."

"You're despicable," she said.

"It gets better," Richy said. "Not only is your anthropologist not an anthropologist, but your minister here ain't no man of the cloth. Isn't that so, Vinny?"

"Haven't you said enough, already?" Vinny said. "Madeleine hasn't done a damn thing to hurt you or, for that matter, anyone else. Why don't you let this be?"

"I'm just trying to be of service to the pretty young thing. She needs to learn to be on the lookout for scumbags like you two."

"Look who's calling who scum," Tim said.

Clearly entertained by the melodrama, Sir John directed a sickening grin at Madeleine. "Now, now, let's not resort to bloody name calling, mates."

"From where I sit," she said, "there's enough scum in this chamber to smother all of Haiti. I don't want to hear anymore. You people, including these two I'm tied to, make me sick." She spoke to Ti Bon in his native language, her voice now soothing.

Richy strode over to the toolbox, flipped it open, grabbed a handful of gold artifacts, swaggered back, and foisted the shiny objects in her face. "We didn't come here for clay pots, sweetheart, and neither did your two pretend friends."

Chapter 47

Love Lies

An hour of group-imposed silence passed as dawn approached. Richy glanced at his watch. "It's time to get this show on the road. Marcel, untie Tim and that dumb-shit farmer."

"What about the girl and Vinny?" Sir John asked.

"Neither of them will be of much use to us for hauling out the gold. Marcel can keep an eye on them while we take care of more important business." He directed a menacing stare at Marcel. "If they give you any trouble, kill 'em."

Marcel grinned.

Richy swaggered over to Vinny and kicked him in the thigh. "You're lucky this Haitian peasant showed up or you'd be dragging up the gold, too."

"What do you intend to do with us?" Madeleine asked.

"Sorry, sweetheart, I only give out information on a need-to-know basis." He shoved Ti Bon into a dark corner of the chamber where an empty trunk rested against the damp wall. He gestured for the Haitian to pick it up and take it to where Sir John and Tim waited. Once there, Sir John jabbed the barrel of his rifle into Tim's spine. "Let's get a move on, old chap."

"Don't blame Tim for any of this, Madeleine," Vinny said as the others disappeared into the corridor leading to the pool and its *Taíno* treasure. "I'm the one to blame."

"You're the one to blame? No one held a gun to his head. Tom, Tim, whomever he wants to call himself, lied to me. How long was he going to continue with this charade? I thought he loved me."

"He does love you."

"Love starts with trust and honesty. Everything about him has been a lie. I don't even know who I fell in love with."

"You fell in love with the person. Not the name. Not the profession."

Madeleine's anger dissolved into sorrow and confusion. "You're both such damn liars."

"Tim only lied to you because I convinced him it was best for all concerned."

"Best for all concerned?"

"Yes, the best for all concerned. I want you to hear me out on this, Madeleine. Tim ran the dive operation a few years back at the beach club in Saint-Marc. His wife drowned and afterward he went on a two-year drinking binge."

"That part is true?"

"It's very true. The club couldn't keep a drunkard on as a dive master, so they made him a maintenance man. Unfortunately, his road to self-destruction included gambling. That's what got him into this fix."

"What do you mean?"

"Sir John Winston came to me in my capacity as an attorney and—"

"Your capacity as a what?"

"Okay, okay, I'm not really an attorney, either. Nevertheless, that's what I've been doing for the past fourteen years."

Madeleine shook her head in disbelief. "Tell me, Vinny, in your capacity as an attorney, why did you convert Tim, the maintenance man, into Tom, the anthropologist?"

"I knew about the possibility of the gold artifacts in this cave. I told Tim a museum would pay him a nice finder's fee, enough to settle his debt, if he could locate them."

"There is no such museum?"

"Correct, but Tim never knew that."

"So, you were going to steal the gold and leave him to fend for himself?"

"Not at all. I was going to pay off his debt. He earned it. Besides, I've grown quite fond of him."

"He is likeable," Madeleine said with a touch of sarcasm, not sure who, or what, to believe.

"You two falling in love wasn't in the plan. Once it happened, Tim pleaded with me to let him tell you the truth. I convinced him to wait until we had the gold safely off La Gonave and his debt paid in full."

"He should have told me, anyway."

"Maybe so, but you have to realize Tim doesn't hold himself in the highest esteem. I'm sure he thought you would be ashamed of him once you learned his true status—a penniless janitor."

"That's not important."

"Exactly, Madeleine."

"You know, Vinny, I think you missed your calling. You should have been a minister."

"Yeah, I would have made a damn good minister."

After a brief pause, she posed another question. "Do you think they'll let us go after they get their gold?"

"Madeleine, listen very closely. These are extremely dangerous men. If you get the chance to escape, I urge you to take it."

"Are they going to kill us?"

She found his answer in the deafening silence that followed.

Chapter 48

Murky Water

Richy and Sir John stood at the opening of the cave, intently watching as Tim and Ti Bon worked their way down to the pool.

Richy turned to his partner. "I think you ought to climb down there with them and make sure they get all the gold out."

"How do you suppose I accomplish that little feat? I'm not exactly the athletic type, you must know by now."

"Christ, Sir John, sometimes I think you're as worthless as a Haitian."

"Let's not bicker amongst ourselves, my good man. We can't, in any event, take more than a trunk's worth of gold. We can both remain here in the shade whilst our two acquaintances top it off for us."

"Yeah, I guess that's the best we can do under the circumstances. Keep your rifle aimed at the Haitian's mangy head. I won't stand for anymore funny business."

****

Tim stared into the pool. Its bottom appeared murkier than before. He wondered how it became that way, but with Madeleine in danger and likely to hate his guts for all eternity, he refocused his attention to the matter at hand.

"Let's get a move on, chaps," Sir John hollered from above. "We don't have all day."

He dove into the pool and rapidly descended to the bottom. Once there, silt swooshed up and clogged his eyes. He groped about to locate the artifacts solely by touch. He clutched several items and then surfaced every couple minutes to hand them to Ti Bon, who tossed the gold objects into the trunk as if they were nothing more than worthless rocks.

The trunk remained only half full an hour later. Worn out and gasping for air at each surface interval, he continued to dive to the bottom to search for more artifacts, hoping Madeleine might be released once Sir John and the others realized they possessed more wealth than they could have imagined in their wildest dreams. He blindly groped about and squeezed a large, scaly object.

It moved.

He bolted to the surface and pulled himself onto a flat rock at the edge of the pool. "I think we have it all now." He said it loud enough for Richy and Sir John to hear.

A bullet ricocheted off the far wall and echoed for several more volleys. "I don't think so," Richy said. "Get your ass back down there or your Haitian buddy is going to be sportin' a nice hole in his head."

He exhaled, took in a deep breath, dove into the pool. He prayed he'd simply disturbed a big fish.

Chapter 49

Damn Good Minister

Over an hour passed since Richy and Sir John led Tim and Ti Bon away at gunpoint. Madeleine, not one to accept being bullied lightly, hatched a plan to escape. "Marcel, I'm dying of thirst. Could you please get me some water?"

"Water? I have no water."

"There's clear water dripping off the wall into a pool only twenty feet away. Please, Marcel, I'm very thirsty."

"I have no cup for the water."

"You can use one of those clay vessels over there on the rock ledge. Rinse it out in the pool."

"Why not get the lady some water?" Vinny asked. "We're not going anywhere."

Marcel got up and trudged over to the terra cotta vessels, grabbed the smallest one, and carried it to the pool. Apparently too dark in that corner of the chamber to see, he came back in a huff, snatched one of the lanterns, and returned to the pool.

"What are you up to?" Vinny asked under his breath.

"Just a hunch. Be quiet and let's see."

Seconds later, Marcel's "ugh" reverberated off the chamber's walls with the accompaniment of screeching bats. The Haitian loped back with the lantern in hand, but no water.

"Where's my water?" she asked.

"You get no water."

"But my throat is totally parched. Please, can't I have some water?"

"I said, you get no water."

She noted Marcel's trembling demeanor and his gaze shifting about the cave. Beads of sweat emerged upon his forehead. "How did they convince you to enter this cave, Marcel?" She felt confident the skull at the pool's edge spooked him. "You do know it's inhabited by spirits, don't you?"

"The spirits have all been chased out. Otherwise, you wouldn't have been able to enter yourselves."

She nudged Vinny, hoping he caught onto her scheme. After her second, harder poke, he did. "The only reason we could enter this cave is because we had our souls cleansed at Saut d'Eau," he said.

Marcel's eyes widened and showed more white than brown.

"*Damballah* must be very angry," she said.

"Silence," Marcel said. Above, the bats unleashed a resonating chorus of screeches.

Madeleine sat still several minutes. She then began to shake and convulse. Marcel's eyes appeared ready to burst.

"What's the matter with her?" Vinny asked.

"Nothing. She's fine."

"She's not fine. What's happening to her?"

"She's fine, I said. Be silent…the both of you."

Madeleine began chanting in *Créole*, her voice eerily growing louder and deeper, almost masculine. Marcel sprang to his feet and bolted down the blackened corridor leading to Ti Bon's farm. Seconds later, a loud thud echoed back to the chamber.

"What do you think happened, Madeleine?"

"It sounded like he hit his head, probably on one of those dips in the cave's ceiling. Hopefully, he's unconscious."

"What do we do now?"

She glanced about the chamber. "We need to cut ourselves loose. Let's squirm our way to where I dropped the machete."

Tied back-to-back, they leaned hard against each other and rose to their feet. They spidered their way into the corridor and kicked around in search of the machete.

"It has to be around here somewhere," she moaned.

"Let's go back into the chamber," Vinny said. "Maybe we can find something there to cut us free." He kicked something that clanged. "Wait a minute, I think I found it."

After feeling with his foot that he had indeed bumped the machete, they straddled the long blade and bent down until able to pick it up with their joined hands. They shuffled back into the lit chamber.

Vinny held onto the handle of the machete with the blade pressed against the twine binding her hands together. She moved her hands up and down until the twine snapped, took the machete from Vinny, and cut the rest of the twine wrapped around herself before cutting him free.

"What should we do now?" she asked.

"Are there any police or soldiers in Anse-à-Galets you can trust?"

"I think I know a couple."

"Good. Let's get the hell out of here and see about getting some help."

"We can't just leave Tim and Ti Bon behind."

"What do you suggest? Richy and Sir John have guns. All we have is a machete."

"You're right." She slowly nodded. "Let's get some help."

Vinny grabbed a lantern and hurried to the corridor, Madeleine a few steps behind. Richy's "son-of-a-bitch" rang out across the chamber before they reached the entrance. Unnerved, she stumbled on the same rock that tripped Vinny earlier and fell to the floor.

"Keep running," she shouted to Vinny. She struggled to her knees.

Vinny had always been quicker with his mouth than his feet, but not this time. Ignoring her plea, he thrust himself between her and Richy to form a human shield, and released an echoing, "No."

Richy pulled the trigger. Vinny slumped to the cold floor. Even the bats became too shocked to utter a sound.

With the gun blast still resonating through the chamber, she dragged herself next to Vinny, propped his head onto her lap, and cradled him in her arms.

Tim and Ti Bon dropped the trunk of gold and raced over to their fallen companion.

"Reverend, are you hurt?" Tim asked. He dropped to his knees beside Madeleine.

Ti Bon, tears streaking down his face, repeatedly mumbled, "*Père* Burkholder," as if it were a refrain to a sad song.

Vinny closed his eyes. His breathing grew faint. Madeleine ran her fingers through his thinning hair. Her lips moved in silent prayer and a teardrop slid down her cheek.

"Please don't die, Reverend Burkholder," Tim said. "Please don't die."

Vinny managed to open his eyes and force a smile. Gazing at Tim, he gasped his final words, "Reverend. Yeah, I would've made a damn good minister."

Chapter 50

Prisoners

The startled bats repositioned themselves among the stalactites once the echoing gun blast faded into oblivion. The sole sounds in the chamber emanated from the trickling of water and the sobs of Madeleine and Tim. Ti Bon knelt silently at their sides.

Richy stood over them, his revolver pointed at Vinny, as if expecting him to return from the dead. "You must be some special lady. First, you elude Delmar, then you do who knows what to Marcel, and now Vinny Berkowitz takes a bullet for you. Who'd ever think that worthless shyster would—"

"There was nothing worthless about him," Madeleine said.

"He gave his life for you, Madeleine," Tim said.

"He gave his life for us."

"Isn't this the sweetest thing I've ever heard?" Richy said. "Vinny, the hero. Now, get to your feet."

"Should I look for Marcel, boss?" Sir John asked.

"To hell with Marcel. We have two strong men to carry this trunk out and a drop-dead, beautiful lady that's going to drop dead the second either of them gets out of line."

Richy took off his jacket, draped it around Madeleine's shoulders, and buttoned it over her partially-exposed breasts. "I don't know what kind of spells you've been casting on these men, sweetheart, but it's not going to work on me."

Sir John opened the lid to the trunk and marveled at the assortment of gold artifacts inside. "Should we add the gold in the toolbox to this?"

Richy protruded his lower lip. "Sure. It's not like we have to carry it."

They abandoned Vinny's body in the lantern-lit chamber and headed down the corridor to the waiting vehicle. Richy forced Madeleine in front of him, holding her shoulder with one hand and a flashlight in his other. Tim and Ti Bon, straining to maintain the pace, carried the gold-laden trunk. Sir John followed close behind and simultaneously pointed his rifle and flashlight at the two of them.

They came upon Marcel after a couple hundred yards. Richy made a quick inspection, noted his lack of pulse, and kicked the Haitian's body to the side. He shined his light in Madeleine's face. "I don't suppose you have an explanation for this?"

"I guess he hit his head."

"Yeah, he hit his head. He hit his head real good. That's one less monkey on the payroll."

****

The sun shone directly overhead in the cloudless sky when they exited the cave. After loading the trunk of gold behind the back seat, Richy ordered Sir John to take Ti Bon back to the chamber. Madeleine rattled a few words in *Créole* as the Haitian passed.

"Hey, what did you say to him?" Richy asked.

"I asked him to say a prayer for Vinny's soul."

Forced back into the cave, Ti Bon knew he had little time to devise a plan. Madeleine's message had been clear. *Escape or he'll kill you.*

When he saw the dim light from the burning lantern left inside the chamber, Ti Bon slowed his pace, knowing the *blanc* would feel obliged to jab him in the back with the barrel of his big gun. The moment the cold steel made contact, Ti Bon yanked at the rifle and spun himself around. Sir John pulled the trigger an instant too late. Ti Bon kicked him in the groin, buckling him over, and darted down the corridor toward the lit chamber, stopping a few paces beyond Vinny's body to locate a place to hide. Finding none and hearing Sir

John in heavy-breathing pursuit, he raced down the corridor leading to the pool. He crouched along the streamside as best he could, not wanting to meet the same fate as Marcel.

A rifle blast thundered from behind. The bullet ricocheted inches above Ti Bon's head. He increased his pace with the encouragement of two additional blasts and called upon all his strength and energy when the spot of light signifying the end of the cave came into view. Once at the edge, he grabbed the rope, slid rip-handedly down to the bottom of the gorge, and concealed himself behind a big boulder.

A moment later, he spotted a rifle barrel protruding from the opening of the cave. It swung back and forth, aimed across the length of the gorge. After several long minutes, the barrel retreated out of view and the rope dangling from the mouth of the cave rose like a braided snake slithering away.

Ti Bon's initial relief at having escaped the *blanc* instantly turned to panic. He now found himself imprisoned in an open-air dungeon.

Chapter 51

Special

Richy drummed his fingers on the steering wheel. Madeleine and Tim awkwardly sat in the back with their hands bound tightly behind them. Nearly an hour elapsed before Sir John emerged from the cave.

"Did you take care of him?" Richy snapped.

Sir John hopped into the front passenger seat. "He won't be bothering us again."

Madeleine lowered her head and sobbed.

"You're both blood-sucking assholes," Tim said. "You have your gold. What possible harm could Ti Bon have done to you?"

"Nothing personal," Sir John said. "It's simply not good business to leave loose ends."

"I suppose the same goes for us," Tim said. "Just two more loose ends?"

"Not to worry, old chap. After we get this gold off the island, we'll be so grateful we're likely to just let the two of you go. Isn't that so, Richy?"

"The rich can be merciful," Richy said. His ugly grin said otherwise.

They drove past Ti Bon's hut and onto the rocky washboard road leading over the mountains. About one hundred yards up the steep climb they came upon a rusty pickup partially hidden in a thicket stand. Richy slowed down. "Shit, we'll leave that damn thing here," he said. "We have plenty of fuel in this baby."

Madeleine and Tim leaned against each other to maintain balance as they bounced over the rutted road. "I know you must think I'm the scum of the earth," Tim said to Madeleine, "but you have to believe me. I wanted nothing more than to tell you the truth almost from day one."

"I know, Tim. Reverend Burkholder, or whoever the heck he was, told me everything. You couldn't have known things would turn out like this."

"I should have told you the truth."

"The truth is you love me and for now that's all that matters."

Tim's guilt for his lies transformed into guilt for the grave peril in which Madeleine had become immersed because of him. He seemed to be failing her exactly as he failed Sarah. He resolved, no matter what, to find a way to protect Madeleine from these bastards.

They arrived at Pointe-à-Raquettes after a prolonged, bone-jarring, dust-filled journey. An imposing yacht silhouetted in the setting sun anchored a short distance offshore. They pulled up to the shoreline where a beached fishing boat waited, along with two partially-clad boys standing at guard. Richy handed the boys a few *gourde*s, after which they lit off. Neither boy glanced in Tim and Madeleine's direction.

"Okay, you two, get out," Richy said.

"Can't you at least untie our hands?" Madeleine asked.

"Sure, but no funny business. You saw what happened to Vinny. We don't want anyone else hurt, now do we?"

The second his hands were untied, Tim said, "I'm not lifting a finger to move the gold until you set Madeleine free."

"I'm not leaving without you," Madeleine said.

"Yes, you are."

"Wait a minute," Richy said, crinkling his face in disbelief. "No one's going anywhere. You two are not in a position to be making any demands."

"Fine, then shoot us both," Tim said.

Richy calmly pulled out his revolver and pressed the barrel against Madeleine's temple. "You sure this is what you want, sonny boy?"

"I'm sure," Tim said. "I prefer Madeleine go first."

"Okay, then—"

"Wait, boss," Sir John said. "You and I can't carry the gold alone, not with my bad back. Why not let the young damsel go? We're almost home free. What can she possibly do to us at this point?"

Richy paused a moment and then turned to Tim. "We'll set your lady free as soon as we load the gold onto the boat."

"No dice," Tim said. "Let her go now. We'll load the gold as soon as she's out of sight. Otherwise, shoot us both."

Richy pressed the revolver harder against Madeleine's temple. "You're mighty brave with someone else's life."

"You've already killed my two best friends. I'm no fool. I know what you have in store for Madeleine and me. Let her go and I'll totally cooperate. I don't care what you do to me so long as I know she's safe."

"No," Madeleine said. "Let them kill us both."

"You heard the lady," Richy said to Tim.

"I'm not listening to the lady."

Richy released his hold on Madeleine. "Okay, you've got a deal."

Tim glanced at Madeleine and then at Richy. "Can I?"

Richy nodded his head.

Tim reached out to Madeleine and blocked her tears with his index fingers. He gazed into her eyes and cupped her cheeks with his hands. "Madeleine, I'm so sorry I got you into this mess. You didn't deserve any of it. I don't deserve—"

She placed her right hand over his mouth and stopped his words midstream. "I love you, Tim. I always will."

"I'll always love you, Madeleine." He reached into his front trouser pocket and pulled out Madeleine's leather charm he found on the floor at the clinic. He tied it around her neck and kissed her. Not wanting to pull away, but knowing he must, he released his embrace.

"Run."

She grasped the *ouanga* with her right hand and cried out, "I love you."

Tim retained his composure and repeated his order—this time more firmly. "Run!"

She closed her eyes and slowly turned around. After a brief pause, she ran without looking back.

"Damn, that must be one helluva special lady," Richy said.

"She's as special as they come." He watched Madeleine disappear, little-by-little, into a darkness creeping upon them.

Chapter 52

Mercy of the *Loa*

Ti Bon paced about the bottom of the chasm like a caged panther searching for any means to escape. Over one hundred feet above his head, the cave entrance looked like nothing more than a blotch of ink on an otherwise vertical, gray wall. The rocky slopes surrounding the other sides seemed less steep, but no less formidable. He resigned himself to doom. Only the *loa* could save him now.

He wandered to the pool and became entranced by his reflection in the still water. Memories of when he first spotted Marie Joseph, the prettiest girl in the village, spun through his mind. It had taken him several weeks to muster the courage the first time he spoke to her. When he did, he found himself at loss for words and spitted out some ridiculous comment about the weather. *What is there to say about the weather? It's hot.* He managed to expand upon the topics of their short interchanges over the course of several months and, after overcoming his fear of rejection, asked if she might join him for a soda at the single store in Anse-à-Galets. Cocking her head to the side, she released the most delicate "yes" he ever heard. In like manner, she repeated that response exactly six months to the day when he asked if she would become his bride. Eight years and five children later, Marie Joseph remained the prettiest girl in the village.

His thoughts returned to the present as he clenched his eyes shut and prayed aloud. "*Damballah*, please protect my family and save my two friends. Do unto me as you wish."

Opening his eyes, he found his reflection in the pool distorted by a mass of ripples. Feeling the presence of the *loa,* he stepped into the crystalline water, waist-deep at the edge. He closed his eyes and offered himself as a sacrifice. "*Damballah*, it is I, Ti Bon Baptiste, your faithful servant. Take me and spare my family and friends."

A lone cloud cloaked the sun. Shivering in the cool water, he accepted his fate, fully prepared to be taken into the other world. Several minutes passed. The intense sun returned, radiating and rejuvenating warmth into his core. He opened his eyes to the water, now still. The *loa* had been merciful.

He climbed out of the pool and marched to the boulder where he had hid from Sir John. He wondered how he missed seeing them. *Perhaps the loa blinded me and now have given me back my sight.* Partially obscured by loose rocks, rested the tools Tim had previously emptied from the toolbox. He picked up the hammer and admired it as if a work of fine art. He treated the screwdrivers and wrenches in a similar fashion. Caressing a large chisel, the last implement discovered, he held it to his lips and offered praise and thanks to the *loa*.

Chapter 53

Santa Maria

Madeleine sat cross-legged on the sandy beach, resolved to retain her composure in the face of the dire plight in which she found herself. She ran away only because she thought Tim might have a better chance to escape without being burdened by her. It didn't make abandoning him any the easier. Despite being miles from home and anyone she knew, she concentrated on finding a way to save Tim from the greedy madmen who ripped him away at gunpoint.

She heard the rumbling of the outboard motor over the pounding of the surf and stood on her toes to get a glimpse of the fishing boat heading out to the yacht. She dropped to her knees once the skiff reached its destination, fearful Richy and Sir John would do away with Tim once the gold was unloaded. A single tear fell from her left eye as her gallant effort to remain in control momentarily surrendered to emotions.

Minutes later, she spotted lights and movement aboard the luxury boat. *No gun blast so far.* She released an extended sigh. A long hour of silence passed. She concentrated upon spotting further activity. The puttering of a beamless motorcycle approaching from behind went unnoticed until almost upon her. Startled, she jumped to her feet. About to run for cover, she froze when she recognized the driver.

Ti Bon drove past without slowing down, the cycle picking up speed as it headed down the beach. He jumped off the instant before it cruised into the surf. The powdery sand cushioned his fall. He rose to his feet and stared at the submerged motorcycle, its engine dead in the water. He turned to greet Madeleine, who instantly engulfed him in a tackling embrace.

"Ti Bon, I thought you were dead. How did you escape?"

He spat out an abridged version of how he overcame the funny-sounding *blanc,* escaped to the bottom of the gorge, and how the *loa* provided him with a hammer and chisel to punch holes into the soft, limestone cliff. He pounded his way, step-by-step, up to the mouth of the cave.

"How did you know how to drive the motorcycle?"

"No problem," he said. "I learned by watching you, but I forgot how to come to a stop. Now, the motorcycle is drowned. Where is Mister Jamison?"

She pointed to the yacht. "He's out there."

"These are very bad men. We must save him. But how?"

She fixed her eyes upon the yacht and grimaced. "Maybe we can borrow a canoe from a local fisherman. We could paddle out there."

Ti Bon agreed and suggested she wait on the beach while he ran to the nearby fishing village. Once he disappeared into the darkness, she returned to her vigil, her concern growing with the passing of each pulsating minute. Nearly thirty minutes elapsed before she spotted Ti Bon paddling up to the shoreline in a dugout canoe. She ran to the water's edge and squeezed herself in front of him inside the tiny craft. With their combined weight depressing the canoe to an inch or two of freeboard, they paddled across the breaking waves, hardly taking on a drop of water.

They pulled alongside the fishing boat a few minutes later and tethered the canoe to it. She held onto the gunwale as Ti Bon slipped aboard.

"*Soeur* Madeleine, please wait here while I search the big boat for Mister Jamison."

"I think—"

Her thoughts of dissent turned to concurrence upon seeing the resolve in the Haitian's eyes. For now, Tim's best chance at escape rested with Ti Bon, not her. "Be careful, Ti Bon. They have guns."

She hopped into the boat to conceal herself. She noted the nameplate on the yacht—*Santa Maria*.

****

Ti Bon climbed aboard the yacht, crept along the aft, and froze in place when voices arguing in a language he once heard from natives of neighboring *Republique Dominicaine* broke the silence. He spotted someone climbing up the steps from the belly of the boat and retreated to where Madeleine waited for any word of Tim, her face pale with apprehension. Before he could speak, the yacht's engine suddenly rumbled to life and, with the fishing boat and dugout canoe in tow, the *Santa Maria* set out to sea.

Chapter 54

Loose Ends

Tim lay face down on the bunk of the cramped forward cabin with his hands tied behind his back. He overheard the fate awaiting him. Either Richy and Sir John didn't know he could hear their conversation in the adjoining cabin or, more likely, they didn't give a damn.

"I know we're not supposed to kill this chap," Sir John said, "but what possible purpose does he now serve?"

"Why don't you quit whining?" Richy said. "I didn't get to where I am by leaving loose ends. I made an exception for the pretty dame, but that's it."

"What do you suggest?"

"First of all, do you really think I'm going to let this mega-asshole call the shots much longer? We just need to bide our time a bit longer. When the time's right, we'll rid ourselves of the entire lot, one by one. That has been my plan since day one."

"Who do we eliminate first?"

"Does it really matter? They're all goners in my book, but we do need someone to navigate the yacht back to the beach club's marina. That leaves either the captain or our *sweet-baby Mister James.*"

Both men snickered.

Willing himself not to be incapacitated by panic, Tim fully fathomed he had to get to the captain or, better yet, the *mega-asshole* in charge, the person Richy and Sir John conspired to betray.

Sir John's sickening chortle came to a halt. "I need to get my rifle before we cut the fishing boat loose. I left it in the front compartment."

"You wait here," Richy said. "I need to catch a smoke anyway. I'll get your rifle."

****

Ti Bon and Madeleine remained crouched on the floor of the fishing boat, spying on Richy as he stood on the stern of the yacht taking deep drags at a cigarette. They sighed with relief when he finally tossed his butt overboard, but to their shock, instead of returning to the mid-hatch the bulbous-nosed *blanc* approached the ladder leading down to where they hid.

Ti Bon gestured for Madeleine to get inside the canoe and lay low. He slipped over the opposite side of the skiff and held onto the gunwale, retaining his precarious hold as he dangled in the passing water.

Richy climbed down the ladder, hopped into the fishing boat, and fumbled around in the forward compartment. He picked up a rifle, placed its strap over his shoulder, and climbed back aboard the yacht. Richy glanced over his shoulder and then swiveled around. "What the fuck?"

He jumped back down into the skiff, grabbed the spotlight attached to the gunwale, and shined it directly at the canoe dragging behind. "What do we have here?"

Madeleine poked her head up.

"So, we meet again, sweetheart." Richy began to untie the tether.

"Please, let Tim go," Madeleine said. "Please."

"Sorry lady. No more loose ends." He stopped untying the line, pulled the rifle off his shoulder, and took aim.

Ti Bon thrust all his weight on the side of the skiff. Richy lost his balance and sailed headfirst into the choppy water. He also lost his grip on the rifle, but managed to grab the canoe's partially untied tether, which instantly came unfastened from the skiff.

Ti Bon's eyes widened in helpless horror as the canoe and Madeleine slipped away. Richy groped at the line still attached to the canoe and attempted to pull himself aboard. Water poured in and Ti Bon thought the canoe might topple. Madeleine grabbed one of the paddles and held it above her head.

"Please," Richy said, almost appearing to be worth pitying.

Madeleine paused only momentarily. "Sorry buster, no more loose ends." She whacked him over the head with all her strength and he disappeared into the dark water. She closed her eyes and grimaced.

Ti Bon prayed to *Agoué Royo* to watch over Madeleine, there being nothing else he could do for her now. On the other hand, he could still help his blond friend. He climbed aboard the *Santa Maria*, tiptoed to the hold, and peeked below. He couldn't hear voices over the rumbling of the yacht's engine.

****

Waiting for Richy to return, Sir John's edginess grew with each step he paced within the cramped cabin. His patience now exhausted, he grabbed the revolver, burst into the adjoining cabin, and motioned for his bound captive to move to the deck.

Confused when he discovered no sign of Richy on the top deck, he forced Tim aft and peered over at the fishing boat. He saw no sign of his boss there either. Deciding to take matters into his own hands, he pushed Tim to the starboard gunwale and jabbed the revolver into his spine. "It's high time to get on with this, old chap."

Before Sir John could pull the trigger, Ti Bon leapt out from the shadows and jumped on top of him, sandwiching him to the deck. The gun fired after a brief struggle. Both men lay motionless for an extended moment and then Sir John rolled Ti Bon off to the side.

Tim, nearly helpless with his hands bound, spotted blood spewing from Ti Bon's temple. Sir John struggled to get up. Tim kicked the revolver out of his hand and booted him in the midriff. Sir John rolled in the direction of the gun. He grabbed the revolver on his second rotation and clumsily rose to his feet. He pointed the gun at Tim. "It's all over now, chum."

A gun blast followed his prophetic words. Sir John slumped onto the deck in a puddle of blood.

Tim instantly recognized the bearer of the firearm. *How can this be? Am I hallucinating?* A blunt blow to his head from behind left questions and answers for a later time.

Chapter 55

Hispanic

Tim regained consciousness in the same cabin that held him captive earlier. Ti Bon, a bandage wrapped around his head, lay motionless on the opposite berth. On a chair between the two bunks sat a stranger, a male Hispanic about forty years of age. He spoke with impeccable English. "Welcome to the *Santa Maria*. I am Jorgé Ortíz. I would normally be your host. However, tonight I find myself a prisoner very much as yourself."

"What happened?"

"You were hit over the head."

"Was I unconscious?"

"Yes. You've been out for a couple hours."

"I guess that explains my throbbing head. Ti Bon, how is my friend, Ti Bon?"

"Your friend was shot. Lucky for him the bullet only grazed his head. He's unconscious, but he should be fine, at least for now."

He noticed Jorgé's hands, like his and Ti Bon's, were bound behind his back. Jorgé looked familiar. "Have we met before?"

"Yes, we've met. I am ashamed to relate the circumstances, though."

"Ashamed? I don't understand."

"I dove with you the night you thought Sarah drowned."

"What? The night I *thought* Sarah drowned? What are you fuckin' talking about?" Memories of seeing Sarah on the deck of the *Santa Maria* flashed before him. He struggled to clear his head, barely able to utter a sound. "Sarah's alive?"

"Sarah is very much alive."

"Holy shit. Sarah? Alive? How can that be? What kind of sick joke is this? Sarah would never do anything like this to me. You're lying. You're fuckin' lying."

"It's not a lie, but it is a very sick joke. First, it was played on you. Now, the joke's on me."

Tim's head spun, his pulse raced, and his hyperventilation maintained the pace. He shut his eyes to stop the spinning and kept them closed until he could control his breathing. His pulse continued pounding uncontrollably. Forcing his eyes open, he said, "Tell me. Explain to me. What in hell is this all about?"

"Let me explain from the beginning."

"Yeah, please, from the damn beginning."

"As I said, my name is Jorgé Ortíz. I'm from Venezuela. I come from a very wealthy family, a long line of aristocrats—"

"What the fuck does that have to do with anything?"

"It has much to do with it, if you will allow me to continue."

"Go on." He shook his head to clear his thoughts.

"I am a collector. I collect fine art, antiquities, properties, anything of enormous value. I also collect beautiful women."

"What do you mean you collect beautiful women?"

"I collect beautiful women, like Sarah."

"Give me a break. Are you saying you collected my Sarah?"

"In a sense, yes, but truth be known, Sarah collected me. Do you want me to continue?"

"Yeah, go on."

"I met Sarah, your Sarah, at the beach club. She was the activities director for Hispanic guests."

"Yeah, I know that. Get to the fuckin' point, will ya."

"The point, yes, the point. The point, Mister James, is I was totally captivated by your wife. Yes, captivated. That word takes on new meaning for me, considering my present circumstances. I knew I must have this woman the instant I laid eyes on her. Her beauty is beyond comparison. When she spoke her first words to me, in perfect Castilian Spanish, I was stunned."

"I thought you were going to get to the point."

"Yes, I am. Sorry. Excuse me for digressing. It's a Hispanic trait, you must know."

He nodded his head.

"I was determined to win over your wife. She was to be another trophy. You were always occupied with your diving, leaving us much time to be together. It's funny. I actually thought she was in love with me."

"Yeah, that is funny. It seems like I had the same idea."

"I know now your wife only loved what I could provide for her. She never loved me."

He shook his head. "Why in the fuck the fake drowning?"

"That was Sarah's idea. I preferred she simply divorce you. She convinced me this way would be less cruel."

"Less cruel? How can anything be crueler than what she did? What you did?"

Jorgé looked away. "I'm not proud of what I did. Sarah has a way with me. I give her…do for her, whatever she desires."

"She desired for me to think she was dead?"

"Yes. That is what she desired."

"Who else knew about this?"

"It was planned with your assistant, Marcos. I paid him a handsome fee."

"I'm sure you did. That son-of-a-bitch sure played his part well. Anyone else?"

"Sir John Winston was also involved in the deception. It's my opinion he was also enthralled with Sarah."

"Yeah, she's quite enthralling. Sir John, that asshole, knew Sarah wasn't dead all along. Do you have any idea what kind of misery I went through these past two years?"

"Until this evening, I never gave it a second thought."

"Damn you both."

"I am damned. That's for certain."

Despite the shocking revelation, lucid thoughts fired through his mind. "I have two more questions for you."

"Yes?"

"Why are you a prisoner?"

"I'm a prisoner because your Sarah, our Sarah, no longer has need of me. She plans to keep the gold for herself. She has grown tired of me, as she did of you. Your second question?"

"Why did she save my life?"

"That's a question you must ask her."

The cabin door swung open. Sarah stood at the threshold. She stared at him and then at Jorgé. "It looks like you two became acquainted."

Neither man responded.

"You look good, Tim," she said.

"You're not looking bad, either…for a dead babe."

"Would you prefer I told you I didn't love you anymore? That I found someone else who was more exciting? Someone who could give me everything you couldn't?"

The shock of seeing Sarah alive became dwarfed by the shock of what she became. She trashed his life and now insinuated she did him some sort of favor. "I hope you're not offended if I'm slow to show my gratitude."

"You haven't changed, Tim. You're still judgmental."

Too dumbfounded to respond, he lowered his head and stared at the floor. He'd been certain she drowned. He and his fellow dive masters had search the area where she went missing for weeks, but never found a trace of her. Night after night he'd suffered the same nightmare—Sarah consumed by some deep-sea creature. *Shit…she's the fuckin' creature. Motherfuck…she's the mega-asshole.*

"Look, this rendezvous wasn't something I planned," she said. "I never wanted you to know I was alive."

"Then why did you save me from Sir John's bullet?"

"I felt I owed you at least that much."

"I guess we're even, aren't we?"

"Look, Tim, the captain said a squall is coming in. We're heading back to La Gonave, to the protective harbor at Anse-à-Galets. I'll let you and your Haitian servant—"

"Friend."

"Okay, I'll let you and your Haitian friend off there. You can go your merry way and I'll go mine."

"What about your other ex-lover?" He motioned with his eyes toward Jorgé.

"He's no concern of yours." She glared at Jorgé before storming off, slamming the door behind her.

"Sounds like Sarah has plans for you, Jorgé."

"I suspect those plans will have a certain, should I say, finality to them."

"Sarah may be a ruthless bitch, but she's surely not capable of cold-blooded murder."

"Sarah's capable of anything, as am I. If she lets me live, she knows I'll track her down like a wild animal. She won't let that happen."

He reflected upon the Hispanic's words, wondering what kind of she-devil witch Sarah had become. *How could I have not seen any sign of it? How much of our marriage was nothing more than a sham?* His thoughts turned to Madeleine. *She is nothing at all like Sarah. Her beauty, unlike Sarah's, extends into her very soul.*

"What about the captain?" he asked. "He must be in your employ. Surely he'll protect you."

Jorgé shook his head. "The captain answers to Sarah, not me. Sarah convinced me to fire my regular captain prior to this voyage. She told me he made lewd advances at her. I'm sorry to say, I believed her."

"Who's the captain?"

"He's a Haitian Sarah somehow knew. He has apparently plied these waters all his life. It made perfect sense to hire him. As I indicated, I obliged Sarah on her every whim."

"We have to figure out a way to get you out of here."

"I don't understand. After what I did to you, why would you risk yourself for me?"

"Let me put it this way, Jorgé. In my book, anyone Sarah has tired of can't be all bad."

Chapter 56

Squall

Madeleine's arms ached from hours of paddling the tiny canoe toward the scattered bonfires flickering in the La Gonave hillsides. The *Santa Maria* had long passed from her sight. Resolved to reach the shore and get help to rescue Tim and Ti Bon, she remained oblivious to the immediate threats, even the murky swells mounting all around. She struggled to maintain the tiny craft upright as the wind abruptly changed direction, blowing her further out to sea. After fighting the insurmountable forces of wind and water into a state of exhaustive delirium, she plopped the paddle into the belly of the canoe and collapsed.

She regained consciousness when countless raindrops stabbed her exposed flesh, finding herself engulfed in a raging, compassionless tempest. She and the canoe proved no match for the chaotic, towering waves. The canoe toppled and both paddles floated out of her reach. The salty water burned her eyes, throat, and lungs. As she struggled to stay afloat, her thoughts remained unchanged. *I love you, Tim.*

****

The *Santa Maria* failed to outrun the squall and veered off course, striking a reef while rounding the northwest point of La Gonave. The engine instantly died and, a moment later, so did its electrical generator. The trapped men could hear Sarah's screaming voice over the roar of crashing waves, whirling winds, and bursts of thunder. The *Santa Maria* rumbled across more hard coral and began listing to starboard.

"We're sinking," Tim exclaimed.

"Yes, we're sinking," Jorgé said.

Ti Bon's wide eyes made it unanimous.

The door to the cabin swung open. Sarah stood at the entryway. She held onto the threshold to keep from falling inside. "We're taking the fishing boat ashore. It can only hold the weight of one more. Tim?"

He had no doubt as to Sarah's priorities and surmised the gold had already been loaded onto the skiff. "I'm not leaving anybody to drown in this fish trap."

"This is no time to be self-righteous, Tim. I'm giving you a chance to save your ass."

"There are three asses here that need saving."

"Well, that's three asses that are going to have to fend for themselves. *Adios, pendejos*." She abandoned the three men, their hands still bound behind their backs.

The open porthole bobbed merely inches above water level and the frothy ocean surged inside the cabin with each wicked wave. He and Ti Bon scampered to the doorway as best they could. Tim turned around, expecting to see Jorgé a step or two behind. Instead, the Hispanic remained up against the far wall, still seated with the water rising to his neck. "Jorgé. Get the hell up. This boat's going to sink any second."

"I'd very much like to, but I am fastened to this chair, which is affixed to the wall."

"Holy shit. Maybe I can free you." He hurried back to Jorgé, Ti Bon close behind.

"It's no use," Jorgé said. "What can you do with your hands tied? Save yourself and your Haitian friend."

Before he could refuse Jorgé's offer, the *Santa Maria* lurched forward and down, fully submerging Jorgé. Tim took a deep breath and lowered himself underwater in hope of saving the drowning Hispanic, only to discover why the man resigned himself to his pitiful plight. He'd been handcuffed to the metal chair with Sarah undoubtedly holding the key. The aristocratic Venezuelan, who lived a life of taking whatever he so desired, had now been taken by the sea.

He and Ti Bon stumbled up the steps and through the hatch, plopping onto the deck an instant before the front cabins became fully submerged. They crawled to the stern of the yacht, now poking up in a balanced counter to the sunken bow. Having only seconds to react, they backed up to each other to untie themselves. Ti Bon, realizing the futility of their efforts, turned around and chewed the rope binding Tim's hands together. Once freed, he untied Ti Bon. They leapt into the churning water as the gurgling *Santa Maria* joined its original namesake in the unforgiving Haitian sea.

Tim struggled to keep Ti Bon afloat—the Haitian's buoyancy being that of a sack of rocks. When he thought he would have to let him go, lest they both drown, the fishing boat pulled up alongside and a life ring landed next to them. He grabbed the ring with one hand while holding Ti Bon with the other. To his shock, Ti Bon had lost consciousness again. He slipped the life ring over the Haitian's head and shoulders. He then pulled his friend's limp arms through. Still unconscious, Ti Bon floated with his head bobbing above the violent sea.

Lightning illuminated the sky for the briefest of moments. Even as the fishing boat sped away, the flash proved sufficient for Tim to recognize Sarah's accomplice. The captain of the *Santa Maria* could be none other than the Ebony Man.

Chapter 57

Boats

Simone, the best fisher in Pointe-à-Raquettes, invariably paddled out first each morning, particularly after a storm, to check his traps. If he happened across someone else's trap, purely by mistake, their catch would also be taken. After all, more fish could swim into those traps by the time their lazy owners chose to check them.

He spotted a log floating amongst the flotsam in the calm sea that morning. A stroke of good fortune. Since it floated, the wood must still be good and could be sold. If it proved to be a very fine piece of wood it could be used to make boards. Worse case, it could always be turned into charcoal. He hoped the log could be cut into boards since that would fetch him a higher profit.

He paddled closer and noticed something white draped over the log. After further inspection, it appeared to be the arm of a *blanc*. What he hoped to be a log turned out to be a canoe floating upside down.

He paddled alongside the toppled canoe, touched the arm, and jerked back when it moved. The head of a female *blanc* emerged over the half-sunken canoe. To his amazement, she spoke perfect *Créole*. "Please sir, help me to shore. I've been hanging onto this canoe through most of the night."

He pulled her into his canoe and righted the other one to float back with them. He would give it to his eldest son if it originated from some other village or collect a reward if it belonged to someone in his own. "Who are you?" he asked.

"My name is Madeleine, Madeleine McCoy."

"*Soeur* Madeleine?"

"Yes, *Soeur* Madeleine."

"Your father saved my son, Philippe, two years ago. *Père* Thomas was a great man. If your father had not passed away, he could have saved Philippe again. I lost him to an infection last month."

"I'm so sorry."

"I have four more sons. I am still blessed."

He paddled toward the village. As they approached the shore, Madeleine insisted upon being taken to the vehicle parked near the beach. It made no difference to Simone as long as he got to keep the canoe.

Once they reached the shore, Madeleine thanked the fisherman and promised to return another day to bring him a reward. He refused any such notion, but instead agreed to accept a gift.

****

Madeleine exhaled all the air in her lungs upon finding her key still in the Jeep's ignition. Exhausted, but not defeated, she resolved to return to Anse-à-Galets to inform Marie Joseph of the grave danger that had befallen Ti Bon and Tim. Next, she would plead to the Nazarenes to allow Cristophe to take her out in their boat to search for the *Santa Maria*. She prayed the squall had forced the yacht to seek a safe harbor within the confines of one of the numerous coves of La Gonave.

The rugged drive seemed to take longer than ever and provided ample time to agonize over Tim. *Is he still alive? He has to be.* She would not allow herself to think otherwise. She drove past her home and headed to Ti Bon's sister-in-law's hut. There, she found Marie Joseph cradling Ti Ti in the shade of the thatched-roof overhang.

Marie Joseph eyed Madeleine's filthy clothes and matted hair. "What is wrong, *Soeur* Madeleine?"

"Ti Bon's in danger. He's possibly been taken prisoner by hoodlums."

"Were these hoodlums riding blue motorcycles?" Marie Joseph asked, her voice crackling.

"No. Those men are no longer a danger to anyone. White men are the danger now."

"What do they want with Ti Bon?"

"They made Tim a prisoner. Ti Bon went after them to save him."

"Tim? Who is Tim?"

"Tom. I meant to say, Tom—Tom Jamison."

"Tom. Yes, your blond-haired companion. What of the minister?"

A pool of tears welled in her eyes. "They killed the minister."

Marie Joseph's eyes widened. "What should we do?"

"I'll go to the Church of the Nazarene. They have a boat. I'm sure they'll help us search for Ti Bon and Tim, I mean Tom. Can you send word to *La Reine* Memmene? Maybe she can help."

"Yes, *La Reine* Memmene will know what to do. I will go to her at once." Marie Joseph embraced Ti Ti in her arms and departed without further word.

Madeleine rushed to the Church of the Nazarene. The usually bustling compound appeared deserted. She sprinted in and around buildings and finally located an old woman sweeping some outside steps. "Where is everyone?"

"They have gone to a big meeting in Port-au-Prince."

"Did they take their boat?" She sunk with despair upon hearing the old woman's affirmative reply.

Her last hope rested with Mildred Sponheimer. She raced to the mission and screeched to a halt at the outside gate. She ran to the administration building, scurried past Rachelle, and barged into the director's office.

The startled mission director looked up over her bifocals. "Madeleine, I've been so worried about you. Mister Jamison and the minister thought you might have been kidnapped. My God, look at you. Have you been defiled? Did that handyman—"

"No Mildred, I haven't been defiled. There's been much trouble, though. The minister's dead. Murdered. Mister Jamison's been kidnapped. Ti Bon Baptiste may have been, too."

"The minister is dead? Murdered?"

"I'm afraid so."

"I don't understand. Who would do such a thing? And Mister Jamison and Mister Baptiste kidnapped? What sort of criminal activity has been going on around here? The authorities must be informed at once."

"There's no time to inform the authorities. What can they do? I'm begging you to let me use your powerboat to go after Tim, I mean Tom, and Ti Bon."

"Our powerboat? What on earth for?"

"They're on the yacht that was anchored at Pointe-à-Raquettes."

"How can you be sure?"

"I saw them there. It's too long a story to go into now. Is your boat available?"

"I'm afraid our boat is under repair. We're waiting for parts from the States."

Madeleine dropped her head into her hands and squeezed her eyes shut. All options to save Tim and Ti Bon vanished.

"Is there anything else I can do?" Mildred asked.

Too distraught to respond, she shook her head and wept.

Mildred put an arm around Madeleine's shoulder. "I know it's not a good time for me to be bringing this up, but you must realize now more than ever, Haiti is no place for you to be."

Chapter 58

Pool

Octave Polynice, his ebony skin glistening in the late afternoon sun, stood over the pool below the cave where for centuries the *Taíno* treasure had remained hidden. At his feet rested the latched trunk filled with gold artifacts. He summoned all his strength and lifted the trunk to the level of his massive chest.

"I return to the spirits that which belongs to the spirits. I ask only that I, Octave Polynice, be granted the power that is my birthright."

He released his hold on the trunk. When it hit the water, the swooshing sound eerily echoed off the cliffs and continued long after the trunk plunged into the pool's silent depths. Concentric rings of water rippled throughout the pool's previously glassy surface.

Helpless to prevent the *bocor's* offering to the spirits, Sarah stood a few paces behind in shocked silence. When he approached, she nudged up to him and pressed her breasts against one of his bulging biceps. She gazed up at the towering Haitian.

"Octave, together we could have it all."

His returned glare forced her to lower her eyes. "I have no desire for a woman such as you."

"The gold, we can share the gold."

"I have no interest in material wealth. You know where to find the gold. You are free to take as much of it as you wish."

With no further words, he climbed up the cliff using the steps Ti Bon had pounded out two days before.

****

Sarah remained alone in the gorge and stared into the pool's mirror-like surface. She spotted the trunk through the clear water. It had landed in an upright position no more than twenty-five feet below. Tim had taught her well. Certain she could dive to that depth while holding her breath, she hatched a plan to carry out as much of the gold as she could that day and return another time for the remainder.

She stripped off her clothes and stood on the same rock where Tim had previously made his entries into the pool. With a textbook dive hardly making a ripple, she descended to the trunk, unlatched it, and opened the lid. She peered inside, became transfixed by the sight of the glittering treasure, and failed to perceive the shadowy presence looming from behind.

The hungry crocodile's usual diet of small fish and unwary rodents quenching their thirsts along the bank would not suffice today.

****

Octave Polynice stood vigil at the opening of the cave where the stream cascaded to the pool, comforted by the realization he could now meet his mother, the *Vodou* queen, on his own terms. His powers would be equal to hers. The crimson bubbling in the pool below signified that *Damballah* had, indeed, accepted his gift. Once the spectacle reached its merciless conclusion, he unleashed a devilish grin. His gold-capped tooth glittered in the Haitian sun—as did the gold amulet adorning his broad neck.

Chapter 59

Vodou Queen

Marie Joseph feared too much for Ti Bon's safety to let the midday sun torching La Gonave slow her ascent to the mountaintop temple of *La Reine* Memmene. All hell had broken loose ever since these latest *blancs* arrived upon their peaceful island. The men who accosted her were Haitian, although she suspected they'd been fouled from living in the States. In addition, the minister, a *blanc* himself, was murdered. Surely, *Soeur* Madeleine would not allow herself to become mixed up with common criminals of any color.

She covered Ti Ti with a white cloth to protect him from the blazing sun. Snuggled next to his mother's bosom, the baby boy remained content, only whimpering every now and then. She reached the temple in a little over two hours, spotted one of the *mambo's* followers, a girl in her late teens, and demanded to be taken to *La Reine* Memmene.

The girl nodded and motioned toward the *houmfort*. "Come with me."

She found *La Reine* Memmene and three other women sitting at the base of the altar. The *mambo* raised her eyes to greet her.

"Welcome, Marie Joseph. I pray a fever has not struck your son again."

Marie Joseph paused a second to collect her thoughts. "Please forgive my intrusion, *La Reine* Memmene. Ti Ti remains in good health, thanks to your intervention with the *loa*. It is Ti Bon and his friend, the one you call the White King, who are now in danger. Much danger, I fear."

"Tell me of this danger, my dear one."

"I know very little." She lowered her head in a show of respect. "*Soeur* Madeleine came to me with information that Ti Bon and the blond-haired white man have been taken prisoner by evildoers. White men. These men killed the minister."

La Reine Memmene's eyes showed no change in emotion. "I have felt an evil presence on our island for some time now. I am much saddened to learn of the minister's death. *Soeur* Madeleine...she is safe?"

"Yes, *Soeur* Madeleine is safe. Please, you must save Ti Bon and the white man."

"I will do what I can, but please understand, it is within the spiritual world where my powers reside."

"The *loa* can save them. I know they can."

"You are aware, as well as I, my dear Marie Joseph, the *loa* often refuse to intervene when men do evil unto themselves."

Streaks of tears rolled down her cheeks. She nodded her head in agreement.

"I will send messengers to every village on the island," *La Reine* Memmene said. "Thousands of eyes will search the countryside and the shorelines. If Ti Bon and the holy white one are still alive and on the island they will be found. I must tell you, there is more danger, more evil, lurking amongst us."

She pulled her infant tighter to her chest. "What is this evil of which you speak?"

"I do not know. I have never felt such evil before. A stranger has been visiting my dreams these past few nights. He exudes evilness beyond any I have ever experienced, and yet, I also feel an urge to hold him. I have been very troubled by these dreams. Now you bring me word of the minister's death and possibly more tragedies."

Her confidence in *La Reine* Memmene's powers remained undaunted. "You are our *Vodou* queen. You will save Ti Bon and the white man. The *loa* will not fail you. The *loa* will not fail La Gonave."

****

293

Drums rumbled throughout the night amongst the hilltops of La Gonave. Two of its men remained missing. One man was black and the other white. *La Reine* Memmene's *Vodou* temple served as a central point of communication. Runners constantly arrived and departed with whatever scraps of information had been gleaned from near and far. All news proved worthless, with the possible exception of a shipwreck off the northwest point of the island. Fragments of the ship had been found strewn about the shoreline. Upon hearing this, *La Reine* Memmene sent a party of six men to further investigate. Meanwhile, she continued to beseech the *loa* to provide a safe return for Ti Bon and the white man, who now calls himself Tim.

Several *houngans* from scattered parts of the island arrived throughout the evening to assist the *mambo* in conducting the impromptu ceremony. Drummers beat with their usual fervor. White-clad women, *hounsis*, gesticulated around the numerous blazing bonfires illuminating the night. The growing congregation joined in the chants. Animals were prepared for sacrifice.

The ceremony came to a premature halt. The dancers stopped first, followed by the chanters, and then the drummers. Everyone faced a towering intruder standing near the edge of the temple grounds. His piercing glare shot fright into nearly all the congregation, the young women and *La Reine* Memmene being the lone exceptions. No one dared approach the ebony-skin stranger—no one except *La Reine* Memmene.

The source of the evil enveloping La Gonave stood before her. The *mambo's* apprehension dissolved the moment the imposing figure spoke the words she longed to hear.

"Mother, it is I, Octave Polynice."

Chapter 60

Ouanga

Madeleine slumped in her rocking chair as the last remnant of the Haitian sun melted into the horizon. She sent Yvette home early, leaving herself alone, isolated. The day passed with no word or sign of Tim or Ti Bon. She did everything she could to save them, but failed at every turn. Mildred's stinging comment about a life in Haiti not being meant for her ran amuck through a mind already frazzled by recent events. Through it all, her resolve to remain and serve the children of La Gonave had not faltered. Perhaps, continuing her father's work by herself was the way it was meant to be.

She lit a lantern and placed it on the small table by her rocking chair, purposely keeping the wick low. The porch remained otherwise shrouded in darkness. A short time later a faint rapping sounded upon the screened door. At first she failed to register it. Another volley of raps, this time louder, broke her stupor. She suspected it to be Yvette returning to comfort her, or worse, Mildred Sponheimer returning with more unsolicited advice. Prepared to make the necessary excuses, she pulled herself from the rocking chair and opened the door.

He stood outside, banged up, but very much alive.

"Ti Bon." Catching herself by holding onto the door, she blew out her breath, inhaled, and then hugged her Haitian friend. "Please come in and tell me everything you can remember. Is Tim, I mean Tom, safe?"

He recounted the ordeal of the terrible night from the beginning. He repeatedly interrupted the story to ask Madeleine the particulars of hers. The last thing he remembered was jumping off the sinking *Santa Maria* with their mutual friend, still Tom to him. The sun blazed directly overhead when he regained consciousness. Some of *La Reine* Memmene's followers found him lying face down on a sandy shore. Near him they found an orange life-ring, about three feet wide, floating back and forth with every frothing wave.

When he made no further mention of Tim, Madeleine scraped up the courage to ask what remained most on her mind. "Do you have any idea what happened to Mister Jamison, any idea at all?"

He lowered his head. "I saw nothing of Mister Jamison. I fear he gave his life to save mine."

Her heart sank. "Why do you say such a thing?"

He placed an object in her right hand. "I found the Spanish sea-god's cross tied around my neck. As you know, *La Reine* Memmene proclaimed no harm could come to the one who wears it."

She clenched the cross and raised it to her quivering lips.

"I think Mister Jamison would have wanted you to keep the cross, *Soeur* Madeleine. It has already protected me."

She wept. Ti Bon placed his arm around her.

She regained some composure. "Does your family know you're safe?"

"No. I came straight here to see if you had survived."

"Please, go home. I'm sure your family's worried out of their minds about you."

He nodded his head, kissed her on the forehead and, without further word, disappeared into the blackness that had overtaken the night.

She wandered to the living room and picked up the carved mask Tim had left there the night of the big storm. She took it to her bedroom, removed a primitive painting, and hung the carving in its place. She took a step back and recalled Tim saying the wooden mask was his sole keepsake of his parents. Now, it would seem, it represented her sole keepsake of him.

****

Madeleine stared at the silver cross and visualized Tim taking it off and tying it around Ti Bon's neck—such a noble gesture being exactly what she would expect of her missing lover. She doubted Tim believed the cross actually possessed any special powers, but felt certain he realized Ti Bon believed in such things. She sunk with guilt after wishing he had kept the cross safely fastened around his own neck. It seemed whatever words *La Reine* Memmene voiced always came to pass. Ti Bon was safe and, it seemed with all the more certainty, Tim was not.

She placed the cross on the table where the lantern's flickering light danced across its shiny surface. She closed her eyes, squeezed her leather charm, leaned back in the rocker, and listened to the rhythmic beat of *Vodou* drums echoing down from the mountains. A curious comment of *La Reine* Memmene's replayed in her mind. "You may only look inside the *ouanga* at a moment of total despair."

She removed the leather charm from around her neck, opened the pouch, and found inside an assemblage of seeds, leaves, and twigs. Nestled in the midst of the botanical concoction, she discovered a miniature braid of hair, half the strands being auburn and the other half blond. She clenched the pouch in her fist. Torrents of tears poured down her pallid cheeks.

****

The midnight hour had come and gone when two brawny hands gently cupped her chin. Madeleine opened her watery eyes to a blurred image kneeling in front of her. She could not believe it to be real—would not believe it to be true—until she joined her hands with his.

"I thought I lost you and would never see you or feel you again, but you're here…alive…with me."

Tim's eyes brightened. "I'm alive, thanks to some of *La Reine* Memmene's followers. They found me washed ashore in the middle of nowhere, barely conscious, and brought me here to you. I crave nothing more than to stay here for so long as you'll have me."

"That could be a long time. A very long time."

"How does eternity strike you?"

"Perfect. Absolutely perfect."

"Then eternity it is."

Epilogue

Two men woke in the shadowy night to the resonating pulse of island drums. One man was black and the other white. Both found solace in the rhythmic beat.

Comments from the Author

I am compelled to make the traditional disclaimers regarding any resemblance to actual events, locales, persons, living or dead, as being entirely coincidental. However, I must confess this statement is not entirely true. My goal was to write a work of fiction that captured as a backdrop the beauty, magnificence, and sorrowful plight of Haiti, a country and culture that left me with an indelible imprint. I am not an anthropologist or historian, so I do not claim to have written a novel describing all events, places, or cultural underpinnings with absolute accuracy. Hopefully, I managed to capture some of the pride, color, and mysticism that are the fabrics of Haiti.

The geographical locales described in *Cracked Island* are real, although my descriptions include a sprinkling of fictitious license. Many of the specific places and structures also exist, although sadly, *la Cathedral Nationale* and many other historical buildings are now in ruins. Victims, along with, and even more sadly, countless numbers of innocent Haitians of the ravaging earthquake striking Port-au-Prince on January 12, 2010.

I developed many scenes depicted in *Cracked Island* by modifying events I read and heard about, or personally experienced. For example, in one of my opening scenes I re-enacted an incident where a former graduate student from Ghana, West Africa, had been involved in a car accident in which he was knocked unconscious and pronounced dead. He regained consciousness in the city morgue with a large tag tied to his toe. Amy Wilentz's non-fictional book on Haiti—*Rainy Season* (Simon & Schuster, Inc., 1989)—served as a springboard for several scenes. She presents an account in her opening chapter in which a white powder, actually crack cocaine, is innocently used to whitewash mud huts. Columbus certainly found Indians wearing gold ornaments when he first arrived to Hispaniola (Haiti and Dominican Republic today). The discovery of gold *Taíno* artifacts in Haiti by a *real* anthropologist is described in an article in *Time* (October 10, 1960) entitled "Columbus Vindicated." Dr. Frank Roberts, a former professor at the University of Maine, told this story to me while we once journeyed together from Fort Liberté to Port-au-Prince. This story became the spark for the entire novel. Incidentally, Columbus' flagship, the *Santa Maria*, is believed by experts to have sunk somewhere off the coast of Haiti.

Vivid memories are etched in my mind of a *Vodou* ceremony I witnessed many years ago. Such ceremonies are also described in a number of books. I primarily drew upon William Seabrook's *The Magic Island* (The Literary Guild of America, 1929), Hugh Cave's *Haiti: Highroad to Adventure* (Henry Holt and Company, Inc., 1952), Alfred Métraux's *Voodoo in Haiti* (Shocken Books, 1972), Wade Davis' *The Serpent and the Rainbow* (Warner Books, Inc., 1987), and Wilentz's *Rainy Season*. I attempted to capture the *spirit* of these ceremonies. The *cleansing of souls* at Saut d'Eau is described in a National Geographic article ("Haiti's Voodoo Pilgrimages of Spirits and Saints," March 1985) by Carole DeVillers. Once again, I took considerable literary license in describing these events. The ceremony at Les Arcadians to appease the sea gods is described in the book, *The White King of La Gonave* (Garden City Publishing Company, Inc., 1931) by Faustin Wirkus and Taney Dudley. Yes, there really existed a White King of La Gonave, a marine sergeant stationed on the island during the United States occupation in the early 1900s. I apologize to any of his real descendants if they do not find Tim James worthy of their heritage.

I found the *Créole* spelling of words to differ significantly in everything I read about Haiti. I chose spellings, whenever possible, that seemed consistent with recent writings. In particular, I used *Vodou* instead of the Hollywood version *Voodoo* to reinforce the efforts of Haitian scholars and depict the term as representing one of several religions combining West African deity worship and elements of Roman Catholicism. *Vodou* is practiced today in several islands of the Caribbean, parts of Brazil, and parts of North America, in particular, Louisiana.

In *The Magic Island,* Seabrook describes the tale of a great cave beneath the mountains of La Gonave where in a pool underneath a waterfall a sacred crocodile dwells. The *Taíno* Queen, Anacoana, along with her entourage, would travel in long canoes from Leogane, a village on the coast of the main island, to bathe in the pool. Such a pool, it seemed to me, would be a logical place for her to hide treasures when Columbus returned.

Haiti is a wondrous country steeped in colorful culture and tradition. The next time you hear or read about a public ferry sinking between the main island and La Gonave, sadly an almost annual event, the devastation wreaked by hurricanes and, even more unimaginable, an earthquake, think of Ti Bon, Marie Joseph, and their five children. Those are the sorts of gentle and proud people who lost their lives.

About the Author

Chris Kohler, Ph.D., is a professor emeritus of zoology at Southern Illinois University-Carbondale. He has published extensively in the scientific literature, including co-editing a popular college textbook, *Inland Fisheries Management in North America,* first and second editions. The international focus of much of his research and development work thrust him in the midst of exotic locales throughout much of the Caribbean, Central America, and South America. One of his more memorable endeavors occurred in the colorful and mystical island nation of Haiti. *Cracked Island*, his first novel, draws upon his personal experiences, stories conveyed by friends and colleagues, and fragments of story lines gleaned from the many fine books and articles written about Haiti, its people, and its rich culture. Chris lives in North Carolina with his wife, Charlee Sue, and the fond memories of two rather large tabby cats.

For more information,
www.Chris-Kohler.com

Find more books from
Keith Publications, LLC
At

www.keithpublications.com

CPSIA information can be obtained
at www.ICGtesting.com
Printed in the USA
LVOW04*1921271215

467669LV00032B/1256/P

9 781628 821123